The

LAKE CLUB

Advance Praise for *The Lake Club*

"A fast-paced, twisty, delicious debut, *The Lake Club* explores long-buried secrets, burgeoning romance, and the gossip that fuels small towns and exclusive clubs. A juicy mix of rich people behaving badly and love in all its forms, Lina Patton reminds us that, no matter how convoluted things have become, the truth really can be a clean slate. I'll be first in line to read Patton's next novel!"

—Kristy Woodson Harvey, *New York Times* bestselling author of *Beach House Rules*

"I'm a sucker for lakes (especially in an unfamiliar part of the country), rich people behaving badly, outsiders to an insular world, summer parties, and a hot but approachable leading man. *The Lake Club* has all of this and more—its twisty, propulsive plot hooked me early and kept me turning the pages until I reached the unpredictable end."

—Meg Mitchell Moore, author of *Mansion Beach*

"From *The Lake Club*'s opening pages, I was captivated by the intoxicating prose and immersive summer setting. Patton's debut is juicy and tense, insanely readable, and surprisingly tender—you need this one in your beach bag."

—Carola Lovering, bestselling author of *Tell Me Lies* and *Bye, Baby*

"With its lakeside glamour, elegant prose, and simmering secrets, *The Lake Club* is the ultimate summer escape. Stylish, smart, and utterly unputdownable—Patton's debut marks the arrival of a thrilling new voice in fiction."

—Georgia Clark, author of *Play It Again*

The LAKE CLUB

A NOVEL

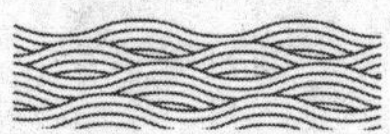

LINA PATTON

wm
WILLIAM MORROW
An Imprint of HarperCollins*Publishers*

HarperCollins books may be purchased for educational, business, or sales promotional use. For information, please email the Special Markets Department at SPsales@harpercollins.com.

hc.com

FIRST EDITION

Interior text design by Diahann Sturge-Campbell

Water wave line illustration © shamanviiii/Stock.Adobe.com

Library of Congress Cataloging-in-Publication Data

Names: Patton, Lina, author
Title: The lake club : a novel / Lina Patton.
Description: First edition. | New York : William Morrow, an imprint of HarperCollins Publishers, 2026.
Identifiers: LCCN 2026011440 | ISBN 9780063447295 (paperback) | ISBN 9780063447271 (ebook)
Subjects: LCGFT: Novels
Classification: LCC PS3616.A9268 L35 2026
LC record available at https://lccn.loc.gov/2026011440

ISBN 978-0-06-344729-5

Printed in the United States of America

26 27 28 29 30 LBC 5 4 3 2 1

To M + D

What we want
is never simple.
—Linda Pastan

Prologue

There was something romantic about brand-new, empty houses. The delicious, acidic smell of fresh paint. The way the sun fell in crisp geometric shapes across the wide wooden floors. The gleaming silver of fridges and dishwashers and sinks—the general air of promise.

When they stepped inside 91 Sycamore Lane that morning, it felt as if they had stepped into a different life. The tension from the night before lingered, a desire they were both struggling to ignore, and the beauty and quiet of the house only heightened the words unsaid.

Nothing can happen. Nothing can happen. The refrain played silently, simultaneously, inside their heads. Still, a low harmony echoed in the background: *What if?*

They weaved through the house measuring each room's dimensions, pressing tape measures to crown molding and across doorframes, meticulously tracking widths and lengths. They moved slowly as they worked, catching glances as they shifted around each other, studying the place: for the design, for the marketing, for making money, they told themselves. They talked in empty phrases:

"It's going to be another hot one. Record temps. Can you believe it?"

"I just love those skylights. That sky."

"Can you hand me the pencil? Can you move a little to the left?"

It wasn't until an hour in, kneeling along the wall of the main bedroom that, finally, their hands overlapped. It was accidental at first—they'd been shifting the ruler when their knuckles hit, their pointer fingers brushed—yet neither pulled away. Their eyes met. And then they were kissing, moving up against the wall.

Had they been anywhere else, maybe the kiss never would have happened—maybe the affair never would have started. Maybe they never would have become such expert liars, the type who could go about their days and routines interacting as normal, as if this other plane of passion did not exist, as if they did not know the taste and feel of each other's sweat, tongue, teeth.

But that day, the house and the world were on their side. The summer was set in motion.

Everything was about to change.

1

Every plan is more exciting when you're the only one who knows it.

This was Danika Crawley's first thought as she entered the Club's main dining room, immediately plucking a glass of champagne from a passing waiter's tray. She took a sip and studied the room over the rim of the glass, pretending she didn't notice the flutter of eyes moving over her like hummingbirds across a flower. Not that she minded. It was expected. After all, she hadn't been to the Club in a full week—not since the incident—and she was prepared. *Let them look.* She shook back her dark blond hair and straightened her spine.

Danika and her husband, Bill, walked together toward their table. While the staff always shifted the dining room for events—including tonight's Champagne and Caviar Happy Hour—they left the tables on the perimeter untouched. That was to say, they left the old money's standing reservations, untouched. Danika was relieved to have a destination as they crossed the room, splitting the sea of boring blue ties and midi floral cocktail dresses.

She was also relieved to see Frank and Holly Fravel already at their table as they approached. Despite the facts that Frank was their lawyer and that Danika didn't have any real friends, she did like

Holly best; they were both from California and hated all the same people.

"Hello, bombshell," Holly sang as she grabbed Danika's hand and raised it as if to twirl her in a waltz. "Is this new?"

"Ninety-nine percent off." Danika smoothed her new indigo silk jumpsuit down her thighs. This was one of their inside jokes: making fun of the way Minnesotans downplayed compliments, shoving their humility toward you like a gift you didn't want.

"I like this, too." Danika nodded to Holly's billowing black pants and fitted black vest.

"Must continue my reign as the Gothic Queen of Aldon Lakes."

Danika lifted her drink in a cheers. She appreciated how Holly only wore dark colors and sharp lines, which suited her jet-black hair, thick eyebrows, and angular checkmark cheekbones.

Danika took a long, unsteady sip as she turned to the room, trying to quell the adrenaline coursing through her. Part of her wished she could've told Holly, or Bill even, her plan for the evening, but it would have been too embarrassing to admit how desperate she was to regain power over the narrative—how eager she was to take control of the gossip that had surely been floating through the hallways and locker rooms and out onto the golf course over the past week. It wasn't that she had been hiding; she simply hadn't wanted to face any questions or flat expressions of concern until she had a tangible solution.

Now, as she glanced at her Rolex and registered it was just after six—one hour to go—the buzz felt better than the drink.

"Upgrade?" Bill said as a waiter arrived with a new bottle of champagne. Bill's thick chestnut hair caught the light of the chandelier as he draped one arm around Danika's waist. They always acted more intimate at the Club than at home, though neither would acknowledge such a thing. Even now, his touch felt foreign and awkward. It'd been so long.

"Always one step ahead of us, my guy. The stuff they're passing is shit." Frank Fravel clapped Bill's shoulder as he swiveled toward them, his large stomach swinging to the center of their group like a compass.

As Danika registered the six-hundred-dollar bottle, it warmed her to know Bill would not offer anyone else a splash. Despite his decades in the Midwest—his family started one of the oldest dairy cooperatives in the state—Bill had never caught on to the practice of Minnesota Nice. This was one trait she genuinely loved about him: He had always been straightforward, honest.

"You spoil us," Holly said as the waiter filled her glass.

"Only the best for the best." Bill winked.

This was one of Bill's less desirable traits: He had always been a flirt.

The four continued drinking and chatting as they nestled the bottle on ice. Yet as the string quartet switched to a cello-heavy cover of Justin Bieber and everyone's conversations grew louder, Danika heard two familiar voices nearby and took a deep breath. She'd been preparing for this moment, aware that as soon as she laid eyes on Robin Greene and Mallory Harrison, she'd feel a flash of unease, instantly plunged back to last Wednesday, with all the embarrassment and chaos.

THE DAY HAD started normally enough. She and the boys were still getting used to their summer schedule, shuffling from Cooper's art camp to soccer camp to tennis lessons at the Club. Cooper had more energy than the average five-year-old, and he loved bouncing from activity to activity. It was less ideal for Danika and two-year-old

Max, but at least Max loved riding in the car, and all around, they were making it work.

Cooper's lessons were at the lower courts from four to five, which meant that when Danika and Max went to pick him up that afternoon, the women's pairs were about to kick off. This was why Robin and Mallory were stretching nearby. At ages sixty and thirty-five respectively, they were the unique, dynamic duo to beat.

The sun was strong, and Danika had pulled Max toward the shade of the snack shack as they waited for Cooper to finish. They'd only been there a moment when Robin and Mallory appeared beside them, ordering waters.

"I wish they would push these matches back a half hour," Robin said. She wore a fitted white tennis dress that was age appropriate but slightly sexy all the same. "I know the Cities are close, but it still takes me thirty minutes to get out here and change. It's a rush."

Mallory nodded sympathetically as she adjusted the zipper of her similar, yet shorter, white dress. "I know, I'm spoiled the hotel is so close."

Behind her sunglasses, Danika rolled her eyes. Everyone knew Robin Greene was the CFO at U.S. Bank and that Mallory ran the Hotel Harrison, her family's famous lakeside hotel. Both were always bragging about their jobs as if little "boss bitch" charms dangled from their bracelets of accolades. Danika often felt all women at the Club wore these metaphorical bracelets, showing off markers of pedigree, family, money, beauty, career, tennis or golf prowess. Danika never used to mind. When they had first moved to Aldon Lakes six years ago, she'd had charms of her own! She was worldly. Younger. Prettier. Edgier. She used to revel in looking down on all the sheltered, incestuous people of Aldon Lakes. Though now, at thirty-two, she was beginning to feel like one of them. And worse: one they kept on the outside.

"Oh hi, sweetie," Robin said as Max weaved around their legs.

"Sorry," Danika said as she grabbed Max's hand.

"I just love his white blond hair." Robin ruffled it. "Such a beach babe."

Danika focused on Max, pained to know Robin had lost one of her own sons years ago. That was a confusing emotion for Danika: feeling sympathy for people you didn't like.

"He's so big for two," Mallory said with a smile. This was another confusing reality: how everyone in Aldon Lakes knew everything about one another—the ages of sons, their birthdays, even—yet otherwise acted like strangers.

"You all off to a fun summer?" Robin interjected, still petting Max's head.

"Yes, busy as always." Danika glanced to Cooper loitering about the courts. "A bit stressful, actually, because I'm headed back to work, and I need to find a nanny."

Danika didn't know why she had said this. While it was true—Bill had asked her at the last minute to help with his new housing development—she had wanted the news to filter slowly. Saying it now felt desperate, even to her. Regardless, she enjoyed the surprise falling across Robin's and Mallory's faces.

"I'll be designing a model home." Danika locked on to Mallory's doe eyes. Years ago, she had offered Mallory a design consultation for the Hotel Harrison's revamp, and while Mallory had been as fake-polite as ever, she had never followed up. Danika knew what she thought: Danika's run-of-the-mill design certificate meant nothing. Danika couldn't wait to blow everyone away. The model home would be perfect. Stunning.

"That's wonderful," Mallory said. "But, gosh, Danika, I'm not sure what to tell you about the nanny. I wish I could help. It's already

June." She grimaced. "Everyone qualified was snatched up months ago."

Robin commiserated. "It really is hard to find good help these days. I swear everything was easier back in my time. I feel for you young mothers. I really do."

Danika's jaw tightened. Condescension dripped from each of them like sweat.

Of course, soon the day's drama would eclipse these remarks—everything that happened next was far worse.

Cooper had always had a knack for wandering. Danika had lost him several times, including at the Galleria two months prior. While she had been extra careful since, as she watched the other children clear the courts, dread seeped into her bones. She immediately sensed what was happening. She turned around and around, calling his name.

Nothing.

Naturally, everyone began to help. The tennis coaches swore he had just been there; the tennis ladies were aghast with worry. Danika felt self-conscious at first, but ten minutes later, all she felt was fear. Highway 15 ran beyond the Club's parking lot—and Cooper, who'd follow anything from a wandering butterfly to a stray ball, was rarely aware of his surroundings. *Will this be it?* she suddenly thought. *The next tragedy to define my life?*

Time blurred from there. The general manager appeared. The lifeguards were alerted. Danika called Bill, who was out of town. She called Holly, who was also out of town. Then, as Max stayed with a coach, she searched every room in the Club—from the main dining room to the ballroom to the library. There was a bridal shower in the library at the time, and everyone had glared at her as she burst inside, but thankfully, the events manager, Aida, had quickly ushered her away. "Don't worry, we'll find him," she had repeated, squeezing Danika's shoulder. Aida's kindness had felt so sincere, and for the first time that day, she felt less alone.

The search continued another half hour until some waiter finally heard crying from inside a storage closet and found Cooper sitting among boxes of decorations. He had a cut on his cheek from trying to climb the shelves to reach the piñatas, but overall, he was no worse for wear.

When Danika saw him, she cried. She was too relived to feel embarrassed. The shame only returned later as she struggled to fall asleep that night. She had imagined the ladies gossiping after tennis, talking about Danika's new job, her inability to hire a nanny—how she couldn't even keep track of her own kid. *Some mother*, they'd think, unclasping one of her final charms.

"You okay, darling?" Bill followed her line of sight to Robin Greene. Despite their issues, Bill still knew her best. He reached for the bottle and topped her off as Danika said, "Of course."

Bill leaned closer, whispering, "Once again, the power suit swings and misses."

A smile tugged at Danika's lips. They often joked that Robin Greene always showed up to the Club in her signature pantsuits to remind everyone how important her job was—how important she was. Danika pressed her cheek quickly against Bill's.

The night moved on predictably: The quartet played more pop covers, everyone ordered extra bottles, they brought out the flat cheese plates. It wasn't until the sun waned, turning the sky to a blur of peach and purple and pink, that people made their way out to the deck.

Perfect, Danika thought as she noticed Robin and Mallory slip through the patio doors.

Danika and Holly followed suit and settled outside, hips kissing the railing as they stared out at the course. While much of the Club's decor was outdated and traditional—all classic, patterned carpets and dark wood paneling—Danika would admit the golf course was stunning. She loved how the patchwork quilt of green and moon-white sand traps extended for miles to the east, slipped into the lake to the west. The way all the vibrant colors turned silver in the dimming light. It was peaceful, quiet. You could barely even hear the party inside—or the pool out front. Still, Danika could picture it perfectly: her boys and their new nanny swimming about, getting in their last cannonballs before heading toward their towels at the seven o'clock close. Yes, it was almost showtime.

Danika studied the horizon, feeling Zen and ready—yet, as she looked toward the top of the deck's stairs, she realized it might be better to move farther down the railing. This way, when the boys and nanny arrived, they'd have to weave through more people to find her.

"Let's scoot down a little." Danika touched Holly's elbow. "The idiot." She nodded behind her toward Joshua Mike—the rich, handsome, drunken asshole everyone despised. Even now, he held a bourbon in each hand while slurring Danika's name. At least this time his presence worked in her favor.

Danika took a few sideways steps through the crowd with Holly on her heels, but as she glanced over her shoulder to make sure Joshua Mike was not following, she collided with someone. It happened so fast, she barely registered the tray of glasses crashing to the ground, the girl in the white-and-black uniform exclaiming—the cool liquid splashing her neck. She scoffed as the liquid began collecting in her cleavage and seeping to her navel, leaving a dark line down the front of her jumpsuit.

"Oh, shit," Holly said as she pushed a single cocktail napkin to Danika's skin, which was growing red with rage.

Danika glared down at the girl. She was crouched beneath them now, picking up large pieces of broken glass. Her dark brown ponytail swung to the ground like a broom.

"I'm so sorry," she said as she glanced up. Her face was pained and sweaty, but her eyes were a brilliant aqua blue. They were so bright, Danika paused before her anger rushed back in.

"Why don't you watch where you're going." Danika rounded her shoulders and pulled the silk away from her body.

"I'm so sorry," the girl repeated as she stood, her tray filled with chunks of glass. Danika noticed a trickle of blood running down her left index finger and, on instinct, she thought, *Good*.

"It's just water," she said. "I'll get you a towel."

Danika felt people staring now, but she couldn't bring herself to look. This was not how the evening was supposed to go. Still, her seething was cut short when—right on cue—her phone rang. She flicked her hand at the girl, dismissing her.

Danika's chest seized as she turned away to answer. But within seconds, she loosened—the conversation unfolded exactly as hoped: first, the nanny apologized, then explained that while the boys were dressed and ready to go, the keys to the Range Rover were nowhere to be found, and did she happen to have a spare?

Danika felt a little bad inciting any panic in her new hire, but stealing the keys from the pool bag had simply been necessary.

"Oh, please don't worry." Danika pushed the phone against her ear, its screen clinking her diamond stud. "It happens, and yes, I do have a spare. It's no problem. Come find us around back. Yes, follow the walkway to the pro shop and up the deck stairs. We're already outside." She tilted her chin toward the lowering sun, the sheen of gold across the lake. "See you soon."

As she hung up, Holly squinted at her, but Danika kept her head down. She tucked her phone into her bag, strummed the keychain with her fingers.

"Oh, it's nothing, just the new nanny," Danika said as she finally returned Holly's gaze.

Minutes later, she heard them before she saw them: First, Chat's low, raspy laugh as he said, "Giddyup, hold the railing!"; next, Max's sweet, goofy cackle; and lastly, Cooper's voice as he yelled, "Race you to Mom! Mom? Mom?" She felt their presence, too—the hungry love she held for each of them.

Then, there they were, spilling out onto the deck in a flurry of colorful pool bags and floaties. The boys were tanned and blond, just like Danika, and Max sat in Chat's arms while Cooper clung to his side. And Chat, beautiful Chat, stood tall in his dark-hair, six-four, megawatt-smile glory. Danika softened as she looked at him, shaken back to an old version of herself.

"Sorry to interrupt," Chat said as they bumbled toward her. There was no way not to notice this trio—as expected, every head turned—and Danika felt buoyed by the attention. Soon, this seed of gossip would take off, planting and spreading through all of The Lake Club. "Did you hear?" people would say. "The Crawleys hired a nanny. A male nanny! A twenty-two-year-old living with them for the summer! Can you believe it?"

Danika would once again be different and intriguing. There'd be a new, shining charm on her bracelet. Everyone, in their heart of hearts, would be jealous.

"This is fancy." Chat unabashedly surveyed the party, nodding in approval.

Danika laughed and folded the keys into his hand, letting her palm linger on top of his knuckles. "Oh, no, it's nothing. But thank you so much, Chat. I'm sure the other set will turn up. Don't worry about it." She squatted to kiss Cooper, the smell of chlorine and sunscreen clinging to his skin, and rose to fake bite Max's chubby hand. "We'll see you at home. I'll call a car soon." She leaned in. "This is wildly boring."

"Whatever you say." Chat flashed another perfect smile as he looked out to the party, up at the string lights. "Enjoy yourself. And thanks again." He raised the car keys, jingling them in the air. "I'll protect these with my life."

Danika felt like she was floating as she watched them go, and she couldn't wait to turn and face the crowd—but then, someone else appeared in Chat's place: that clumsy waiter. She pushed a white monogrammed towel toward Danika.

"Apologies," she mumbled before scurrying away.

Holding the towel, Danika felt irritated all over again. Her jumpsuit was dry. What was she supposed to do with this prop now? At this point, it felt like one more barrier between absorbing into the party and fielding question after question about Chat, her new male nanny—her *manny*, she'd tell them. They'd eat that up.

Danika moved to drape the towel over the deck railing. Yet, as she glanced down the banister, she tilted her head, surprised to see Chat still standing at the top of the stairs. His eyes were locked on something—or someone—at the party.

Danika felt a strike of panic. Did he *know* someone here? She had only allowed herself to hire him because he had zero ties to the community—well, zero idea about any ties to the community or their shared history. She intended for it to stay that way. She'd even made him sign a slightly unorthodox contract, citing horror stories about other nannies as an excuse: He'd agreed to withhold details of their private life (Danika valued anonymity); to remain extra alert when at the Club (Danika had told him about losing Cooper and the other mothers' judgy eyes); and finally, not to bring any significant others around the boys (the Clines' daughter really had walked in on their nanny and her boyfriend, and Danika didn't want any distractions). He'd brushed it all off, said he was good at secrets, that he'd be on alert 24-7, and "Don't worry"—he'd laughed—"I haven't had a girlfriend in years."

Now, though, as he raised his hand in a wave, it was obvious he was trying to get someone's attention. Danika bobbed her head, desperate to see over the tops of people and find who he was looking at—but, a second later, Cooper yelled to Chat from the bottom of the stairs, and he was gone, rushing down the steps and out of sight.

Danika pulled back, confused. She didn't have much time to ruminate, though, because before she knew it, people were flocking to her. Everyone wanted to know who he was, where he was from, where she had found him. *Finally.*

Danika straightened and focused, answering each question with enough information to satisfy and avoid suspicion while retaining intrigue, as was her practiced nature. Still, the more she spoke of Chat, the more she found her limbs and heart growing instinctively heavy. She scolded herself for this—she had promised herself that his presence wouldn't derail her—but it was proving easier said than done. Everything about him sent her mind careening back in time—back to a world and life she'd run from all those years ago.

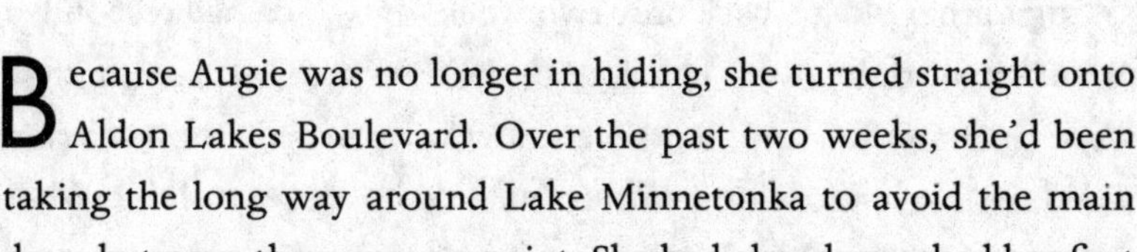

2

Because Augie was no longer in hiding, she turned straight onto Aldon Lakes Boulevard. Over the past two weeks, she'd been taking the long way around Lake Minnetonka to avoid the main drag, but now, there was no point. She had already worked her first shift at the Club, and word was out. Everyone knew she was back in town. That she had failed.

Augie clenched the steering wheel tighter as she drove along the lakeside street, which anchored the area everyone referred to as "downtown." Having just returned from New York City, Augie found it ridiculous. It was only one short stretch of road with one side built up. The other gave way to sidewalks and the bike trail that ringed the lake. The area was more developed than in years past (the suburb had benefited from the pandemic and subsequent shift away from the Cities), but still. As Augie and her mom had noted when they'd moved from Maine nine years earlier, Aldon Lakes was a wealthy suburban bubble.

Augie focused on the pavement as she drove, ignoring all the white manicured coffee shops and steak houses and overpriced boutiques glowing in the summer sun. She barely even looked up at the crosswalks, not wanting to recognize anyone and force a pathetic wave. She hadn't even returned her friends' messages—hadn't reinstalled her social media.

Augie couldn't help but glance out at the lake. Despite how much she hated it there, the town was undeniably beautiful. The water shimmered like spilled glitter, the trees were full and lush with green, the sky overhead cloudless and calm. Augie always found it frustrating when the weather didn't match her mood—how exhausting it was to feel depressed under a bright, beaming sun.

At least today she was helping Aida out. While she had dreaded asking for her old job back only two weeks ago, Aida had responded to her email right away. Thank god, she'd written, explaining they were understaffed and had seven new people with the Harrison wedding fast approaching. What did I do to deserve this? What happened to New York? Xoxo.

Sitting at JFK, eyes puffy from crying, Augie struggled to respond. She'd sent back a simple See you soon.

Augie reached the end of the boulevard, passed the Hotel Harrison, and turned into the Club's employee lot. She hated that this was part of her muscle memory, though it wasn't exactly surprising. Augie had worked summers at the country club since she was sixteen. Now, at twenty-two, she'd made this drive six summers in a row. Augie reminded herself not to dwell on this today; it was high on her list of "Things Not to Think About." Of course, now that she was thinking about what she was not supposed to think about, the memory of him landed in her mind: the guy from the weekend boat party—the third person she'd ever slept with.

Augie didn't remember his name, and while she did not regret sleeping with him (or the way her stomach flipped as she remembered kissing him in the cramped boat cabin), she needed to let him go. As her best friend, Leah, had said, he was a rebound, nothing more. She'd always encouraged Augie to sleep with at least three people. "It's like a science experiment," she'd said, "you need three trials to even out the flukes." Augie would admit, it had helped dull the memories of New York Fuckboy, as they'd taken to calling her heartbreak from earlier that year. As usual, Leah was right. Number three: It had been worth it.

Augie walked fast across the employee lot, sweating by the time she reached the rows of Range Rovers and Audis and brand-new M5s. The day was hot and humid—typical for a Minnesota summer—and she wiped her upper lip as she climbed the final hill to the Club. Augie was grateful for her sundress in that moment, for the loose ponytail that gathered her thick dark hair, for how, in those last seconds, she looked as if she could be anyone: here to relax at the pool, or meet her parents for lunch on the patio. Soon, she'd be back in a fresh, starchy banquet uniform. She'd returned her old one last summer in what was now an embarrassing show of goodbye.

Augie paused as she reached the entrance, staring up at the massive building that reminded her of both a wedding cake and the White House. She swallowed and gave herself one last pep talk: "Everything will be fine," she whispered. "Everything will be fine!" she said again, louder.

Yet, cutting through it all was another, stronger voice, the one she couldn't quiet, the one that kept hissing: *You deserve this, this is what you get*. She didn't know how to respond to that voice. It was the truth.

THE WEDDING WAS at three that afternoon, and though it was only ten, Augie felt a rush to reach Aida. She knew her boss was stressed. This was one of their largest weddings of the season, and Aida was still trying to impress Mr. Dryer, the new general manager, who was hired last year for their first summer fully open since COVID. Mr. Dryer was as stuck up as the guests, but Augie recognized he was only trying to do a good job. When he'd started, she'd imagined him going home at night, making note cards to memorize members' names so he could greet them on the golf course, saying, "Mrs. Cline, Mr. Anderson, it's so good to see you both!"

Augie undressed quickly in the locker room, pausing only briefly to admire her tan lines in the mirror. She'd been amazed by how quickly white lines had bloomed beneath her bikini straps at the boat party, forming an X across her back. She was unable to fight another memory, then: the boy from the lake kissing the lines up and over her shoulder blades, down her back.

Augie shivered, buttoned her uniform, and rushed upstairs, breaking into the Club's golden light. She was relieved she didn't see any members as she snaked down the hall and turned into the cavernous ballroom, which opened like a giant clamshell, everything opal and pearly white. Immediately, she saw Aida in the center, the maintenance staff to her side. They were rolling tables on their edges as if directing wild, unruly animals—almost comically small under the massive chandelier, which hung directly above them, beautiful and bored.

"Aug!" Aida opened her arms and hugged her tight. "I'm so happy to see you. I'm so sorry we didn't get to catch up properly at the happy hour. That was such a shit show. Did you know we went through a whole month's supply of caviar?"

"Of course we did. People probably brought to-go bags." Augie smiled. She and Aida always joked that the richest members were also the cheapest, hoarding the fanciest food.

"I'm sorry I didn't stay till close. I was so wiped." Augie left out the fact that after the incident with Mrs. Crawley, she couldn't wait to get out of there. Breaking a tray of glasses was the last thing she had needed during her first shift back. She knew it was pathetic, but that simple mistake had sent her over the edge. She had cried the whole way home.

"Oh, don't be sorry. I get it. And you'll have to tell me about New York later, maybe at family meal?"

Augie fought a lump in her throat. "So, it's all ten tops, then? Twenty-five total?" She put her hands on her hips, studying the room. "The Harrisons are *so* popular."

"I know, right? I don't know how they think they're going to fit. Sorry, Dr. Harrison, but the room will not become larger, no matter who you are."

Augie laughed. While they both genuinely liked Dr. Harrison—he was retired and sweet and loved to hum Sinatra at all hours of the day—all the Harrisons were divas.

"At least it's only his niece's wedding. Mallory's was a nightmare. Only daughter and all. Be glad that was before your time."

Augie could barely remember a time when she wasn't working at the Club. "I do think you could push those tables a little more into the bar area," she finally said, pointing. "It's going to cool off tonight. Most people will stay outside." Augie instinctively looked out the glass doors, colorful stripes of golf course, lake, and sky stacked like a trifle cake.

Aida nodded down at the circles drawn and redrawn on her clipboard. "Yeah, yeah, that makes sense. Let's move sixteen and seventeen. Hector?"

Augie started toward the kitchen, but Aida suddenly grabbed her hand, looking straight at her. "Thank you, Aug. We really appreciate having you back."

As usual, Augie was caught by Aida's beauty. Aida was Somali, and her irises and eyelashes were so dark and striking, it felt almost physically good—comforting, like touching silk—when she looked at you.

"It's nothing," she said. "I'll start on the dinner plates."

"That would be amazing, thanks. We're having surf and turf tonight, and Chef will kill me if we mess up the numbers. Don't even get me started on the kids' meals. Did I tell you there are kids tonight? I guess she's a kindergarten teacher. Can't get enough, apparently."

"Hope they got the lobster." Augie grimaced jokingly as she turned. "It'll be okay, I got you," she added—eager to be kind and good and useful.

To get the universe back on her side.

Even with the new staff, and though the party was more grandiose than normal, the wedding went off without a hitch. The weather was perfect. The meals were well timed. The decorations—from the Waterford votives to the draped organza to the bursting blue hydrangea centerpieces—felt surprisingly special. And before Augie knew it, they'd reached the dancing part of the evening, and it was time for first cuts.

"Augustus Gloop!" TC sang as Augie kicked her way into the florescent lights of the kitchen, sliding her tray onto the metal table that served as the staff's home base. TC hugged her while lifting her off the floor. "Glad to see you've got your groove back." He picked up a glass from her tray, studied it, and turned it upside down into a rack at their side. "Intact. Well done."

Augie smacked him, aware he was teasing her about dropping the tray at the happy hour.

"I had to shake off the dust, Thomas Charles." Augie knew he hated his formal name. It was part of the reason he'd given her a nickname.

TC dipped his hand in a stray cup of water and flicked it at her.

"Oy," Aida said as she approached, followed by a line of new servers, who gathered in a half circle. On instinct, Augie looked away. She didn't want to be rude, but she didn't have it in her to make friends. Plus, they all seemed so young. Augie knew she wasn't old at twenty-two, but she felt older than these kids. *They* probably thought she was old, too, which somehow made it worse.

The only people she could stand to look at now were Aida, TC, and Liss, all of whom she'd worked with since she was sixteen. She'd gotten especially close with TC and Liss during the pandemic when, for two summers, they'd organized extra take-out orders and golf-side catering. With more downtime than normal, she'd learned how TC struggled with drugs in the past, and how Liss was raising a two-year-old daughter with her mom. They didn't talk as deeply when the schedule was back to its usual chaos, but Augie still felt bonded with each of them.

"Okay, I think we're in pretty good shape," Aida said. "We should only need five of you to stay. So," she exhaled—Augie knew she hated this part—"any takers?"

Everyone looked down at their feet, shifting uncomfortably. If people didn't volunteer to stay through breakdown, they were forced to pull straws. Augie raised her hand.

TC and Liss volunteered, too, and Augie blew her friends a kiss. For a second, she felt a flash of déjà vu, back to a wedding from last summer. All the guests got so drunk and stayed so late that she, Liss, and TC felt like a part of the party. They'd sneaked a bottle of prosecco and danced behind the doors, screaming silently along to "Mr. Brightside." Augie remembered twirling so fast that she'd spilled a cup of bubbly from one hand and dropped a fork full of wedding cake from the other, slipping on the frosting and landing on her ass like a cartoon. Liss had laughed so hard she'd peed her pants, and they had to find an extra pair in Aida's office. Augie looked at the floor now, the exact spot. The memory felt like a different life.

Aida finally waved off the first cuts and turned to the late-night crew, sighing as she announced a small crisis: Mr. Schmidt had seen someone vaping outside. "He's complained to Mr. Dryer and, because it's likely a wedding guest, he wants us to take care of it. I don't need to remind you about our very strict no-smoking policy."

TC laughed. Everyone knew it was only enforced when it came to those who were not actually important. "I feel like Terry Schmidt wants a hit. That guy definitely smokes some pot."

Liss pretended to take a drag and blow it his face. "I could see it. I'd need to chill out too if I were married to Liza." Liza was notorious for always matching her BMW to her outfit.

Aida suppressed a smile. She hit TC and Liss with a napkin. "Regardless, can we divide and conquer, please? If two of you could check the pool and lower patio, that would be great. I can let Mr. Dryer know we're on it."

"All right, let's do this." TC saluted Aida as he turned to Augie. "Join me, Watson?" He held out his hand. "Let's find this mystery vaper on the loose."

It felt strange to be on the Club's lower level at night. Augie was used to men brushing past her in golf shirts, women scurrying by on their way to tennis. In the dark, it was unnerving, like being in a deserted airport or mall.

TC said he'd check around the pool. Drunken guests sometimes had the habit of going for a swim. It'd happened twice last summer, and Mr. Dryer talked about imposing a fine. Augie figured it was just one more way for the Club to make money. They tried to hide prices from the staff, but Augie knew it cost almost one hundred thousand to apply. She tried not to think about how most of her high school friends, including Leah, were members. Like the Harrisons, Leah Greene's family was also old money—legacies.

Augie loved the Greenes. Since she'd moved to Minnesota when she was in eighth grade, she'd become part of their family. They always invited her up to their cabin, or on vacations. Leah's mom, Robin, and Augie were particularly close. Robin was high up at U.S. Bank, and having grown up in Boston, she loved that Augie was from Maine. She'd been the one to link Augie with the New York job—though Augie could barely think about that now. It all made her sick.

Leah's dad, Wyatt, was also a star. In addition to being a silver fox and one of the best golfers at the Club, his family was famous for their banking empire. But the Greenes were more down-to-earth than most members. They'd lost their oldest son, Leah's brother Lyle, in a tragic boating accident twelve years ago. He'd been accused of stealing the boat that had crashed and killed him and a friend, which added more pain to the situation. Augie sometimes felt this was why the Greenes were so humble—and why they liked having Augie around so much. Their other son, their middle child, had moved to Colorado, and Leah was only home in the summers. Their mansion was too quiet, the photos of Lyle around the house too loud. Augie got the sense they felt antsy at home, and that this was part of the reason they were always jetting two hours north to their cabin on Gull Lake.

Leah didn't like boating on Lake Minnetonka, so she and Augie often went to the cabin together instead. She'd once told Augie she hated swimming in the same water where her brother had drowned. She never mentioned it again, but ever since, Augie thought of Lyle anytime she swam in the lake. She'd dunk underwater, look up at the blurry surface, the distant sun, and, without meaning to, she'd imagine what it would feel like to drown.

THEY'D BEEN AT the cabin the previous weekend when they decided to go to the boat party. Leah's latest fling from St. Cloud State had invited her. Leah always had a different boy, a different party invitation. It's what happened when you looked like a Midwestern princess—golden blond hair, lanky tan limbs, a perfectly freckled nose—and had the charm to match.

Augie loved to tease Leah, particularly about this boy. He was a hockey player, and given he was two years younger and still a sophomore, Augie called him "The Babe." She knew he wouldn't last. None of Leah's flings did. Neither Augie nor Leah had dated seriously in high school or college. They often joked about their fear of commitment, yet avoided discussing the reasoning: Leah was scared of losing another person close to her, and Augie was scared of getting trapped. She was terrified to think she'd choose the wrong partner and end up on the wrong path—in the wrong life. Just look at her mom and dad.

Augie hadn't been in the mood to go to the party that Saturday. She was still in hiding. Leah had worked hard to convince her as they sat on the cabin's upper deck, clouds wisping into the blue sky above like swirls of blown glass.

"You're working on Wednesday, anyways," Leah had whined. "That's in only four days. It's not like this is Big Island. None of these guys are from Aldon Lakes. You won't know anyone, I promise."

"You and I both know that doesn't matter. Word will travel. I'd like to enjoy my last days of peace, please."

Leah didn't bother fighting that point; in Minnesota, everyone was connected. Word traveled *fast*. Even a famous reality dating series that had once filmed in the area was a bust because the cast ended up having so many friends in common that as soon as taping wrapped, everyone's secrets were exposed. There was even a viral article about it that explained how "due to the tight-knit nature of the Cities—where most singles grew up, went to college, and settled close to family—outsiders disrupted the relationships in a way locals say was inevitable." Augie had sent the article to Leah, hoping it might motivate her to move, but Leah had only laughed.

"I just know you'll have fun at this party. It's time to stop wallowing. And hey"—Leah smacked her hands on the table—"you can use your alias! Let's bring back Allie Von Braun!"

Augie couldn't help but laugh remembering how, when vacationing with Leah's family in Aruba, Augie and Leah had made up fake names at the resort, teasing boys at the pool. Leah had been Lydia Clausewitz, Augie: Allie Von Braun, both from London. They'd talked in British accents the whole trip, often becoming so hysterical, they gave themselves away.

"Look, I even made a list." Leah slid her phone to Augie. Augie leaned forward, smiling at the way Leah was using her own weapons against her. She had outlined clear pros and cons: Pros: hockey guys are hot; boat parties are fun; you need a palette cleanser (RANDOM hookup!); I want to go (and you love me). Cons: N/A.

Augie was touched, though she didn't have the energy to explain that she no longer felt like her old, reasonable self—a person who followed logic and lists.

Still, after two mimosas and more pleading, Augie finally agreed. She'd go—but only as Allie Von Braun.

Augie meandered through the lower level of the Club, but she didn't find anyone. The only other person she saw was herself, suddenly catching sight of her reflection in the darkened pro shop windows. She cringed.

Despite her tan, her eyes were sunken. Her cheeks narrowed. Her hair tight and flat in its low service industry bun. Her white tuxedo shirt and bowtie didn't help.

It was a sharp contrast to how she'd looked when she left for New York that January—when, dare she say, she had looked better than ever. She had chopped her dark waves to her shoulders, gotten a new set of business casual clothes at Macy's post-Christmas sale, and had even started curling her eyelashes to make her blue eyes pop. As a summa cum laude early graduate en route to a job at a major ad agency in New York City, she had never felt so confident—or so good at pretending to be confident. That false confidence, she realized later, was the reason Micah had been drawn to her in the first place. He had loved her combination of conviction and cluelessness.

Augie took a sharp breath and turned away from the windows. *Just keep working*, she told herself. She walked to check the lower patio one last time. Empty.

Augie was ready to give up when, as she took a step up the stairs and flicked off the lights, she heard a noise. She paused with one hand on the banister, picturing herself in a horror movie, the slow, doomed turn. She lunged for the switches and whipped around.

As the lights bounced back on and she looked across the foyer,

Augie wondered if she had fainted. Fallen. Blacked out. Because there, out in front of her—it couldn't be, could it? But it was, wasn't it?—there he was.

Boat guy. Sex guy.

Augie stared, blank and blinking, waiting for the mirage to disappear. But he was squinting back at her, his expression shifting from confusion to recognition to, finally, delight.

"No way," he said, a wide white smile breaking across his face. "Allie?"

Augie's stomach dropped.

He looked different, yet the same. To be fair, she'd only seen him once, in a bathing suit, then naked. Still, he was unmistakable: tall, scruffy but handsome, strong but soft—the type of guy who didn't have a six pack, but still looked perfect shirtless, with defined pecs and the sexy kind of chest hair. He had a head of thick dark hair and slightly too-long sideburns. The deepest golden tan. His eyes were a bright copper that reminded Augie of pennies. She'd told him this at the lake. Driven by cocktails and the honesty you only have with strangers, she had grabbed his face, looked back and forth between his pupils, and said she wanted to see if Abe Lincoln was hidden in his eyeballs. She felt a fresh sting of embarrassment.

It wasn't until he started moving toward her that Augie noticed all he was carrying. Two teal backpacks, a swim bag, a teddy bear, a tennis racket. It weighed him down, the straps pulling on his broad shoulders. Augie stood in shock as she watched him approach, taking in his black Rainbow Kitten Surprise T-shirt and silver gym shorts. It wasn't until he dropped the bags right in front of her and went in for a hug that she came to, the smell of him sending her back to the boat and making her feel weak.

"Sorry," he said, registering the fact that she hadn't hugged him back. "Hope that wasn't weird." His smile flattened but rose again as he held her gaze.

Augie didn't know what to think. Was someone playing a joke on her? Was this all an elaborate plan? A reckoning? A punishment? All she could do was stare at him. He raised his eyebrows as the silence pulsed between them, and Augie suddenly realized: He didn't seem as surprised to see her as she was to see him.

"No, it's okay, I'm sorry, it's just"—she felt her face flush—"what are you doing here? You aren't from Aldon Lakes, are you?"

"Oh, no, definitely not. Are you? Didn't you say you lived in New York?"

"I'm . . . only here for a bit," Augie stammered, taking a step back up the stairs. "But really, what are you doing here? Were you looking for me?"

He laughed the laugh she remembered, like dice shaking in a tin. "Okay, so, this is a hard question, because the answer is both yes and no. I wasn't stalking you, I promise—I had no idea you worked here—but I did see you at that happy hour Wednesday, so, yes, since then, I have been looking for you. Hoping to run into you. Maybe . . . lightly stalking." He tugged the side of his hair, still smiling. "I tried to get your number from the guys at the party, but they didn't have it, or wouldn't give it to me. And I couldn't find you online. So, I'm super excited to see you now, seriously. I really thought you said you lived in New York." His voice was both confident and vulnerable in a way Augie found refreshing.

She pawed at her bowtie, chewing her lip. She couldn't believe her lies were coming back to haunt her. It had felt so easy—so liberating—to be someone else that afternoon: Allie Von Braun from New York City. Of course she couldn't get away with it.

"What do you mean you saw me Wednesday? At the Club? Why were you there—why are you here now?"

"Tonight, I'm the best man, can't you tell?" He held out the sides of his T-shirt.

"Seriously." Augie forced one unconvincing laugh. "You're not supposed to be here."

"All right, my apologies." He pressed his hand to his chest, faux offended, as he stepped forward. "But I work here, too. Kind of. Okay, I guess that's a stretch. I don't technically work *here* here, but we're at the pool all the time. I think it counts for something."

Augie studied the bags, the pile of junk between them. "Who's 'we'?"

"Well, if you'd like the full job description"—he crossed his arms and pulsed his elbows in the air, his biceps pressing to his sides. That chest, those arms, Augie could feel them around her, the way his hands had climbed all over her—"I'm a manny. I'm here for the summer."

Augie's cheeks flushed deeper. The *summer*? He was supposed to be her one-night—day—stand. To mean nothing. Be no one. Number three. She was never supposed to see him again.

His face clouded as he finally seemed to process her stress.

"I thought I'd mentioned that before, but maybe not. Telling girls you're a manny isn't exactly the best pickup line."

"I don't understand. What even is a manny?"

"Manny," he repeated flatly. "Nanny, but male. *Man*-ny."

Augie tried to recall their conversations on the boat. They hadn't talked much. They'd met late in the day, and she'd assumed he was like the other guys: a hockey player sophomore at St. Cloud. Still, she remembered the moment she first saw him.

Augie and Leah had been at the party about two hours when the guys decided to tie all three boats together in the center of the lake. They were silly and tipsy from endless sun and margaritas, and they'd been dancing on the back of the smallest boat when the wave of a passing pontoon made Augie stumble. As she fell backward, someone had caught her. He'd introduced himself as he helped her to her feet, but she'd been too busy laughing with Leah to pay attention. She'd barely looked at him as she replied she was "Allie Von Whatever." It wasn't until the sun shifted and he pulled up his sunglasses that she did a double take, instantly sobering. Those eyes. Penny eyes. That's when she'd made the joke about Abe Lincoln, grabbing his cheeks to look closer as his smile pressed into her palms.

"If that's a compliment, I'll take it," he said, still grinning, their faces inches apart. When the boat rocked again, Augie grabbed his arm for balance.

"Of course it is. Who doesn't like Abe?" Augie didn't add that she had always been obsessed with pennies—that she and her dad used to collect them, constantly searching for glints of copper on the sidewalk.

"All right, Mary Todd. I'll take it." He'd laughed then—that rasp!—and Augie was so charmed that as the boat swayed again, she let herself bump into him. He didn't push her away. Instead, as the music switched to an old middle school hit, he slid both her arms up around his neck, and they started dancing—laughing and joking as he grabbed her hips, spun her around. At one point, she caught sight of Leah over his shoulder mouthing, "SO HOT," and Augie had to smile. It was the most fun she'd had in months. She loved being Allie Von Braun.

Augie wasn't sure how many songs had passed after that, but eventually, they started dancing closer, the space between their bodies dissolving. She felt the heat of his skin on hers, his breath on her neck, and a new pull took over. So, as the boats started toward shore, Augie grabbed Leah and asked for a pep talk. Asked for The Babe's keys. As the sun lowered, the boats docked, and everyone made their way to the beach, she'd led him down to the cabin.

"Look, I'm a babysitter, okay?" he said now, bringing Augie back to present. "I know it's not the sexiest summer job, but it's a good gig. Good money. Like I said, we spend all day at the pool. We're here all the time. So." He lifted his palms as if feeling for rain.

Augie gripped the stair's banister, unnerved by the desire she still felt for him. Micah's face flashed in her mind, which made her want to cry.

"I was never supposed to see you again," she blurted out.

They both went quiet. His ears and neck tinged red.

"Okay. Got it." He pointed a finger at her in a way that told her he was trying to make light of the comment.

Augie's throat stung.

He picked up a backpack and let it hang off one shoulder.

"You know, I really am just here picking up Max and Cooper," he said, turning defensive. "I'm not actually stalking you. Before this week, I had no idea you worked here. That you even lived here." His face twisted as he picked up another bag. "I gotta go. The boys are falling asleep, and the Crawleys want to stay later. It sounds like a real party." He looked to the ceiling as the color drained from Augie's face.

"The Crawleys? Danika and Bill?" she choked out. "That's who you work for?"

"Yeah!" He looked excited, as if this was good news. "Do you know them?"

Augie couldn't help it then. She sat down on the stairs. On top of being here, in her life, at the Club, he had to be working for the *Crawleys*? While Augie had never liked them, since that happy hour, she'd resigned herself to hating Mrs. Crawley. Augie didn't usually throw around the word *hate*, but there was no other way to describe how she'd felt when Mrs. Crawley had bumped into her—yelled at her—and made her drop that tray. It hadn't even been Augie's fault, yet of course, she was the one who'd had to apologize in front of everyone. This was how the Club worked. This was how the world worked.

"I guess I know them, sort of." Augie could not picture Chat living at the mansion they'd built down the block. While you couldn't see their house from the road, photos from Zillow had been passed around. It was magnificent—all glass walls, modern angles, slate roofs. Augie even remembered the price tag: three and a half million.

"But wait, so how long are you in town? With them?"

"I'm only here for the summer. I'll go to Europe this fall, finally, if I can save as much money as I hope. So, don't worry. I'm leaving the whole country at some point. *You'll never see me again.*"

Augie swallowed, recalling the first time he had mentioned Europe. They had just gone down into the boat cabin, and he'd been rambling on about his travel plans. She couldn't fault him for it—given she'd asked if he wanted to go down to the cabin "to talk." She was still endeared when he took it literally, though. She would never forget his face when, in the small, confined cabin—the bed tucked into the alcove behind them, the swivel table to their side—she'd untied her bikini and let her top fall to the floor. Mid-sentence, he'd finally stopped talking.

"Hey, are you okay?" He dropped the backpacks and came toward her, crouching in front of her as he rested his elbows on his knees like a baseball umpire. Again, the smell of him—new car and soap and grass—engulfed her.

Augie held her head in her hands. She knew she was being dramatic, but she wasn't okay. This wasn't okay. No matter how special the day with him had been, she did not need more distractions or stress. What she really needed was to get it together. She could not fail whatever test this was. She couldn't let another man throw her off course.

Augie breathed in, exhaled through her teeth, and stood up so fast she felt lightheaded.

A second later, he reluctantly rose to meet her.

"I'm sorry," Augie said, her tone forceful. She adjusted her bowtie. "I can't do this right now. I'm on the clock, and I guess you are, too, so let's keep to our jobs. Let's pretend the boat never happened."

As soon as the words left her mouth, she knew he was reliving the memory, too. Silence swelled between them.

"Whatever you want." His T-shirt lifted as he scrunched his shoulders to his neck. "You don't have a boyfriend, do you?"

"No," Augie snapped. "No. I do not." She again fought back thoughts of Micah. "Okay, really, I have to go. Let's just keep our distance. I have a lot going on right now. So, good luck with the Crawleys. Have a good summer."

She took a few fast steps up the stairs.

"Hey, wait," he called after her. "I don't want to overstep, or piss you off, but can I at least know your real name?"

Augie slowed to a stop. She turned around, feeling even more humiliated.

"Because you said Allie before, but your name tag says Augie. I'm still Chat, by the way." He smiled softly, teasing yet kind.

Chat. It was almost as weird as her name. She didn't know how she had missed it. She didn't have it in her to explain, so she simply pointed to her name tag. The lights above reflected off the fake gold.

"Okay. It's nice to meet you, Augie." He raised his hand and pretended to shake the air in front of him. "And I'll assume that while Allie lives in New York, you do live here?"

Augie sighed. Normally, she'd be irritated by such a remark, but something about it felt more flirty than snarky; through and through, he seemed like a good person.

"It's okay if you were trying to impress me," he added while picking up the teddy bear and tennis rackets. "I've never been to New York."

Augie turned back to the stairs.

"You're not missing anything," she said as she reached for the railing. Still, a second later, she looked back over her shoulder. "It's nice to meet you, too, Chat."

She hated to realize it was true.

3

Cooper had lost his crayons, and now they were running late.

Normally, this would send Danika into a frenzy—blood heating up, shoulders pinching—but with Chat on her side, everything came easier. As the clock ticked to noon, Danika even laughed aloud as Chat dropped to the ground in a push-up, searching under the bed.

"You said you had them last night?" His voice was half muffled by the carpet.

"Yes, right before bed, like I said," Cooper whined. He stood over Chat while itching the last of the scab on his cheek. Thankfully, it wouldn't scar.

Chat popped up—he was undeniably athletic—and shrugged his shoulders.

"Did you go in the Big Room?"

Cooper said no. Chat had learned by now that Cooper was reliable, particular, and, like Danika, had a sharp memory. He didn't waste his time rushing to the Big Room, the massive greenhouse that held their toys. He ran one hand through his thick black hair.

"It's okay, Coop." Danika stepped inside the doorframe with Max on her hip. "I'm sure you can borrow some today, and we'll get you a new set for tomorrow, okay?"

Cooper's face twisted in irritation. It was Monday, the start of his second week at art camp, and they'd all heard about how he had to draw five pages a day to finish his fairy-tale books on time. The exact right colors so everything would match: "Pool Float" and "Pizza Crust" and "Dandelion." Last week, Cooper and Chat had made a game naming their own colors.

Chat caught Danika's eye from across the room. She could hear both their silent wishes, a held breath between them.

Cooper was kind but headstrong. Determined and meticulous. He knew all the words to every Selena Gomez hit. He was quick to tell you if you'd miscounted your spaces in Candy Land. He refused to wear mismatching colors. It frustrated Bill, the way he was always "on edge," but Danika admired Cooper's attention to detail. Bill wouldn't admit he was also high-strung. Max, on the other hand, was a ball of goofy sweetness.

Cooper huffed and picked up his backpack. "Fine. I'll do the outlines today. Let's go."

Chat and Cooper moved in a flurry from there: whipping down the wide white stairs and through the expansive, marbled kitchen; disappearing into the cedar mudroom. Danika followed, adjusting Max against her body.

"Okay, so. I'll be back in thirty, I'll take Max, and you'll be home from work by five?" Chat asked.

Danika smiled—she was smiling so much lately, it embarrassed her—and set Max down on the ground between them. As she stood, she suddenly worried she'd flashed Chat a full view of cleavage via her loose linen shirt, but he didn't react.

"Right, exactly." Secretly, she reveled in the question—in the way he saw her as a working mom, as someone who'd be home from work by five. It was one more reminder: This summer would be different.

It also helped that Bill was surprisingly at ease with Chat around, especially after they'd played eighteen holes together and Bill confirmed Chat was an exceptional golfer. "That's some goddamn short game," he'd said as they walked into the kitchen one afternoon, sweaty and sunburned from a long day on the course. How odd it was, seeing them together.

In fact, everything with Chat was going so well, Danika was relieved to know she'd made the right decision by hiring him. She'd felt even more relieved when, after that happy hour, she'd again asked Chat if he knew anyone in the town, and he'd assured her he did not.

Still, Danika knew the real reason she felt better about this summer: She was finally going back to work. While Bill had been supportive of her career at first, since kids, he'd wanted her home. His parents, who'd moved to South Carolina to be closer to his sister, were as old-school as they come. Each time they visited Hilton Head, Danika was jarred by their southern country club. It was a whole new level—stricter dress codes, faker faces, more pearls.

Danika had been okay with staying home at first, so wrapped up in her dream of having a family, but, especially during the pandemic, she struggled. She'd never been overly social, but after being alone day in and day out, she'd started to feel, well, *alone*. At least before, the Club had forced her to interact with people. She began to spiral, questioning her choices and self-worth. As a result, she'd told Bill that once life resumed, she wanted to set up an LLC. "But what's the point?" he'd said. She was already working hard. The boys were a handful.

This had been the impetus of their distance. While they'd always led separate lives, in the past few years, they'd splintered. They barely spoke unless it was about the boys. They slept on separate floors. Danika resented Bill, yet, at the same time, she missed him. So, she was ecstatic when, out of nowhere, he approached her about designing the model home for his new housing development, Briar Ridge. She viewed the invitation as an olive branch—a sign he missed her, too.

Her return to work had been the reason for the nanny in the first place. And while she could not have predicted Chat's sudden, remarkable appearance in their lives, she now felt it was kismet. It had been a long time since she believed in such things—fate and destiny, greater powers and all that—but hell, maybe it was time. Life felt better. *She* felt better. Maybe by the end of this summer, she would feel happy again—because she should, shouldn't she? Despite everything, she'd gotten what she wanted. Right?

Briar Ridge was about twenty minutes west and flanked by farmland, but as Bill explained, it was still close to enough golf courses, lakes, and the Cities to be appealing—especially to Minnesota's upper middle class. Plus, buying it right before COVID, when people started fleeing for the suburbs, was only working in his favor.

Danika grew nervous as she got ready. She reminded herself that she was qualified. Even when studying interior design, she knew you could not teach taste. Taste was what she and Bill had most in common. They both loved their home—their mansion of sleek hygge, Scandinavian meets quiet luxury. It was sprawling, modern but soft, filled with white and gray hues and subtle pops of color: dark blue Lafco candles, pale pink geometric prints, waxy green monsteras and silvery eucalyptus. The ceilings were high, crisscrossed with natural wooden beams and skylights, and the whole first floor was wide open, filled with teak tables and Eames chairs and hallways that felt like rooms themselves. She loved all the other spaces, too: the basement with its double-sided fireplace and wraparound couch; the greenhouse playroom that showcased the sky; the massive outdoor patio and pool, surrounded by stones and stainless-steel barbecues. Her bedroom was heaven on earth, a wash of creamy textures and perfectly balanced light. The whole house had an air of effortless elegance, sophisticated charm. She took a moment to appreciate it, staring out at the glimmering kitchen, up through the skylights, soaking in everything she had worked for, everything she had pieced together. Aside from her children, her house was her pride and joy.

Finally, Danika registered the time, picked up Max and his board books, and headed to her closet. Outfit ideas had been playing in her mind, but as she stepped inside the massive, twinkling space, she paced back and forth. She knew she had too many clothes, but Danika had an exceptional memory, and each piece plunged her back to the moment she'd bought it or worn it. It was exhausting the way so many details were painful portals to the past. Nail polish, bonfires, black dresses, BLTs. While you could always work to remember something, you could not make yourself forget.

Now, as her hands moved across the hangers, she paused on a cap-sleeved dress, the one she'd been wearing the day she met Bill. She'd been twenty-four at the time, and she had followed an entry-level design job to Chicago, where, one sweltering afternoon, she stepped into an elevator with a thirty-two-year-old Bill. She remembered the moment clearly: how after admiring each other in the elevator's 360-degree mirrors, as the doors pinged open to the ninth floor of his office building, he'd turned to face her, introduced himself.

By that evening, they were eating steaks at Carmine's. By that night, they were fucking in his room in the Waldorf. And by that morning, after waking to Bill staring at her, he'd told her she was exquisite, an old soul, like him. He'd asked her to marry him. She'd batted the proposal away at first, but the more she thought about it, the more it felt right: They both wanted to settle down to start a family; Bill was a catch.

Of course, they didn't really know each other. And there was no way she could tell him she'd been married before—his family would not approve. Bill himself would not approve. Instead, Danika promised herself to simply start over. Six months later, she was standing beneath the stained-glass windows of the Basilica of Saint Mary, the refracted light like spilled sea glass across the floor.

By the time Bill directed them to Aldon Lakes, there was no turning back.

Danika eventually decided on a navy dress. It was professional yet casual. Elevated yet approachable. She wore the diamond studs Bill had given her, along with the amber pendant necklace she wore every day. She knew she looked nice, but staring into the mirror while she twisted her hair, Danika frowned, her lips curving down around the bobby pins. Recently, she'd started to notice the first real lines and spots of age in her face. She knew it was inevitable, and that there were ways to slow the process, but it was still terrifying to realize she would not be the same ubiquitous kind of beautiful forever. Now, at thirty-two—the age Bill had been when they'd met—this truth had started to sink in.

Danika was glad to hear the whir of the garage door then—to know Chat was back from drop-off. She took a breath before turning to Max, his mouth opening in a spitty smile.

"Come on, bubs." She squatted as she smoothed her hair and picked him up. "Let's go find Mr. Chat." Her cheeks warmed with anticipation as she headed down the stairs. She hoped he'd tell her she looked nice—or at least, that he would think it.

Danika blasted the AC as she drove. She wanted to arrive crisp and cool, rather than succumb to the humid heat. Having grown up everywhere from North Carolina to DC to Germany, she was none too pleased by these Minnesota summers. Everyone else loved them—the lakes, pools, escape from the winter tundra—but she enjoyed the snow and ice, the way sharp air could fill your lungs, shock you alive.

Danika was glad to have learned this about herself. She was glad to have lived so many places, too. Her whole life, she'd tell people she was from different cities based on where they were from or what might most impress them. For example, with Holly Fravel, she'd claimed Monterey because Holly was from LA. She hadn't bothered to explain her family had only lived there for two years—and that the army houses on the Presidio were some of the oldest and mustiest of all. Let Holly imagine Carmel.

The army housing from her childhood was one of the main reasons she could never live in a place like Briar Ridge. Both felt too stereotypically suburban with their rows of generic houses and little to zero privacy. Danika's mother had especially hated living on base—pressed up against senior officials, forced to play nice and kiss ass. Danika's father had been a staff sergeant (though Danika told everyone he retired a lieutenant colonel), and her mother resented having to suck up to the women who wore their husband's rank as their own—the WOs, or "Wives Of." Danika realized later in life this was probably why her mom became such a good decorator. Even if their home was small and standard, she was creative, thrifty. Too bad she was such a bitch.

Danika checked the GPS, surprised she was close. The development didn't feel as far away as she'd expected. She figured this would help in appealing to all the families who pretended they wanted proximity to Minneapolis—yet really just wanted a Big Room and fake-wood floors and a fenced-in yard for their goldendoodle.

Danika slowed as she approached the complex and, as instructed, took a right on Poplar Street (in a move both clever and tacky, all the streets were named for trees). Then, finally, there it was: the model home glowing above her like a prize. The driveway was long, and as she curved along the asphalt, she felt relieved. The house had a wide wraparound porch, neat black shutters, and neutral, authentic-looking cobblestone. It didn't feel as cheap as expected.

Danika's relief quickly snapped to irritation when she noticed three other cars parked outside in addition to Bill's Porsche. Bill had implied it'd be only them, that they'd go for a drink at LÅK after. Danika parked behind the M5 and killed the ignition, squinting at the license plate in front of her: "JSH MKE." She groaned.

In addition to never trusting anyone with two first names, Danika thought Joshua Mike was slimy. He'd made millions in private equity, married into the Cargill family, and, after his wife died of cancer, inherited more money than he—or anyone—deserved. He went wild from there. Quite literally. He bought the Minnesota Wild hockey team, the famous Lake Minnetonka marina (now aptly "Mike's Marina"), and the marina's accompanying restaurant, The Manor. He was often drunk and crass, and Danika didn't think anyone genuinely liked him, but with his money and power, he still had lots of "friends."

He had a particular affection for Danika. He always followed her around the Club, asking about their house, their cabin, their architect—who'd grown famous over the years. He invited them to *his* house frequently, too, bragging about his Himalayan salt room, living green walls, the marble he had imported from Italy. Danika knew he was fishing for a reciprocal invite, but she refused. On several occasions, he'd also told her she was the most gorgeous woman in the room.

"Danika, darling," Bill called from across the living room as she pushed through the front door. He stood in front of a huge wall of windows that revealed the sloping backyard and, down the hill, about ten other houses.

The other three men turned to her. She recognized them all. Along with Joshua Mike, there was Malcolm Mitchell (Mallory Harrison's husband) and Wyatt Greene (Robin's husband). Instantly, she felt thrown; while Bill had mentioned he'd partnered with shareholders, she had not imagined this group. Her face went hot with embarrassment as she remembered how she'd bragged to Mallory and Robin about the job at Briar Ridge.

"Malcolm, Wyatt, Joshua." She walked to each of them, gliding confidently as she shook their hands hard. "It's great to see you all."

"As you can see, we have the A-team." Bill gestured to the group.

Danika grimaced. Why hadn't Bill told her who exactly was involved? Bill and Wyatt—despite being golf rivals with a twenty-year age difference—were old friends. Their families went way back. Bill *had* explained how expensive this project was, that he needed investors with deep pockets. So on second thought, it did make sense to Danika that here, around them, were three of the richest members at the Club.

"Danika, darling indeed." Joshua Mike leaned down to kiss her on both cheeks. "Did you have fun at the wedding?"

Danika leaned against the counter, folding her hands on top of each other. "I did, it was lovely. I hope Miriam had a good time," she said to Malcolm, Miriam's new cousin-in-law.

"Yes, absolutely. Paid for it yesterday, though," Malcolm said. "Irish flu, as they say."

"Speak for yourself," Joshua Mike cackled. "I felt great. That Dom went down easy."

"It's nice to see you, Danika," Wyatt said. He had always been a gentle soul. He wasn't bad to look at, either, with that thick, silver hair and perfect square jaw.

"You too." She dipped her head to him, then looked out to the room. "So, this is it? I have to say, it's nicer than the photos. I think we have a lot to work with."

"Absolutely," Bill said. "Good space, right? Good air."

Joshua Mike came around the counter, standing next to her. "You think you can work your magic?" He crossed his arms. "I've got to say, Vicki was very impressed, and jealous, when we came over last year. Remember that night? That last tourney of the season when we forced our way back with Mr. Hole-in-One?" He jabbed his finger toward Bill. "God, that was a good night. We haven't been back at your place since. What gives?"

Danika remembered that night—as much as she'd tried to put it out of her mind. The men had shown up unannounced, drunk and wild after a tournament, piling half-thawed steaks onto the poolside grill and blasting "Country Roads." Joshua had even invited his girlfriend.

Bill nodded politely. "She'll work her magic indeed. But yes, absolutely, we'll have you all over soon. Count on it."

Danika's blood ticked up a notch.

"Perfect," Joshua Mike said, still with that stupid grin. "Although Vicki's long gone. I'm sure Jackie will be just as impressed. You'll like her, D. She's got style."

He wiggled his eyebrows, and Danika felt a wave of disgust. Was he really calling her *D*?

Bill clapped his hands. "Okay, so, darling, shall we take a proper tour? Gentlemen, you're welcome to stay or go. It was great to see you all. I appreciate your time."

To Danika's relief, they all mumbled excuses and made their way to the door. Danika ignored another muffled call from Joshua Mike as she moved into the dining room.

As they left, Danika pressed her hand to the cool, freshly painted wall. "It's nice," she said to Bill, the house now quiet, the air tinged awkward.

"Right? I knew you were expecting worse."

"Well, yes. But it's wonderful. Thank you. For not setting me up for failure."

"Oh, you're never one to fail."

He was right. She wanted to tell him more—how she was going to aim for a commercial version of their style; how she was going to give each room an exclamation point; how, as always, she would get the lighting right. Still, she held her tongue. She didn't want to look overenthused or flippant. Despite his current mood, things were still off between them. She wasn't so delusional as to think they'd fall back into some fantasy, but still. Bill used to love to show her off, to wine and dine her, and lately, it seemed as if he was living on a separate island. It made Danika feel cast aside, which made her feel needy, which—in turn—made her feel pathetic.

"Remind me, how many bedrooms?" She walked to the staircase.

"Four." Bill pulled his phone from his pocket.

"Right." Her heels clapped each step as she climbed toward the mezzanine balcony. She'd always liked those—how they conjured images of Romeo and Juliet.

"But, hey, *D.*" Bill craned up at her, teasing. Danika paused and stared down at him, feeling an unexpected flash of affection for him. "We'll still get a drink after?"

"Yes, sure, *B*," she said as she continued down the hall, reveling in the sound of Bill's laughter echoing off all the empty walls.

4

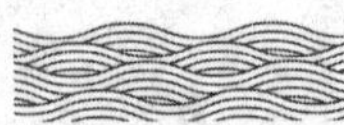

New York, January

Augie often wished she could go back to that first week in New York and skip the moment when she first met Micah entirely.

"Augie?" he had said as he opened the door to his and Julia's penthouse, the massive apartment spreading out behind him. Augie had never been in a penthouse. She hadn't even understood what "PH" stood for when she'd gotten on the elevator. "Am I saying that right?"

Julia and Micah had invited her for dinner. Julia was Leah's second cousin from Boston. While she was fifteen years younger than Robin, they both worked in finance and were close. Julia's husband, Micah, was the creative director at the ad agency where Augie would be working; he, by way of Julia and Robin, had been the one to secure Augie the job.

Before that night, Augie and Micah had only talked over email—Augie was interested in brand strategy, so he'd linked her with a different director—and Augie had somewhat forgotten about him up until he opened the door. He was undeniably handsome. Even in his early forties, he looked youthful and striking, tall and strong with muscles visible through his faded T-shirt. His hair was buzzed, and his eyes were a piercing blue. Even as Augie shook off her coat and the cold air, then shook his hand, she felt numb.

Julia had been on the phone when Augie stepped past him into the apartment. She saw her in the kitchen, unloading the dishwasher, still in her work clothes. She had the same blond hair as Robin and Leah, and she looked like the quintessential "Woman Who Does It All" as she put away plates while speaking Mandarin. It had all been overwhelming: the foreign language, the beauty of them both, the penthouse itself. Everything was huge and shiny, a modern floor plan filled with low neon furniture, smooth white carpet and walls, a chair that looked like it had dreadlocks. Beyond, skyscrapers and water towers offered a postcard view of city life.

"Are you settling in okay?" Micah had asked, an air of amusement about him as he hung up her coat. Julia had waved as they moved into the kitchen and he reached for a bottle of wine. She mouthed "Sorry" before disappearing into another room. Micah twisted off the cork.

Augie wasn't sure whether to stand or sit on a stool, so she hovered by the gleaming countertop. She told him she was settling in well, thank you, grasping for confidence.

"My apartment is a little funky. But I like it," she said, glad to have something to ramble about. She told him all about the one-bedroom she was subletting from an artist who only used recycled materials, which meant that while her bedroom was lovely and clean, the living room was packed with junk. There were piles upon piles of boxes, craft supplies—trash.

"Well, as long as it's not filled with rats." Micah smiled with all his teeth. "You're starting with Cheryl on Monday, right? The lottery account? Those guys need your help. They're so out of the loop."

Augie was comforted by his words. She'd been briefed on the

project: The New Jersey Lottery's clientele was dying out, and they needed help getting young people to play. She didn't want to admit she knew nothing about the lottery—the only person she'd ever known to play was her friend Teuta, who had won tens of thousands from a scratch card years ago—but she figured that was the point of market research.

"You'll be a good addition, no matter what," Micah said, as if reading her mind. He handed her a bulbous glass of red wine. "A breath of fresh air, if you will. Cheers."

"Cheers." Augie lifted her wine. He held her eye contact longer than expected—his eyes searching hers intently—and Augie felt the first wave of intimacy pass between them. Their eyes were the exact same shade of blue.

"You know, the Europeans say always make sure you hold eye contact when cheers-ing. Otherwise, it's seven years of bad sex."

Augie blushed, glass hovering at her lips, the word *sex* hanging in the air. Later, she'd come back to this exchange. She'd wonder if he'd been noticing their irises, too—how it was like looking in a mirror.

Micah was charming. Clever. Witty. He asked about her New York bucket list, if she'd ever ridden the ferry, been to MoMA. He gave her a list of restaurants and bars. Every time she spoke, he seemed to really listen, and his insightful comebacks made her feel smart and interesting in a way she hadn't before. She kept laughing, impressed by her own banter, this version of herself—and by the time Julia emerged, Augie felt as if his wife was intruding. But she told herself to grow up. That whatever chemistry or attraction she'd felt radiating from Micah was in her imagination. She was being immature. Everything was harmless—they were all adults.

* * *

After the Saturday wedding, Augie was glad she had Sunday and Monday off, but she was disappointed Leah wouldn't be back from her cabin until Monday afternoon. All Augie wanted to do that morning after seeing Chat was go to Leah's pool and rehash the night.

Still, after the flurry of text messages Augie had sent Leah, first at the wedding and then after getting home at three a.m., Leah called as soon as she'd woken up.

"That is some crazy shit," she agreed as Augie told her every detail. Or at least every detail except for how attracted Augie still was to Chat; she didn't want to admit that to herself. "I feel bad," Leah groaned. "Here I was trying to get you one hot bone to get you out of your head, and now we have this mess. It is kind of funny, though. Kinky. A manny!"

"Yes, obviously, this is all your fault," Augie joked. "But, seriously, I'm afraid to see him again. I need to focus on applications. And can you believe he's with the *Crawleys*?"

"Danika probably treats him like the pool boy. 'Chat, go fetch me a Chardonnay! Chat, take off your shirt!' Poor guy. We'll make a plan tomorrow. Don't overthink it."

Augie said she'd do her best as Leah apologized and said she had to go—that her cousins were dragging her to the lake. Augie said no problem. She knew Leah had family in town from Chicago, which was why she'd stayed at the cabin since the party. That, and because she didn't start work until the next week. Not that it was real a job. Leah was doing yet another unpaid internship at the Hotel Harrison, working as Mallory Harrison's right-hand woman. Augie tried not to resent the fact that she had the option to work for free.

When Augie woke up Monday morning, she looked forward to Leah returning and finally spending all afternoon at the pool. She pushed herself out of bed and headed toward the smell of coffee.

"Couldn't sleep in?" Her mom, Lilly, sat at the breakfast nook with her laptop, wearing her typical teaching outfit: black slacks and a silk tank top. While she never bought trendy clothes, she was so naturally beautiful with her shiny dark hair, angel wing lips, and perfectly symmetrical face, everything looked good on her.

"Curse of a day off." Augie poured coffee as Lilly pointed beyond her.

"Byrek's on the counter, by the way. I went to Hyla this morning."

Augie opened the box of cheesy, flaky pastries. She loved the Balkan delicacy from their friends' bakery down the street. She stuffed a piece in her mouth.

"Zami and Teuta were asking about you. You should go say hi."

Augie sat down, grateful she was chewing and didn't have to explain she wasn't ready to face them. They'd thrown her such a nice goodbye party.

Augie folded her knees up on her chair and soaked in the green of the backyard. Their house was small, a two-bedroom right off 394, but Augie loved the space, this table especially. It was cozy—exactly the feeling a nook should evoke.

Lilly tilted her laptop screen down and raised her mug. Augie lifted her mug to clink, one of their rituals. When she was younger, she'd become obsessed with saying cheers. She wasn't sure where she first heard it—probably in her dad's restaurant, a seafood dive in Camden—but however it happened, it had stayed with her.

"Are you headed to Leah's pool? Or Hannah's? It's going to be *extra* hot today."

"Leah's. She should be back soon." Augie rotated her mug in her hands. When they'd first moved and her mom had chosen Aldon Lakes for its incredible public schools, she hadn't realized the schools were a result of the town's wealth. They'd both been aghast by Augie's friends' mansions—all their lakefront views and pools.

"I swear, every summer, they say, 'This is the hottest summer on record.' But it really does feel like it," Augie groaned.

"Thanks, global warming. Maybe I should be teaching science and not *Gatsby*."

"Whatever. *Gatsby* is as essential as the globe."

"Right? All hail the green light." Lilly slid her papers and laptop into her tote bag, and Augie felt comforted as she noticed the familiar doodles on the back of a page—the same flowers and stars she sketched when daydreaming. It was one of many traits they had in common—including how they both laughed in a downward scale; loved all the same books, *Little Women* and *The Bell Jar* and every Harry Potter; and said "oofda" ironically. Even if Augie looked like her dad, she was glad that deep down, she was more like her mom.

"So, your summer class is Monday, Wednesday, Friday? Is it in Pillsbury Hall now?"

"Yup. Finally finished the construction. It's so fancy. You'll have to come see."

Augie nodded. She didn't want to go back. It had been strange enough to circle her mom at the University of Minnesota in undergrad. Not that Augie had a choice, given the perk of free tuition from her mom's job.

"I had requested Tuesday, Thursday, but alas. It's okay." Lilly leaned over to buckle her sandals. "I'm only teaching the first two sessions, then I'll be all in on research. We have a good summer team, too. It's not too bad. And I can help you with your résumé anytime." She checked her watch. "Okay, shoot. I have to go." She kissed Augie on the head, slung her tote over her shoulder. "You'll be home for dinner? I'm making pesto."

Augie said of course. Even in high school, she'd always been home for dinner. "Sounds great. Love you. Have a good class."

Alone at the table, Augie felt even more unsettled. While her mom had been supportive through the fallout of her job, assuring Augie she'd find something else and couldn't have controlled the agency merger (which Augie had blamed for her firing, instead of admitting the truth), Augie felt horrible. She knew her mom had once dreamed of living in New York. While she didn't talk about it often, Augie had learned that after she'd finished graduate school at Bowdoin, she'd hoped to work at a publishing house in the city. That was the summer she got pregnant. Instead, she'd stayed in Maine, married, gotten a job at the local college, helped with the restaurant. It wasn't until years after her dad left them that she even started applying to better teaching jobs, which landed them in Minnesota.

Augie was glad when her phone suddenly chimed, the screen filling with Leah's name and the words En route!!!

IT WAS A bright day, and Augie soaked in the winking waves and boats bobbing in the distance as she curved along the bays to Leah's. While she couldn't stop thinking about Chat, she was glad to be out of the house, passing the mansions that felt like old friends: the Lincoln Log castle with its four floors and flagpole; the cottage-core palace with its wavy roof and six-car garage; and Augie's favorite, the pale yellow mansion that looked like a hotel in New England. The homes you could only see from the lake were even more sprawling and jaw-dropping—one could watch endless videos online of Lake Minnetonka estates—but Augie enjoyed these roadside homes all the same.

It was busy for a Monday. Everyone seemed to be outside, escaping the heat and carrying colorful beach bags along sidewalks—especially as she passed Mike's Marina and its sister restaurant, The Manor. Augie and Leah tried to avoid The Manor. Crowds filtered in and out on boats and Jet Skis all day long. People were often coming from Big Island, too, the nearby party spot where everyone anchored their boats and turned the shallow water into a drunken rave. It unsettled Augie, how frivolously these big machines were treated on the lake, how people pretended BUIs weren't real. Everyone seemed to ignore the reality that there were over a hundred boating accidents each summer.

Augie rolled down the window, enjoying the sun on her face, and wondered what Leah would tell her to do about Chat. Augie was notoriously bad at making decisions, so afraid to make the wrong choice that she'd get lost in a web of reasoning—even when ordering from a menu. As Leah said, she was bad at following her gut. Leah was the pragmatic one.

With Micah, though, Augie hadn't been thinking at all. Now, she hated that no one could know the truth, especially not Leah. Or Robin. They would never speak to her again. She was grateful Robin was up at the cabin today; she wouldn't have to face her yet.

Augie whipped her car around the Greenes' driveway (barely reacting to the white-and-black house that spread the length of a football field), parked, and rushed around back to the pool. She felt instantly better as she dropped her bag on her favorite lounger, the water shining like ice before her, its infinity edge dissolving into the lake view beyond.

"There she is, the manny magnet!" Leah emerged from the basement carrying towels.

It was cathartic to recount everything again as they settled into their usual tanning positions, heat draping across their bodies. This was at least one perk of being back: her favorite routine.

"So do you think I should ignore him?" Augie finally said, flopping her arms on the sides of the lounger. "Do you think that's even possible if they're at the Club all the time, like he said? I don't want it to be weird. I don't want to be a jerk, either."

"Oh, you're never a jerk." Leah sat up. "Okay, don't hate me, but I have to confess something." She grimaced as she adjusted her swimsuit straps, exhaled, and twisted to Augie. "The Babe . . . Danny . . . asked me for your number Wednesday. He said the guy you were flirting with at the party asked *him* for it. It must have been after Chat saw you at the happy hour."

"What?" Augie sat up fast, matching Leah.

"I didn't know the details! I swear." Leah raised her hands. "You know Danny's clueless, and Chat didn't explain. I figured he just wanted your number to keep in touch. That you were that good in bed." Leah poked Augie's side. "Obviously, I said he couldn't have it."

Augie was sweating. "Did he say anything else?"

"No, it was only a quick thing, seriously. Danny did say he gave Chat *my* number in case he wanted to ask me directly for yours, but Chat never texted, so I figured he got the hint. I really didn't think he'd pop back up like this. I'm sorry, though. I should have told you earlier."

Augie reclined back into the cushions. Here Leah was apologizing for a tiny white lie while Augie was hiding so much worse.

"It's okay. It's just odd, right? What are the chances?" She stared up at the sun. "Of course he's working for the Crawleys, of literally everyone. Mrs. Crawley is such a nightmare."

"Indeed." Leah cleaned her sunglasses with her towel. "I honestly can't imagine him with Danika every day."

"Do you really think she treats him like a pool boy, like you said? Do you really think she thinks he's hot? Do you think he thinks *she's* hot? I mean, she *is* hot. I'm grossed out." This had been bothering Augie more and more over the past two days: the fact that Mrs.

Crawley was only ten years older than they were—that Micah had been almost twenty years older than Augie. She hated to imagine Mrs. Crawley and Chat flirting. She knew she was a hypocrite.

"Yes, they're all objectively hot. But I doubt she's after him. It'd be too Mrs. Robinson. Too on the nose. Humiliating. Nah. I'm sure she just likes having someone to boss around. I don't think Bill gives her a whole lot of attention. My mom says she feels bad she's so closed off. Has such a stick up her ass."

Augie tapped her fingers over her stomach, feeling her silent laughter. She always loved hearing Leah say anything bad about members. It was always the ones who deserved it.

"I don't know. Whatever." Augie turned her head, the cushion warm against her cheek. She wished she had a better way to describe her true feelings: excitement, panic, shame. She hoped her feelings of attraction wouldn't be linked with self-loathing for the rest of her life.

It went quiet, and Leah lay down, too. Augie watched her adjust on her chair, and her eyes instinctively landed on the white-ink tattoo of her late brother's initials on her wrist. The way Leah moved around the loss was like the tattoo itself: You couldn't often see her grief, but the pain was there. There had been an investigation after the boating accident, but despite the money the Greenes poured into the case, it wrapped quickly. Law enforcement focused on the evidence and the clear story it painted: Nineteen-year-old Lyle and his friend Grant were out drinking with teammates at The Manor at the end of training camp, and while the other boys left before midnight—with alibis to prove it—Lyle and Grant had stayed until close, after two a.m. Everyone knew Lyle was obsessed with speedboats, and that the new $400,000 Cigarette X42 had just arrived in the marina next door. The lockbox that held the key had been broken into. The boat had crashed into the railroad bridge dividing Crystal and Smith bays. The boys were thrown from the boat. Both suffered blunt force trauma to the head and drowned.

Of course, Augie hadn't known this when she first met Leah. It had happened three years before she moved to Aldon Lakes. Augie would never forget the night Leah told her. They were having a sleepover, and Augie had made the mistake at dinner of asking where her oldest brother went to college—having noticed all the pictures of him, his handsome square jaw and movie star smile. He looked like Leah's dad. The entire table went quiet.

Later that night, in the safety of the dark, Leah had let everything out. She showed Augie the shoebox she kept under her bed filled with printed articles about the accident, the investigation reports, photos of Lyle from his summer training camp—the last of him alive—and all the birthday cards he'd written her. He never would have stolen a boat, she insisted. He was the kind of guy who never let her cheat at board games. He always bought everyone ice cream. He never forgot a birthday. But what could she do? The investigation was over. Her brother was gone.

Leah didn't bring him up anymore, but Augie sometimes wished she would. She knew it still tugged at her friend, that neither Leah nor her family had real closure. Leah sometimes cried after drinking too much, her buried feelings surfacing, and Augie wished she could do more to help. Instead, Leah always seemed to be the one helping her.

"Okay, so here's what we do about Chat," Leah said as she moved her hair from one shoulder to the other. "Nothing. I think your instincts to ignore him are right. I mean, you don't have to pretend he doesn't exist . . . just be friendly and professional if you see him at the Club. It's not worth anything more complicated. It will only stress you out."

Augie rolled in her lips, disappointed. Despite everything, part of her had hoped Leah would tell her to go for it.

"I will ask Mallory about him, though. Chitty Chatty Bang Bang. I'm too curious."

Augie stretched out her legs and bounced her knees. Mallory Harrison knew everyone and everything in Aldon Lakes. She probably did have answers.

"Just promise not to tell me anything. You're right. I need to forget him."

"My lips are sealed." Leah pretended to lock her lips and throw away the key.

The gesture sent a pang through Augie's heart. She was again reminded that she was lying to Leah, building a chasm between them. The tension in her chest ballooned into guilt.

"I'm baking," Augie said, suddenly hot and overwhelmed. She pushed up off her chair.

"All right, but beware. Robin said they were keeping it colder this year. She read all about how polar plunging was just oh so good for you." She danced her hands in the air.

"Oh, it can't be that bad." Augie walked to the shallow end, dipping in a toe before inching down the first step. Instantly, goose bumps climbed over her whole body as her shoulders scrunched to her neck.

"I'll take that as a yes?"

"Colder? This is freaking glacial." She hugged her elbows closer before splashing Leah. Leah screamed, but within seconds, she bounced up, threw her sunglasses on her chair, and headed toward the deep end.

"*That's* your problem." Leah raised her hands in a perfect V, the candy blue sky behind her, her pink suit glittering in the sun. "You just have to jump."

AUGIE COULDN'T STOP thinking about Chat.

She tried to train herself. Every time he popped into her head, she asked herself a math question: *What's 79 times 30? 145 plus 912?* It was a habit she had before presentations or getting shots at the doctor's or taking off in an airplane. Usually, it was an easy way to switch her focus.

She'd looked for him at the Club all week, but there was no sign of him. It almost seemed like she'd made him up. Regardless, she promised herself that if and when she ran into him again, she would be purely friendly and professional, as Leah had advised. She'd be *normal.*

It helped that she was busy. The luncheons all went long, and the parties were all crazy, everyone hyped up on summer, cocktails, and AC. She was relieved Aida had assigned her the Saturday swim meet instead of the wedding. She thought she could make plans with Leah for the evening, but when she called, Leah had been reluctant to tell her she was going to a party. While their friends knew Augie was back, Augie hadn't seen them. She didn't want to answer any questions about New York. She'd felt so proud—and a little smug—to leave.

The day of the swim meet, Augie sat under the gazebo at the lower snack station—grateful it was one of the rare positions where the staff was allowed to sit—and yawned. It was only eight a.m., but everyone had arrived early, rushing to claim chairs and set up tents for the kids. Parents took the sport too seriously, but her job was easy enough. Augie was also glad she got to wear the outdoor uniform for meets: blue polo, khaki shorts, tan tennis shoes. The polo matched her eyes, and years ago, Leah had given her a pair of old Coach sneakers. Augie felt more confident in that uniform. She always felt the members registering her expensive shoes, unnerved.

Augie stared across the pool and gave TC a thumbs-up. Despite the early morning, setup had been easy. The only snag was the bees. The day before, there'd been yet another poolside birthday party—this time with a cotton candy machine—and sticky, webbed sugar was everywhere. The bees were having a field day. Augie had never been bothered by bees, but she scooted her chair to the side as a few flew into her domain. "I come in peace," she whispered while they buzzed about her feet.

"Could we get two bagels and two waters, please?" she heard a second later. Even amid her distraction, the voice sounded familiar, and when she sat up, there he was. Finally. A reminder that she wasn't crazy. That he was real. Relief and excitement flooded her body.

Chat smiled wider, his cheeks folding like parentheses. She didn't know what it was about him—one sentence, and they were back in their own little world.

"You scared me," she said, her tone light—and, she hated to admit: flirty.

"Were you talking to the bees?" The creases around his smile deepened.

"They have all the good gossip."

She soaked in his laughter as she studied his tan Modest Mouse T-shirt and red gym shorts. "Where are the boys?" she asked, trying to be nonchalant.

"Cooper's over there with the Birch kids, and Max is with his mom. They're coming later. We ran out of time to eat breakfast this morning, so here we are."

Augie picked up her pencil, remembering his order.

"And look"—he lowered his voice as he dipped his head to her—"I know we're keeping our distance, but it's good to see you. Even if you were never supposed to see me again." He studied her, repeating her words from the night of the wedding. "So if this isn't okay, I get it. I can grab stuff from the other station. It's no worries."

Augie ignored the warmth in her face as she took two wrapped bagels and cream cheese from a cooler. *Be normal*, she reminded herself, reaching for the waters.

"It's all good. Is this everything? Do you need anything else?" Without thinking, she scribbled the Crawleys' member number. Over the years, she'd accidentally memorized lots of member numbers—especially easy ones like theirs: 9119. It was basically an emergency.

Chat loosened and angled away from her, leaning against the table as he looked out at the pool. The sun bounced across the water's surface, trapping wiggly rhombuses of light.

"So, are these meets a big deal? Olympic status or what?" As he faced away from her, Augie noticed he'd had a haircut since the wedding—the hair on the back of his neck was buzzed so short, it looked like black velvet. She had the sudden urge to touch it.

"I guess." She scooted forward and folded her arms. He smelled the same as always and it was so intoxicating, she pulled back as if burned. "All very important. All very official. There's even a podium at the end."

"Man, it's too much. The Crawleys' calendar is so packed, I'm tired *for* Max and Cooper. I swear I've never seen so many activities in my life: swim meets, karate, art camp. All I ever did was play hockey and sneak onto the golf course."

"Gotta make sure they get into a good college." As he turned back to her, Augie again thought of the boat, the taste of his mouth. *What's 112 times 3?*

"Seriously. It's crazy. Like that even matters, at the end of the day.

I mean, for me, college was honestly kind of a waste of time. I should have at least taken the gap year I wanted. I shouldn't have listened to my dad."

Augie tapped her pencil on the table, pausing as she remembered the St. Cloud guys from the boat. Most were sophomores. "Aren't you still in college?"

"Me? No, no, no way. I graduated this spring, thankfully. It was miserable. I did the last two years online . . . COVID, fun . . . and I also had to quit hockey. It's kind of a long story."

He seemed melancholy, and while Augie felt a little bad, she also felt defensive. She had loved college—pandemic and all. Switching to online classes had even allowed her to graduate a semester early. College was the last time she'd felt like a success.

"Well, I don't know. I don't think you can say college is a waste of time. Although don't get me wrong, I do agree these activities, the whole application process, pressure"—she gestured to the meet—"can be a bit much."

Chat bobbed his head back and forth.

"Okay, but bear with me for a sec," he finally said. "Because I've been thinking a lot about this lately: I just think it's kind of crazy to act like college is the only path forward. My dad was so insane about it. He was always telling me to be realistic, that if I wanted to travel like I said I did, I had to be smart about it. Get a scholarship, play hockey, save money. Then go explore. Do this and this and this. But it's not that simple. You can kill yourself trying to do the right things, and sometimes, it still doesn't work out." He pushed on his jaw with the back of his hand. "I know it seems dramatic. I guess I'm just frustrated. I tried to 'be realistic,' to use hockey as my ticket to Europe, the international leagues, but even though I was close, it didn't go my way."

His face fell.

"All I'm saying is I wish I'd gone off script earlier. That I hadn't listened to anyone. But I'm going to travel now, so, that's something." He shrugged one shoulder. "Thank you for listening to my new life perspective," he joked, leaning down. "It's copyrighted."

Augie tried to smile, but everything he was saying hit a nerve—and mostly because it made sense. She had done everything right, too.

"Okay, but what's the alternative?" she heard herself say. "You skip college and bum around the world with no education? You have to follow at least some rules. Make at least some plans." While she hadn't intended to argue, she felt if she could just win this debate, nothing he was saying could be true.

"Maybe." Chat looked amused. He stretched his fingers against the table, leaning down on them. "I don't know. Who knows where I'd be if I'd done what I wanted from the start? I wouldn't be *here*, that's for sure."

A lifeguard blew a whistle, a group of kids splashed into the pool, and Augie felt suddenly embarrassed by her surroundings—as if she were responsible for the "here."

"Yeah, I guess. I just don't think you can say college is a waste of time." Her mouth was dry. "Even if things don't go as you hope, even if you fail. It's okay to make mistakes. You need a degree to get a job. And you need a job to make money, right? Trust me, I'm not saying you need country club, megamansion, Range Rover money. But still. There's some reality to reality."

Chat went quiet as he looked out to the parking lot. Augie felt desperate as she waited for him to say something, the pencil sweaty in her grip.

He paused. "I do kind of like driving the Range Rover."

Relieved, she leaned back and used one hand to smooth her ponytail, her hair hot on her palm from the sun. "I prefer the 3 Series."

"This is a weird world, I'll give you that. People are *rich* rich. I'm still getting used to it. I guess it doesn't faze you anymore."

"I guess."

"You've also probably gotten to know the members pretty well by now, too, huh? Have you been here a long time? You know the Greenes, Crawleys?" He paused. "Joshua Mike?"

Augie felt confused by his tone, which felt suddenly unnatural—but before she could respond, a trail of bees zoomed between them.

"Oh, shit." Chat waved an arm as another swarm whooshed past.

"Oh, god." Augie pushed away, her chair falling as she stood. And then—because she deserved it, she'd later tell herself—she felt a searing pain on the back of her neck.

"I knew that would happen." She bent forward in pain as Chat rushed around the table. Before she could fight him, she felt his fingers against her neck. It was strange how quickly pain could be displaced by want.

"Hold still."

Augie sensed his body behind her, and she wanted to close the inches between them, but she forced herself not to move.

"It's best to get the stinger out right away. I see it, don't move."

Slowly, Augie felt a growing pressure, a quick pinch. The air went cold as Chat moved away, holding up the stinger.

"Got it," he said proudly. "You okay?"

They were both behind the table now, anchoring the spread of snacks and drinks. Augie ran her hand over her neck, feeling the swollen mound. She felt pathetic, flustered, and suffused by an almost nauseating need for Chat to touch her again.

"You know, bees die as soon as they sting, so at least you won."

Augie's throat tightened, a reaction that did not stem from the sting itself. "I'm good."

"You sure?" Chat flicked the stinger onto the ground. "Let me see." He reached to the table to grab one of the waters she'd removed from the cooler. "Come here."

The bottle was cool and crisp as Chat pressed it to her neck, and Augie was disappearing into the bliss of the cold and the closeness of Chat when, out of nowhere, he lurched away, the bottle dropping between them. She stepped forward to regain her balance, grabbing at her wet skin. She watched in confusion as Chat rushed to the other side of the table.

"Sorry." He gathered the food. "I hope you're okay. I have to go. She has rules about being . . . distracted, at the Club—when I'm with the boys." He winced and raised a shoulder as Augie saw what he was talking about: Across the pool, Mrs. Crawley and Max opened the gate.

"Keep icing." He backed away. "It was nice to see you, Augie. Really. I'll see you."

Augie couldn't resist watching him—them. Mrs. Crawley looked even more stunning than usual. She wore a black linen romper, a large straw hat, and designer sunglasses Augie knew cost more than a full week of work. Her dark blond hair was loose and wavy, her smile paper white as Chat reached out and took Max from her. Augie watched their mouths move and noticed Chat gesture to Cooper with the Birch kids while raising the bagels—an explanation.

As the meet continued, Augie stared down at the table, the snacks, her job. *You're fine,* she whispered, willing herself not to look up. She was glad when Mallory Harrison and her daughter, Gigi, suddenly appeared, asking for granola bars, forcing her to be cheerful.

Augie tried to ignore the pull of Chat and Mrs. Crawley across the pool, but she couldn't quell her curiosity. What rules had he been talking about? Why did he seem so indebted to her? Augie couldn't wait to talk to Leah about it. Maybe Mrs. Crawley really did keep him in a cage.

It all bothered Augie on a more personal level, too. It felt like he had chosen Mrs. Crawley over her. She knew that was ridiculous—babysitting was his job, and Augie had heard about how Cooper had gone missing at the start of summer—but it still made her feel second rate. They had finally been talking. Touching. Shouldn't he have wanted to stay?

Stop, stop, stop, Augie scolded herself. It was for the best that he'd left. She was working, too. *Don't look up. What's 49 times 12?*

She only made it three more math problems before, finally, as she lifted a piece of ice to her swollen neck, she also lifted her eyes.

It was unfair how beautiful Mrs. Crawley looked, then and always. She was a stock standard model of beauty: tall, curves in the right places, but she also had something unique about her, an extra-perfect dimension to her eye to nose to mouth ratio—a face like a well-cut diamond. Augie felt a growing sense of envy and disdain as she watched her settle into her pool chair while Chat brought Cooper and Max to the tadpole pool. She looked mesmerizing as she rubbed sunscreen into her long arms and legs, as she shook out the boys' towels and leaned back, raising a knee.

Augie continued watching as if hypnotized, and she had no idea how long she'd been staring—did not even register she still *was* staring—when Mrs. Crawley suddenly sat up, lifted her sunglasses, and, as they locked eyes, Mrs. Crawley raised her arm, fluttering her fingers in a wave.

It was never supposed to happen again, but of course, it did. And soon, 301 Hemlock became their favorite place to meet. It was one of the smaller houses in the neighborhood, yet it was nestled back against the tree line, which gave it an air of privacy. The main bedroom only had one window, and as soon as they were inside, they didn't have to hide. They could embrace as any couple would; they could tumble to the floor in the exact space a bed would be. Like all the houses in Briar Ridge, there was still no actual furniture—not even a stray chair or curtain—but it didn't matter. Here, they were together. Despite the rug burns on their knees, the straining of their thighs, the desperation that fueled each of their kisses, here, it felt the most real. Ah, the Hemlock house, they'd text each other every third week, reveling in the relief. After all, they had to keep a careful rotation—could not be caught together in this space, at the same time, day after day. Theirs was a delicate lie.

5

There were three things bothering Danika that last Sunday in June. First, she did not want to attend mass (as usual). Second, she did not want to host a Fourth of July party at their cabin. And third, she did not want to talk to Chat about flirting with that Club waitress. Each sent a corkscrew of anger through her.

Church was always a pain point. The first time Danika and Bill slept together, his gold cross kept hitting her in the face, falling into her mouth—but she'd held out hope he might be one of those devout Catholics who never actually went to mass. This wasn't the case. Still, it felt like a small price to pay for the life she now had with him.

So that Sunday, as always, Danika sat stoically in the pews of Lady of Our Lake. At least the church was beautiful. It smelled like old books, held a claustrophobic yet serene quality, and you could glimpse the lake from each window. On a good day, Danika could relax there—so long as she could tune out the words of Father Michael and the boys refrained from kicking the pews.

Truthfully, she didn't like forcing mass on her children. Once, early on, she suggested they let them choose their own religion, but Bill had grown defensive as if they'd surely go straight to hell. It wasn't worth the fight. Secretly, she tried to remind Cooper that God was more synonymous with love than anything. It'd been unsettling when he started going to Sunday school and began talking to God as if he were an invisible friend. He'd go around the house saying, "Hi, God!" or "Good morning, God!" or "Did you hear that, God?" It both entertained and terrified her.

Danika stared at the lake as they drove home along Highway 15, tracing the line where the water kissed the sky. She had hoped to feel more relaxed once church was over, but the next item on her list weighed heavier: the fucking Fourth of July.

They had never hosted the Fourth before. They rarely hosted in general—and Danika had been aghast when, as they sat at the dinner table the night before, Bill mentioned it so casually, you'd think he was asking her a simple favor, to pick up more milk or his suit from the tailor's.

Danika was already exhausted and upset from the swim meet, and this was the last thing she needed. She had glared at him as she slowly stopped chewing her arugula salad.

"Excuse me?" she'd said. "What?"

The boys were already in bed, but Chat was sitting between them.

"The Fourth," Bill repeated. "I invited the shareholders, their families. I think it'd be a good idea to spend some time together. Briar Ridge is a big project, and we have some votes coming up, and I want to make sure we're all on the same page. Call it team bonding, if you will." He forced a laugh and cut a bite of steak, his knife scratching through the silence.

Danika took another small, tense bite of salad, remaining poised despite the frustration growing inside her. She could not imagine hosting the Greenes and the Harrisons and that imbecile Joshua Mike. *What the fuck, Bill?* This was out of character, even for him.

He didn't like any of those people personally. He liked the escape to their cabin as much as she did.

"Because what, they'd stay with us all week? The Fourth is on a Monday."

"Never, of course not. No. One night. A party." He raised his wine and studied her through the glass. "I'm going to invite the Fravels, too."

"Sounds fun," Chat said, fireworks practically bursting behind his eyes. "I can't wait to see the cabin. We have to bring badminton, like you said." He pointed his fork to Danika.

Danika's frustration grew to fury. Even if she did like Holly and Frank Fravel—they'd been to the cabin once, years ago—she barely liked throwing a dinner, let alone a holiday event. And the worst part, she realized as she ran her tongue along her teeth: She was disappointed. She loved their cabin. It was sprawling, seated right on Gull Lake, with a huge grassy lawn that dropped into a sand beach. She had so been looking forward to sharing it with Chat—to catching minnows off the dock with him and the boys, roasting marshmallows, playing badminton. Now, that relaxation had been plucked away. She imagined Joshua Mike sitting in one of their Adirondack chairs, staring at her ass as she waded into the water.

Nonetheless, Danika didn't want to make a scene in front of Chat, so she switched the subject curtly. She'd talk to Bill later. She asked for more wine.

She didn't have any luck later, though. Not that night, nor that morning as they got ready for church and she pleaded with him to be reasonable.

"I already talked to Zami," Bill had repeated, matter-of-factly. "He's game. He has a whole menu set. Everyone's excited except you. It'll be fun."

Now, on the car ride home from mass, Danika still felt shocked. But as she leaned her head against the car window, she knew she had to accept it. *Fine*, she finally decided. *If he wants a party, we'll throw the best freaking party he's ever seen, and he'll owe me.* It always felt better to frame things as a challenge. She had a week to prepare. And thank god for Zami. Danika had never been a cook.

Regardless of her new mindset, her disdain for Bill remained. That was one of the strangest things about marriage: how you could love and hate someone simultaneously. It wasn't a new concept, she knew. Yet, like most clichés, once you actually experienced them, they still felt singular—stunning.

At least Chat would be there. Sweet Chat. He'd love the cabin. She'd grown obsessed with sharing these luxuries with him, seeing his enjoyment. It was as if by impressing him, Danika was impressing herself—viewing everything anew. She basked in the way he lit up when she told him to order the forty-dollar steak. To take the Range Rover anywhere he pleased. It made Danika appreciate her life more; it made her appreciate *herself* more. But here was the next item on her list: She needed to remind him of the rules. She needed to remind him that his focus, especially at the Club, belonged only to the boys.

It hadn't been a huge deal, Chat's swim meet tête-à-tête. Not on paper. Danika couldn't deny her mounting fear, though: If Chat proved to be an inept, distracted nanny, she'd be mortified. On top of everything, he'd no longer be her comeback. She hated to think how satisfied the other mothers would be by her failure. They'd all been keeping a close watch.

Danika also hated to imagine Chat getting close to someone else in Aldon Lakes, sharing details about her, their life. She had warned him about members prying for gossip, and he had seemed to understand. "Don't worry," he'd said. "I'll steer clear of the housewives of Aldon Lakes." She hadn't thought to warn him about the staff. But she didn't want Chat to get sucked into *anyone's* orbit. She couldn't risk him sharing something that would embarrass her—or accidentally reveal something they had in common.

It was hard to explain the relief she'd felt when she first confirmed Chat did not know who she was. It was hard to explain how quickly that relief had flipped to excitement, too, something all-encompassing and cosmic, like a wish come true.

After the initial shock of his application had worn off, she'd studied his profile for hours. She'd memorized everything he wrote about his hobbies (hockey, live music, road trips, ice fishing), his education (St. Cloud State), and his experience with kids (he helped raise his younger twin sisters), searching for clues, but eventually, she knew she simply had to talk to him.

She had to know.

She scheduled a phone interview and, through a fit of panic, asked if his family was supportive of his "nanny goals"—if they were okay with him heading to Aldon Lakes, of all places. He'd barely reacted, explaining how his parents were so busy with his sisters heading to college, they were just happy for him to be busy, out of the house. To make some money before he went to Europe that fall.

"That's my goal," he'd continued. "I'm trying to get to Germany by the end of August. I'm going to travel for a year, see the world. As cheesy as that sounds."

Danika had swallowed into the phone, the mention of Europe igniting a supercut of memories—that parallel life.

"My buddy was a manny last summer," Chat explained, "and he said it was a great way to make cash, way better than mowing lawns—I usually work landscaping. I really do love kids, too. Sometimes I think I like them more than adults." He laughed, and his laugh, along with his answers, had seemed so genuine, Chat seemed more real than anyone she'd met in years. And best of all, to him, Danika was a stranger.

Yes, this was the main reason she needed to scold Chat: She could not have him faltering at the Club, breaking the contract.

She didn't let herself admit that the moment at the pool had additionally thrown her because instantly, she'd felt a flash of jealousy. She'd killed that thought immediately.

Maybe she could talk to him on the drive up to the cabin, she thought as they returned home, pulling into the garage. *Yes*. She sighed as she unbuckled, relieved to have yet another plan. *That could work*. Bill was heading up the night before, so it would only be her, Chat, and the boys in the car. She didn't want Chat to feel too bad. Only a little bad. To be warned. That girl, she wasn't worth it. Danika needed him to do his job. She needed him.

6

Augie met Zami Martinaj when she was sixteen, her first summer at the Club. It was Zami's first summer too but because he started after her, he joked she was a veteran. "You were running the place, don't pretend," he teased, flattering her. Zami was magnanimous. He had lake blue eyes with black eyebrows and a gray beard. He always brightened everyone's mood.

Zami was a hit with the Club members. Augie watched him ascend quickly from line cook to grill master to any front of house role, impressed by his ability to shuck oysters and chat business with the bigwigs, prep bruschetta and ask about people's kids, work the pig roast and start sing-alongs. Even the old GM became enthralled by him. Zami also frequently discussed the war he had fled, proudly explaining he was Albanian Kosovar. This was another reason no one challenged him: Say the word *war* and sheltered Midwesterners went stiff. Augie figured most people didn't know where Albania or Kosovo were. But she felt comfortable with Zami, so when she told him she couldn't remember much about the Balkans, he welcomed the conversation. He explained that he and his family had stayed in Pristina the first few months of the war, hiding out at their apartment, but after the night their restaurant was burned, he packed his wife and daughter up. They followed a cousin to Iowa, then to Minnesota.

Zami's wife died from a heart condition soon after arriving in the States, but over the years, Augie got to know his daughter, Teuta. She was twelve years older than Augie, but Augie loved her like a sister. Their bakery was also down the road from Augie's house, so she and her mom visited frequently. Leah and Augie spent a lot of time there in high school, too, doing homework and eating Balkan delicacies—everything from byrek and mantia to Augie's favorite, ajvar, a dip made of charred red peppers.

They especially loved being around Teuta. Like her father, she commanded a room. Additionally, she was gorgeous, with thick eyebrows, a full mouth, and a heart-shaped face.

Fueled by her work ethic and scratch card winnings, she was also determined to make Hyla as successful as their family's old restaurant in Pristina. There was no way she'd go back to waitressing, either, she lamented, bitter about all the years she'd spent at The Manor.

Still, because it was off the beaten path and people weren't familiar with Balkan food, the bakery struggled. This was why, when Augie had to choose a client for a marketing competition in high school, Hyla came straight to mind. Zami and Teuta were all in, and with the help of her mom—who'd picked up all there was to know about owning a restaurant working with Augie's dad before the divorce—Augie developed a campaign that included everything from rebranding to partnering with influencers and farmers markets.

In the years that followed, the bakery took off. Zami was able to follow his true passion of working as a chef; he started a part-time catering business and helped families like the Crawleys with parties and meal prep.

Augie hadn't seen Zami or Teuta since she got home. While they'd heard she was back from her mom, Augie was dodging them—they'd been so excited for her life in New York. Even so, Augie wasn't surprised when, one morning as she was eating cereal, her phone flashed with Zami's name. She dropped her spoon as she read his message.

Love, Teuta and I could use help for a party. A drive north but easy. Good money. The Crawleys? Their cabin. July 4. 9 people. Would love to see you. Would love your help! Call me. Yours, Zami

Augie's ears began to ring. What was the universe doing to her?

If it was all couples, Chat would be number nine. He had to be. She took a moment before responding. Instantly, her mind returned to the last time she'd seen Chat—and Mrs. Crawley—laughing and playing with the boys across the pool.

That stupid, condescending wave.

She hadn't seen Chat or Mrs. Crawley in the days since the meet, and while she knew it was a self-indulgent thought, part of her wondered if they were avoiding her.

Augie turned her phone over and focused. She made a mental list:

Pros: good money, time with Zami, I hate working the Club's Red, White, and Blue party, the Crawley cabin is supposed to be insane. . . .

Cons: Mrs. Crawley, and everything else.

It still sounded too complicated. Yet as Augie picked up her phone to say she was sorry she couldn't make it, she felt suddenly foolish. She stopped.

If her goal this summer was to recalibrate—and not let anyone get in her way—she had to go. She had to make money, support Zami, remain in control. And really, *fuck Mrs. Crawley*. It was time she stood up for herself. These members—she was sick of them all. People like them got away with everything. Just look at Micah.

Augie began typing, not allowing herself to register the way her heartbeat doubled as she imagined Mrs. Crawley seeing her at the cabin. For once, Augie would be the one making the passive-aggressive power play.

She didn't allow herself to register how excited she was to see Chat, either.

Zami!! she wrote before she could stop herself. Anything for you. When do we leave?

7

Before Danika knew it, the Monday had arrived—the lauded Fourth of July. The week before had passed in a blur of shopping, preparation, and harassing their cleaning company to set up the extra bedrooms. As much as she resented their guests, everything needed to be perfect.

"Can't forget these." Chat stood in the driveway in the milky light of morning, the sun casting weak shadows from the trees across the asphalt. He held up the pool noodles they'd bought at Target, gently swinging one to hit Max in the thigh, another to bump Cooper. The boys recoiled, giggling, the neon foam soft against their skin.

"Boys," Danika scolded, though her heart wasn't in it. Chat swung the green noodle her way, hitting her below the hem of her white shorts as she closed the trunk.

Against her will, she was wearing full holiday attire: white shorts, a blue tank top, and red Hermès Oran sandals. Along with the noodles, Chat had insisted on buying the boys Fourth of July T-shirts that read "Red, White, and Cool" and "Star-Spangled Stud." Danika had cringed, but Chat found them so hilarious, he even bought one for himself: "'Merica: Kicking Ass Since 1776." After Chat's pleading, she'd promised to at least wear the colors. No one mentioned Bill.

Danika relaxed as they stuffed the last duffel bags and floaties in the car. She'd always liked early summer mornings, the way the dew gathered in tiny balls along blades of grass, the way the sky looked peaceful and pastel, the way the air turned her skin clammy and cool. The weather today was also falling in their favor: a high of eighty-two, mild humidity. A rare reprieve.

"You sure you don't want to chill in the passenger seat? Take a load off?" Chat said after buckling in Max.

She scoffed as she grabbed the keys from her pocket. "You're too kind, but another day." She knew Chat loved her Range Rover Sport.

As she pulled out of the driveway, catching glances of the boys teasing each other in their matching shirts, listening to Chat hum along to the radio, she began to feel excited. It was not like her to be so festive, especially when forced to play host for such a ridiculous holiday, but once again: Things were different now.

Danika felt confident in her party plans, too. Zami's menu was impressive: honey-glazed spareribs, homemade fennel chicken sausages, jalapeño cornbread, watermelon feta salad, and tabbouleh. They would eat on the screened-in porch, have s'mores by a bonfire, and, when the next town over set off fireworks at nine, head up to the deck to watch.

The guest list had also gone better than planned. The Greenes couldn't make it—thank goodness—and the Fravels had agreed to come alongside the Harrisons and Joshua Mike. Danika knew Joshua Mike would never deny the invite. As she thought about it, she realized he might have been the one to pressure Bill into this whole ordeal. Their cabin was a bit famous in the area due to its impressive deck and design, and Joshua Mike had mentioned wanting to see it on more than one occasion. Maybe Bill wasn't going as crazy as she thought.

Danika always forgot how much land sat between the Cities and the northern border—yet as they sped through the forest, lakes appearing and disappearing like magic, thick evergreens rushing by in a wash of emerald, she enjoyed feeling as if entering a different world. Chat must have felt this, too, because after an hour or so, as the boys fell asleep and Chat stared out the window, he suddenly turned to Danika and lowered the music.

"Do you guys come out here a lot?"

Danika adjusted her hands on the steering wheel. Chat's tone was normal, but with only the two of them awake, it felt intimate.

"We try to. It's a good escape." She slid her hands down the wheel.

"Did you grow up camping? My dad and I used to go out to the Boundary Waters every summer, without my sisters. He wasn't around a lot, got sucked into that whole oil boom up in North Dakota, and we were never close, but it was fun when I was little. We fished all day."

Danika tightened her grip, pretending she didn't already know this.

Even so, her mind surpassed those memories and focused on her own father. She didn't have it in her to tell Chat that she had indeed grown up camping with her dad. Once, when they had been living in North Carolina, they went on a canoe trip outside of Asheville, one of her fondest memories. She was ten years old, and it had been pure joy. It had only been her dad, one of his army friends, and herself, and the men had been so happy slicing salami for sandwiches, telling jokes she didn't understand, asking riddle after riddle. Her dad had loved riddles. She never knew where he got them, but it would take her hours asking the right yes-or-no questions to unlock the mystery. He was always proud when she got the answer.

That trip was six years before he killed himself. Danika wished she could stop pinpointing every memory of him in relation to his death, but when he died, he stuck a maypole in the ground. Every other memory, every other moment of his life, was tied to a ribbon, circling around it.

Danika sat up, correcting the swerve of the car.

"A little, yeah. Although I have to admit, this isn't exactly . . . camping. This house is not a *cabin* cabin." She was glad to change the scenery in her mind. It felt important for Chat to hear her say this, too—to know she could see their wealth for what it was. She knew real camping.

"I know, I know. But something tells me I'm going to like this kind of camping, too."

Danika exhaled and stared ahead, the pavement shimmering and shaking in the heat. They were a little over halfway now, and she thought maybe here, in this closeness, in this fresh silence, she should say something: The pool. The girl. Their *privacy*. But she couldn't bring herself to ruin the moment.

Plus, every time she thought about what to say, it sounded more and more trivial. Maybe she'd been overreacting after all.

The house, indeed, was not a cabin. Not even close. And as they pulled off the highway, looped down into a dense expanse of woods, and hit the gravel road, Chat leaned forward. Danika couldn't help but watch for his reaction as they reached the final turnoff, bumbling across the pebbled driveway toward the house, the boys now awake and chanting, "We're here, we're here!"

"Oh my god," Chat said as the house finally emerged.

Danika tried to see the cabin for the first time. Her chest swelled with pride as she killed the engine.

The house was a rambler. From the driveway, it looked like one story: wide and expansive, a low spread of teak wood, slate shutters, and a big stone entryway. It was built into a hill, and from the back, you could see the walk-out bottom floor and the way the deck twisted and turned above. It was an extraordinary deck; it consumed the whole house, reached every bedroom, had little steps and landings that made it feel like a tree house. There was a circular firepit in the middle, maples shooting up all around, a screened-in dining area with string lights, and a general air of peace. After they'd built the house, the architect had been featured in *Architectural Digest*, and the deck, in all its glory, had gone viral on Pinterest.

Danika didn't mention the deck to Chat. She helped him unbuckle the boys, told him they could go explore around back, green lawn and sunlight engulfing them. Everything was comically bright, like the world was painted in the palette of confetti.

Danika checked her watch as she grabbed the first round of bags, relieved to see it was only noon; the guests wouldn't arrive until three. She'd have time to unpack, settle in, change. Check on Zami and the food.

"Hello, hello." She stepped into the foyer, the smell of oil and garlic mixing with the fresh air and pine trees.

"Welcome home," Zami called from the kitchen.

Danika dumped the bags and stretched her neck, massaging her driving kinks while soaking in the house. Everything looked perfectly untouched. She loved this entryway view: Immediately, the stairs headed down to the lower level, a landing and railings lining the cut-out space above, and beyond that was the immense living room, all Norwegian carpets and furniture, colorful cushions and soft striped throws. There was a modern Contura woodstove in the corner, more high wooden beams above, and, of course, Gull Lake filled the windows like a mural.

Zami grinned. Danika did not like most people, but she'd felt instantly connected with Zami. While he came only twice a month to meal prep and stock their freezers, she had grown to love him and his daughter, Teuta, who ran their bakery. She was also beautiful and charming, entirely up front. It was a nice change from the passive Midwesterners. Danika didn't see Teuta often—Danika rarely visited Hyla, since Zami came to them—but Teuta always helped with parties, and Danika was excited to see her tonight. She'd made sure to bring extra cash for tips. She loved to spoil them.

"The byrek is almost ready." Zami wiped his hands on a towel as she stepped farther into the kitchen, his body framed by the glossy, navy cabinets. He was deeply tan, and while his beard turned whiter each year, he still had a youthful air about him.

"These tomatoes look amazing." She picked one up, the lush vegetable filling her palm.

"The best time of the year." Zami held another to his nose.

"So." Danika put her hands on her hips, then removed them. "I was thinking we'll have appetizers around four, then grill by five thirty? Is that still the plan?"

"Yes, exactly," Zami said.

Danika loosened. How nice, to be *exactly* right about something.

"And"—Zami clapped his hands—"do not stress. We have plenty of help tonight. I brought another waiter from the Club, so we'll be all set. She and Teuta are unloading now. This night will be special. I can feel it. It is in the air. And look, the gods! They sent you a nice day!"

He waved to the window, the open blue sky.

Danika hummed a little. "Right, well, we did get lucky."

They stood side by side, staring out the windows into the wash of blue sky and water. The lake was as smooth as a fitted sheet. Danika wanted to run her hand over it.

"I hope you will enjoy yourself." He nudged her. "Happy Fourth of July."

Again, as she looked at him, Danika felt comforted. Again, she thought of her dad. She caught herself and said Happy Fourth of July. She knew Zami was more patriotic than most. He kept a picture of Bill Clinton in his wallet. She figured she would, too, if she'd lived Zami's life. She'd never told him her dad had been deployed to Kosovo with the army. She didn't feel she deserved his credit. She didn't want to talk about him, either.

"Okay, thanks again." She moved away, explaining she needed to unpack.

As if on cue, as Danika rounded the corner, Bill emerged from the stairs. His hair was wet, and she could see the lines of his comb through his curls.

"Darling." He seemed surprised, as if he hadn't actually expected her to come.

"We made it." She patted his shoulder before walking past him down the stairs.

From there, things continued smoothly: Danika changed into her white AllSaints dress and YSL wedges. She only wished she had more time to talk with Teuta before the evening started; she'd only caught her in the hallway briefly.

"You look amazing," Teuta had said as Danika hugged her three times, alternating each side as was the Albanian custom she'd learned when she met Zami.

"*You* look amazing," Danika had echoed, touching the ends of her long dark hair. "So long." It was another reminder Danika hadn't seen her in months.

"Extensions! You wouldn't know, right? Even though I tell everyone." She shuffled the bowl of peaches in her arms. "My girl over at

Fiftieth and France is amazing. You should see her sometime. Not that you need it. You're aging backward."

Danika tucked her hair behind her ear. It was strange to remember Teuta was two years older than she was; it felt wrong, somehow. "You flatter me. Do you need help?"

"Please, no, no. You go play host. We have it all set." Teuta hugged her again before disappearing to the kitchen. Danika reminded herself then to put the cash out where she'd remember.

If Danika had it her way, Frank and Holly would arrive first; it seemed best to have the core group there before new people. She hoped Mallory, Malcolm, and their daughter, Gigi, would arrive next. She had already prepared to talk about their hotel's new restaurant, which everyone had been gossiping about lately. Holly said the theme was "magical realism," whatever the hell that meant.

Still, even if Danika found the Harrisons ridiculous—and even if she was still bitter about Mallory not giving her a chance at the hotel design all those years ago—she'd play nice. Plus, she sincerely liked their daughter, Gigi. She was mature for an eight-year-old; one time, at a Club brunch, Danika had spent the whole time talking to Gigi about horses, riding lessons, her dreams to own an Appaloosa. She'd been in awe at how Gigi returned all her questions, making more polite conversation than most adults.

Above all, she hoped Joshua Mike and his latest girlfriend, Jackie, would arrive last.

But no matter the order of arrival, Danika was comforted by having Chat there. He and the boys would command the energy and holiday spirit. As such, she made everyone gather in the front sitting room by two forty-five. And now—as the boys sipped their lemonades and Danika poured a glass of Sancerre—she felt ready.

Danika leaned back in a rattan chair, exhaling, as she noticed someone round the corner. At first, she only saw the large silver tray of fruit she'd requested—watermelon and clementines and sliced kiwis—but as she leaned forward, preparing to thank Teuta, she did a double take. She almost dropped her wine. Because it was not Teuta.

Instead, her.

The girl from the Club.

Danika felt dizzy. She gripped the chair tighter, her knuckles straining white. She watched the girl like a laser, tracing her every move. Yet as the girl set down the tray, Danika finally came to and whipped around to Chat, who was also staring at her, surprise and excitement filling his face.

Danika's anger raced through her. *Who the hell was this girl?*

Danika had sensed something between the two from the swim meet, and now it felt confirmed.

Thankfully, the shock on Chat's face was evidence he hadn't expected to see her, either. *She* had to be the one after *him*, tracking him down. Out to insert herself into their lives.

How dare she.

The cabin was her family's oasis. Chat belonged to her.

"Danika," she finally heard, the voice far away and then ringing right next to her. She swiveled to Bill as he nodded harshly toward the window—where, just beyond, the first car was crunching down the driveway.

8

The cabin was more than Augie could have imagined. It was even nicer than Leah's. It felt like a resort, something you'd find in a magazine. When they had first arrived, Augie was glad not even Bill was home as Teuta and Zami punched in the door code. She pretended it was her house and she was returning after a long, stressful year away.

Her favorite part was the skylights. She imagined at night, if you turned off all the lights, you could see the stars floating right above you on the couch. Augie had always loved stars. Her dad had taught her all about constellations when she was young; she could point out the Big and Little Dippers, the Bear and the Bull, Cassiopeia and Cygnus.

"Pretty wild, right?" Teuta said as they brought bags and crates into the kitchen—which was massive and beautiful with its dark blue cabinets and thick slabs of marble. Augie mimed her brain exploding as Teuta laughed.

"Is this what Leah's cabin is like too?" Teuta asked as she slid a bag onto the counter. "The only other one I've been to is the Andersons', which is also totally insane. I'm starting to sense a pattern here."

Augie sighed dramatically. "Insanity all around." She paused.

"You'll have to come to Leah's with us sometime. Just for fun. We go as much as we can."

"Don't tempt me with a good time." Teuta opened the fridge.

Augie smiled as she arranged containers of sauces, imagining Teuta at the cabin. Augie always wished to spend more time with her, but Teuta kept certain walls up. Augie still felt that she and Teuta had a special bond, being Aldon Lakes outsiders. She hoped now that she'd graduated, they could be more like peers.

Leah loved any chance to hang out with Teuta, too—as well as helping her with dating apps. Leah prided herself on her online stalking skills, and she'd conduct a full review of any suitor deemed worthy. Give her a name and job title, and she could tell you what high school someone went to, where they vacationed, their favorite band. This was helpful, because after spending her early twenties working at The Manor—where she was harassed and ogled endlessly—Teuta had a strict No Aldon Lakes dating policy. This was also the reason she despised Joshua Mike even more than most people. She and Augie had already commiserated about his attendance at the party.

The first few hours of work were easy. Even when Augie got word Danika and Chat had arrived—even when she spotted him and the boys by the dock—she forced herself to look away. She didn't want Teuta or Zami to notice her reaction. Plus, Augie had a careful plan: Above all, she would stick to her job.

It also helped to remind herself that there was no real reason to be intimidated by Danika. Augie hadn't done anything to her. She was there to help, for god's sake.

But now, as Augie returned from the sitting room, watermelon juice sticky on her fingers, and leaned against the wall outside the kitchen, she felt all her careful resolve snatched away. If Danika had been cold and condescending at the pool, the emotion emitting from her now was ten times worse. It was pure disgust. Augie didn't understand. She pressed her shoulder blades against the wall, running her hands over her face. *Forget her*, she repeated to herself, trying to think her way around her hurt. She hated how much she hated being disliked.

"Are you okay?" Teuta peered out the doorframe into the hall.

Augie straightened.

"Yeah, for sure. It's just"—she slouched, pointing behind her—"Joshua Mike is here."

"Dirtbag asshole." Teuta pulled Augie back into the warm lights of the kitchen.

Augie tried to calm down as they began prepping for happy hour, arranging spirals of peach and mozzarella and basil, sprinkling salt over freshly baked pita chips.

"You sure you're okay?" Teuta blended the last of the edamame hummus, staring at her. "You look a little off."

"I'm fine. Just hungry." Augie popped a chip into her mouth.

"Hey." Teuta smacked her wrist. "Save yourself for family meal. It's going to be divine."

"You betcha," Zami said across the room, joining in with his favorite Midwestern phrase.

"I can do front of house if you want." Teuta pulled her hair back and slid the elastic from her wrist. "You can focus on prep. But don't eat it all."

Augie thanked her.

"Trust me, I'll glare that asshole down for both of us." She picked up a platter of caprese. "At least the nanny is sweet. Cute too, right?" Teuta stuck out her tongue. "He looks familiar. I don't know which celebrity. He comes in the bakery every week—sometimes twice—

and I always think, this time, *this time* it will come to me, but it never does. Think on that, please."

Augie paused as she left, surprised to hear Chat came into the bakery so often. It seemed odd. Maybe he just wanted to get out of the house? Loved the food? Or, worse, maybe he liked flirting with Teuta, too. Maybe he had a thing for older women?

Augie shook her head, pushing away the thought. She hoped she'd at least get the chance to talk to him that night. She knew if Mrs. Crawley had her way, he wouldn't come within ten feet of her. Augie grabbed a bunch of parsley and began chopping fast, trying to ignore the sinking feeling that this night would not come without a price.

9

I fucking love baked brie." Joshua Mike meandered about the deck. Outside, thick maple trees swayed above, tea lights danced in glass lanterns, and the sky faded to a dusky purple. Everyone circled the gas firepit, a table of hors d'oeuvres to their side.

Danika had been proud when she first planned the spread. Together, she and Zami had crafted a perfect menu: There were his signature byrek and ajvar, a tray of peach caprese, a spiral of edamame hummus and homemade chips, and decadent apricot baked brie. Danika had designed the table tastefully, too: small glass vases filled with black-eyed Susans and Queen Anne's lace and water lilies, candles in colorful hand-blown votives, each tantalizing dish atop precious Polish pottery. Everything was lovely. And now she could not even enjoy it.

"Me too," Jackie said, sidling up to Joshua as she raised her small plate in the air. Her arms flexed with the movement, revealing the thin definition of her muscle.

"Me three," Abby, Jackie's friend—who had arrived alongside them, unannounced—chimed in.

This additional guest was one more blow to Danika and the week. Her unexpected presence was almost as bad as that girl's, *Augie*. She had learned her ridiculous name from Zami. It all made Danika enraged, her body tight. She poured herself more wine.

Danika knew she had to remain collected. So just as the Fravels arrived, she'd retreated to her bedroom, pacing back and forth while shaking her hands at her wrists, trying to release her anxiety. She couldn't stop replaying Augie's sudden appearance, Chat's reaction. While he had been clearly surprised, he had also been clearly *happy*. It was obvious now that Augie was here for payback. Danika *had* bumped her at that happy hour—*had* broken her and Chat up at the pool. Would that make this revenge? Danika felt emboldened by the thought, threatened and defensive. Who did she think she was?

Danika was further annoyed Augie was spending so much time with Teuta. She trusted Teuta's opinion of people—she hated certain members—and Danika thrived off her approval. She felt Teuta, like Chat, was one of the few people who really saw her, who knew she was different. It incensed her to imagine Teuta and Chat and Augie together in the kitchen, talking about how over-the-top the cabin was, how spoiled they all were—talking about Danika herself.

It was unfair how only just after Danika regained her composure, Joshua Mike and Jackie had arrived with an extra guest popping out of their back seat. Danika felt like a firework had gone off inside her—and she'd instantly turned to Bill, looking for someone to blame. He had raised his hands in surrender, a promise he hadn't known. Danika steadied herself once more as she greeted them, as Jackie hugged her and told her she was the "hostess with the mostest!"

Now, Danika forced a smile at the two women over the top of her wineglass. She couldn't wait for this night to end. She was already tired of playing along, pretending not to be bothered by Jackie and Abby, who were feeding each other cheese and crackers. Danika wondered if the three of them were sleeping together. She knew Joshua Mike was part of the Club's swinging crowd—the not-so-secret group that met at the Lakeside Lounge on Thursdays. From the instant the three had arrived, they were always touching one another, elbows and shoulders and chins. Even now, Abby brushed crumbs from Jackie's lip.

Danika wanted to complain to Holly, but Holly was already tipsy and chatty, and Danika couldn't get her alone. Not that she'd know where to start anyway.

"The brie is from Bennington Farms," Danika said mechanically as she turned back to the group, trying to hide her frustration by making small talk. She couldn't imagine Abby or Jackie knew the renowned farm-to-table grocer; she hoped it would make them feel dumb.

"Oh, wonderful," Mallory Harrison chimed in. "We have a standing delivery with them for the new restaurant. The cheeses are divine."

"Never heard of it," Jackie said, indifferent.

"It's all delicious, Danika," Joshua Mike added. "You really do have the best taste."

"We can't wait for the restaurant opening, Mallory," Bill interjected. Danika could feel him working the room, his charm set to full blast.

"You *and* us both," Malcolm said. "Shit is taking forever."

"Is the theme still magic or whatever?" Holly said as she sipped her drink.

"Magical realism," Mallory corrected. "It's the Michelin chef's concept, of course. A blending of Latin flavors. It's whimsical. You'll see. We've all been working really hard."

Holly made a sarcastic humming sound as Jackie asked if that meant tacos.

"Okay, ladies." Bill laughed. "I'm sure it will be fabulous, Mal."

Danika looked to the other side of the deck, where Chat and the kids had set up a board game on the outdoor couch. She felt comforted by their presence. She was also glad she hadn't yet seen Chat with Augie, who seemed to be hiding in the kitchen.

This made Danika more skeptical. *Why* was she hiding? *What* was she hiding? Part of her was glad she was out of sight, though. Unlike Jackie and Abby with their fake eyelashes and fillers, Augie was a natural beauty, all flawless skin and apple cheeks, her youth shining and undeniable. It made Danika depressed, picturing her twenty-two-year-old self. She had been better looking than them all! She again felt her age dividing her from her previous sense of self—a line in the sand. She would never be that person again.

God, this night was hell.

"Did you have any ajvar?" Danika said to Chat as she crossed the deck toward the bar. She knew ajvar was his favorite of Zami's creations.

"Of course." Chat rose from the couch, glancing at Gigi and the boys as he moved to Danika. "I think I had half the bowl. Like I told Teuta, it never gets old. I could eat it every day."

Danika smiled. She was a little surprised Chat and Teuta seemed to know each other so well, but she was glad they were friends. She knew Chat visited the bakery between the boys' activities. *See,* she thought, *she wasn't some crazy, possessive employer.*

Danika traced the thick swoop of his hair, his face—that sharp chin, smooth neck—and suddenly flinched, jarred by how seeing him at a certain angle, in a certain light, sent her through a time portal. She raised her glass.

"Oh hey, give me that." Chat grabbed her wine before she could take a sip. She froze, worried he was commenting on her drinking, but then he reached for a knife from the table. Holding her glass out in front of him, he fished a gnat from the side of the rim. Danika stared at him, the knife, back to him. She felt momentarily numb from his kindness.

"Gotta save room for dinner." He wiped the knife and grinned, handing the glass back to her, their fingers brushing.

"So, are you headed to Hilton Head again this year?" Malcolm asked, pulling Danika back to the group. The men stood close to the firepit, the flames casting shadows across their khakis.

"Yes, sir, wouldn't miss it," Bill said. "End of August, as usual."

Danika took a bitter sip as she watched the fire dance. As exhausted as visiting her in-laws made her, she did love their house in Hilton Head, their yearly end-of-summer trip. Bill's family was reserved to the point of being dull, but this year, she couldn't wait to show Chat the colorful row houses, the wide white beaches. He'd eat it up.

"Oh, I love me some Savannah." Joshua Mike chewed yet another hunk of brie. "Love those open container laws. And all the ghosts." He wiggled his fingers at Jackie, who hooked her arm in his. She was a foot shorter than Joshua Mike—so was Abby. They were both so petite, they seemed like two halves of a whole. Again, Danika imagined them all having sex.

"Have you played Oyster Reef?" Joshua Mike asked.

The conversation turned to golf from there, and as Danika moved away, she realized she was getting drunk. She had hardly eaten, and the alcohol was swimming through her veins.

Danika went inside and headed to the kitchen. She walked slowly as if approaching a crime scene—but felt absurd. This was *her* house. Augie did not deserve her nerves. She fixed her hair and walked faster.

As Danika stepped into the kitchen, she held her chin high, prepared to meet them all, but there was only Zami. She paused, deflated, and went to the sink.

"Everything good?" Zami asked as he whisked a bowl.

"Yup, yes." Danika chugged a glass of water. She stared at her reflection in the windows above the sink. Catching herself in a mirror always sobered her. It was unnerving, like watching yourself cry.

"I'm going to check the place settings and then we can get this show on the road." Her mouth was still thick and dry as she turned to face Zami. "And are you all set? Are you and Teuta, and . . . Augie? All set?"

"Yes, yes, you betcha. No worries, Mrs. Crawley. You enjoy yourself, yeah? We have it all under control. Are you sure you're okay?"

Danika assured him she was fine, then started down the cedar hall toward the screened-in porch, which connected to the far side of the deck, one landing up from the firepit. As she approached, she suddenly sensed another presence.

Augie was focused on lighting the candles, the ashy smell of a fresh-struck match hanging in the air. She moved carefully from one golden candle to the next, her hand gliding between them, forehead scrunched in concentration. Even in the dim light, her eyes shone icy blue. Danika coughed once.

"Oh, sorry." Augie jumped back, flicking out the match. They each stared at the table as if afraid to look at each other. One candle remained unlit.

"Why are you sorry?" Danika straightened her back and stepped closer. She crossed her arms as she looked at the centerpieces. She hoped the intensity of her pulse did not show. She gestured to the single candle.

"You can finish."

Augie inched forward. Danika watched her try to light the match, fail, try again. It took four swipes for the flame to burst alive.

As Augie lit the wick, Danika continued studying the table, walking along the opposite edge. The tension between them was palpable, a heavy, disorienting fog, but Danika pretended not to notice. She leaned down and touched the flowers, adjusted a vase. She stood back to admire the table as a whole. There were delicate vases filled with wildflowers, all of varying heights and colors; there was the linen runner she'd gotten in Malta years ago, a swirl of hummingbirds; throughout, rich dried green vines and golden candles anchoring everything. It was more whimsical than Danika's typical style, but it fit the setting, the occasion. It looked effortless. No one would know she had visited two florists and three home decor stores to find the right pieces.

"It looks really nice." Augie stood back against the screened windows, the gray sky framing her.

"It does," Danika said.

"And we, um, we put the extra setting there, right? That's where you wanted it?"

Danika looked to where they had squished an extra plate and chair for the surprise Abby. Someone had even made her a place setting card, which did not exactly match the gold pen and exquisite cursive of Danika's other placards, but it was close. Danika picked it up.

"I tried to make it the same, but we didn't have anything gold, so." Augie gave a small shrug. Danika noticed her shimmering, perfect skin.

"We don't need it." She crushed the paper in her hand. "Abby will be reminded that she wasn't invited." Danika closed her fist. "She'll know that she wasn't—isn't—welcome here."

Augie looked as if she'd been slapped.

"I'll just check with . . ." She trailed off. "Dinner should be ready soon."

She slid past Danika, angling her body as far away as possible before rushing down the hall, the screen door bouncing closed behind her.

Danika exhaled. She felt both satisfied and uneasy as she leaned on the back of a chair. How could that girl be so simultaneously aggressive and timid? She was the one who had snuck up to the cabin. Why was she acting like some kicked dog? Danika felt even more frustrated, and she opened her hand, the crumpled paper now soft as a petal in her palm. She only hoped she'd sent a strong enough message to keep her away.

Danika held still for one more beat, taking in the solitude, and then walked around the table to double-check the place settings. She knew her guests might be surprised by the assigned seats, but she also knew people liked to be told what to do. It was especially beneficial this evening; Danika could ensure she'd be at the opposite end of the table from Joshua Mike. She needed all the control she could muster.

10

Mrs. Crawley is officially a bitch, Augie texted Leah from the bathroom. She sat on the closed toilet seat, knees bouncing. Even the bathroom was a work of art, with its dark floral wallpaper and glossy ceiling. *Who spends this much effort on a bathroom?* she thought, resentful. Augie stared at her phone, wishing Leah would respond. She felt a little bad; Leah had warned her the night might not be as easy as she hoped—she said Mallory Harrison didn't even want to go—but Augie had been out to prove she could face Chat and Mrs. Crawley head-on.

Of course, Leah had been right. This was worse than she had expected. While Augie had known Mrs. Crawley wouldn't be thrilled to see her, she hadn't anticipated this degree of hostility. Every time Mrs. Crawley looked at her, it was as if she were throwing silent daggers.

Augie had felt so awkward, she'd tried to make peace by crafting that extra table setting—hoping that if she extended one small kindness to Mrs. Crawley, she might meet her halfway, move past whatever was brewing between them. Together, they could have made fun of Joshua Mike, praised Zami's cooking. Any small camaraderie could have set them on a different path. But no. As Leah would say, Mrs. Crawley chose violence. Now, Augie didn't know what to think.

Augie got up, flushed for good measure, and washed her hands. She checked her phone one last time, unsurprised Leah hadn't responded. She was back at the lake with The Babe, probably boat hopping, hair slicked down her spine, shivering in her American flag bikini. Maybe it was for the best she didn't see Augie's text. Leah deserved to have fun. Augie felt so needy lately. She sent one more message: but all good, have fun!!!, feeling more alone.

At least she looked nice, Augie thought as she studied herself in the mirror. Her tan was still going strong, and her black dress fit perfectly: it had an appropriate V-neck and thick straps that held her chest and torso tight before flowing to her knees. *You got this,* she said to her reflection. *Be the bigger person. Be glad you aren't her.*

As she stepped back into the kitchen, she froze as she saw Chat, who was seated with the boys and Gigi at the butcher-block table next to the center island, illuminated under a modern orange light fixture. He tucked a bib into Max's shirt while Zami cut sausages on their plates. As soon as Chat spotted her, he also paused, his shoulders lowering, as if now that she was here, he could relax.

"Augie"—Zami held up the frying pan with a hot pad—"have you met Chat? He is the best. Even if I have to double my grocery trips now." He put down the pan and nudged Chat's shoulder. "He eats like a horse! He likes ajvar almost as much as you."

Augie felt aware of her whole body as she moved closer to the table, briefly allowing herself to look at him directly. He was wearing the same blue Fourth of July T-shirt from earlier, but now he had on nicer shorts and his hair was combed in a way she hadn't seen before. Every time she was near him, she instinctively remembered how natural it had felt being pressed against him, kissing him.

"Okay, ladies," Zami said as Teuta stepped in the kitchen, pinching the boys' cheeks and high-fiving Chat. "Let's bring the salads and breads out now, then each main—and watch the heat there." He pointed to a sizzling tray of ribs. "And after that we can have our own feast, yes?"

Zami moved to open the oven, revealing where he'd saved portions of each dish, ribs and sausages and fresh byrek, for family meal.

"We'll join you soon." Zami pointed his spoon from Chat to the boys to Gigi, who giggled with her mouth full. Cooper danced in his seat, flinging a spoonful of tabbouleh on the floor. Max screeched as he craned in his high chair to look down at the mess. He grabbed a fistful and dropped it on the floor, too.

"Ayeeee." Chat fake-gasped. "All hands on deck!" he commanded as each boy placed their palms down by their plates, grinning at him like obedient puppies.

Chat looked up to Augie, smiling like it was only the two of them—and for a second, everything else did seem to fade away.

"We'll save you a seat."

11

Danika avoided looking at Augie as the staff brought out platter after platter at five thirty on the dot, sweet, peppery smells filling the air. She wanted to keep the night moving.

"This is lovely, Danika," Mallory said as she unfolded her napkin in her lap. "So . . . creative."

Danika knew Mallory was forcing herself to be polite—being a nice little dinner guest. She didn't trust her.

"Really lovely," Jackie repeated, spitting a piece of ice back into her cocktail glass.

"I love hummingbirds." Abby held the runner between her fingers and turned to Danika.

Danika smiled tightly in thanks.

They began to fill their plates, and Danika regretted having Chat feed the kids in the kitchen. She wished he and the boys and Gigi were all there, sitting next to her, not cozying up with Augie and Teuta and Zami. She took another large sip of wine as Bill stood up.

"Friends." He raised his bourbon higher. "I'd like to first thank you all for coming." He glanced around the table in a circle—from Danika to Holly to Abby, Jackie, Joshua, Malcolm, Mallory, and Frank. "Thank you so much for joining us on this festive evening."

Danika studied him, confused as to why he seemed nervous. He was rarely nervous.

"I'd also like to thank my wife, and Zami, for putting on such a wonderful spread and party. We're all so glad you could make it."

"God Bless America!" Joshua Mike yelled.

"Nothing beats good friends and food. God Bless America, indeed. Okay, let's eat. Amen." Bill pivoted his glass toward Joshua Mike and sat down.

Danika didn't speak as she ate quickly and listened to the chatter around her, the music streaming from the speakers above. She wished she could turn it louder and drown out everyone's voices, but she couldn't help but take in each surface-level conversation—endless talk about vacations and weddings, the summer's heat. It wasn't until Abby cleared her throat that the energy shifted and Danika looked up.

"So"—Abby rested her elbows on the table while clasping her hands, roping in everyone's attention as if casting an invisible lasso—"where was everyone last Fourth of July?"

She looked across the table through the candlelight, focusing on Danika. Danika stared back, noticing she hadn't eaten anything on her plate. It felt personal.

"You were in Nashville, right?" Joshua Mike turned to Jackie. "I remember a picture of you in some American flag jean shorts. It was that memorable, trust me." He made an "okay" sign with his hand.

"Yes, good memory, fanboy," Jackie teased. "I'm a singer, you know. I love Nashville. Nash Vegas. I wish I could live there."

Danika tried to picture Jackie singing in flag shorts. She'd hate it if she were any good.

"And you all?" Abby turned toward the table.

"I think we were here, right?" Bill said.

"We were in Spain," Holly said.

"The Costa del Sol," Frank sang, opening his arms like a conductor.

"Yes, we were here," Danika replied. It was silent for a second. "We picked up the new boat." She ignored Holly and Frank, trying to sound casual, to entertain this little question-and-answer session. She turned her attention toward the lake and everyone followed, taking in the falling, softening sun. Danika drew her eyes back to Bill across the length of the table.

"A new boat, this house, and no Fourth of July party?" Joshua Mike said. "I feel like you two need to make better use of this place. I've been to a lot of cabins, and this takes the cake."

He held his glass to Danika until she was forced to face him—to reluctantly lift her glass in return.

"I mean, you could have a band, a full catering crew, everything," he continued.

Danika sliced a tomato, growing more irritated. "It is a good space for entertaining, but we like the escape. Being alone." For a second, she hoped that somehow Augie could hear, too.

"Oh, come on. You don't find it a little *selfish* not to invite people up? What's the point of having a place like this if you're not going to show it off?"

"You're here now, aren't you?" Danika snapped.

Bill cleared his throat as the air above them thinned.

"Maybe you have to be a VIP," Holly bragged. "We've been here before."

"It goes back to the same old question. Are you an introvert or an extrovert?" Jackie looked proud as she cut in. "Because, I'm an extrovert. So is Joshy. So, we'd like to have a party. But I can see that if you're an introvert, you'd want the cabin to yourself. Danika, you must be an introvert? What's everyone else?"

The table went silent. Danika drained her wine, reaching for a refill. While she had been drinking white, the red was closest. Most of the time, the way people described themselves was far from the truth. Danika's mother used to tell people she was "laid-back." Danika poured a heavy glass.

"Oh! You know what this reminds me of, the whole like, 'Would you rather host a party or spend the holiday alone?' question . . ." Jackie grabbed the table, excited, and looked to Abby. "It reminds me of that game. That 'Would You Rather' game, the one we used to play in the car, you remember?"

"I remember," Abby said coyly. "We should totally play."

Jackie shrieked, shimmying her bony shoulders. "Oh my god, yes, we have to."

"What's the game?" Mallory said, uneasy.

Danika kept drinking.

"So, okay." Jackie focused. "It's like we take turns asking questions, and they have to be either-or questions, so like, would you rather do this or that." She bobbed her head. "It's like the 'Who Would You Rather Fuck' game, you know, the one everyone used to play in high school? It's basically the same."

"Should we go around the table?" Abby added, amused.

"Definitely."

Danika eyed Holly, who stuck out her tongue.

Everyone shifted uncomfortably.

"Sure," Bill finally said, rattling the last of his drink. Danika tried to catch his attention again but couldn't. He was staring down into the centerpieces now, a shadow of Queen Anne's lace falling over his face.

Jackie nudged Joshua Mike. "Yay, okay. So, would you rather die tomorrow or live forever? You're up first."

"Live, easy. Well, as long as I have enough money to do it right. Otherwise, fuck it."

Bill was next. He hesitated. "Sure, live forever. Why not."

Malcolm agreed. And Mallory.

"You sorry suckers." Frank shook his head. "You're gonna be in for it. Definitely die. Love ya, dear." He grabbed Holly's arm. "But we've had a good run."

"I'll go down with you," Holly said. "Kill me now. But really."

Next, it was Danika's turn, and as she thought about the question, she imagined her boys at her funeral. This only amplified her anger. "Live."

"Die," Abby said next, not offering explanation.

"Spicy," Jackie said. "But for me, live, live. I just hope I'd stay twenty-seven forever."

"Me too," Joshua Mike added.

Joshua was next to ask a question: Would you rather throw a Fourth of July party or spend the holiday alone? Everyone said party until Danika. She told him to guess, despite Bill glowering.

It was Bill's turn next, and he changed the tone, asking which of the two most popular restaurants on Aldon Lakes Boulevard people would pick if they could eat at only one forever. It ignited a full debate, which Danika found pathetic. Neither restaurant was good. Malcolm followed Bill's lead, asking if people would rather give up alcohol or Culver's (another ridiculous question with a unanimous response); then Mallory asked if they'd rather visit Europe or South America; and Frank asked if they'd rather eat a stranger's toenail or drink their piss.

Finally, it was Danika's turn. And as the attention landed on her, Danika knew she was officially drunk. She blinked a few times, her mind blank. She felt resentful then that she had to be part of this dog and pony show—to host these obnoxious people in her home. She felt her frustration growing alongside her dizziness. She took another sip and smacked her lips.

"Fine." Danika was ready to challenge them, an animal instinct taking her over. "Who would you rather fuck, Abby or Jackie?"

Instantly, she felt the heat of Bill's fury. She didn't look at him. Jackie forced a laugh so loud it hurt Danika's ears. Everyone—including Jackie—knew Abby was better looking.

"You don't have to answer." Bill swung his head. "I think it's almost time for s'mores." He slid back his chair, half sitting up.

"What? Sure you do," Danika said. "This is just getting good. I answered all your questions."

She crossed her arms, relaxing backward, as silence settled in. It was getting darker, and she looked down at her wrists and arms, admiring the way her skin glowed in the candlelight. *The most gorgeous woman in the room.* Joshua Mike's words came back to her.

"I'll take Abby," said Holly. "You're kind of mysterious." She twirled a finger.

Abby said thank you. She turned to Danika, waiting.

She loves me, Danika suddenly thought, her confidence peaking. She sipped her wine and spilled a little on her chin.

"I'll take them both." Joshua Mike draped his arms across their chairs. The three of them looked at one another, exchanging glances, and Danika knew she had been right.

"Who would you choose?" Abby shifted forward, now turning to Bill.

Without missing a beat, Bill finally stood up.

"Okay." He slapped his hands together. "That's enough."

Everyone went silent as if scolded. Then, out of nowhere, Jackie screamed.

It had happened so quietly—in comparison to the screeching of Bill's chair, his loud clap—no one had noticed that as he stood, Bill pushed his place mat forward, which knocked over a glass vase. This in turn angled one of the flowers directly above a candle, and seconds later, the entire strand of dried leaves weaving down the center of the table had caught fire. It spread like gasoline as everyone scrambled backward, screaming.

Danika didn't move—not even as the heat pressed into her face like a suffocating hand. In fact, she felt calm. *How poetic*, she thought as she watched the fire lick the air: The evening was already going up in flames.

12

Before the noise erupted from the porch, Augie had felt surprisingly at peace. Once they'd finished serving and returned to the kitchen, sitting down to eat with Chat and the kids, she felt oddly safe, giddy—she loved listening to Zami tease Chat about his sweet tooth, claiming he ate an entire cheesecake in an afternoon.

"It was two afternoons." Chat raised two fingers while chewing.

"Not to mention you set the record for pieces of baklava."

They continued to talk and joke as they passed plates of food. Augie had forgotten how delicious Zami's cooking was. She was suddenly starving. Without meaning to, she also kept hitting Chat's thigh with her own—lightning bolts of contact that were strong enough to overtake her full spectrum of emotions; in those seconds, she forgot Mrs. Crawley entirely.

When they were done eating, Zami and Teuta went to the van to grab supplies, and for the first time all night, she and Chat were alone. They were both pretending to ignore the energy between them, but she knew they each felt the pull. And as they stood at the sink washing dishes (Chat insisted on helping after setting the kids up with tablets), they didn't speak. But minutes later, as Augie handed him a plate to dry, he lowered his head toward her.

"So, are you thinking it or what?"

"What?"

"'I was never supposed to see you again,'" he said jokingly. "It's kind of your mantra now. Though I'll give you, I didn't see this one coming. I did not expect to run into you here, of all places."

Augie pretended to be unaffected as she grabbed another dirty plate. "How do you know what I think?"

Chat took the plate from her and scraped the leftovers into the disposal.

"Fine." Augie sighed. "'I was never supposed to see you again.'" She matched his tone. "But I wasn't thinking it, because I kind of knew you'd be here."

Chat's face lit up. "I'm going to take that as a good sign. The fact that you came anyway."

"Don't be too flattered. This is still my job."

She felt his eyes move over her.

"I've known Zami a long time. He used to work at the Club, you know."

"Have you known Teuta a long time, too?" Chat said, glancing away.

"Yeah, since I was sixteen. So, six years. God, that makes me feel old."

"So you guys are pretty close?"

Augie hummed in thought. Again, she wondered if he had a crush on Teuta, too. She felt suddenly eager to change the subject.

"We're friends, yeah. Like I said, I've been helping them out for years. That's why it makes sense that *I'm* here tonight. That's why *you* are the one who is"—she tilted her head—"happenstance."

"I'm happenstance?" Chat threw a towel over his shoulder and crossed his arms, smiling.

Augie tried to keep her face serious.

"You are." She dried her hands on the towel hanging off his shoulder. "You are purely coincidence. *I was never supposed to see you again.*"

Chat laughed a big, raspy laugh. "If it makes you feel any better, I never expected to meet you at all. Or to even be here this summer." He picked up another plate. "So, I guess you're right. It is happenstance."

"On that note"—something shifted inside her as she moved against the counter—"how did you end up at this job? Where are you from, exactly?"

Chat nodded as if he'd been waiting for this question, then explained about the Savvy Sitter website, how his friend was a manny last summer, how he was from a town near St. Cloud. Augie sensed a hesitation in his voice, and she was about to pry further when he asked her where *she* was from.

"How do you know I'm not from here?" Augie said.

"Your accent. Or lack thereof. You don't have our cool Midwest *ohs*. You don't go out on the 'boht' or carry a 'bayg.'"

They both looked up and caught each other's eyes in their reflections in the window. Outside, the sky was turning from purple to royal, velvety blue, a color like the inside of a ring box.

"Well, you're right. I'm not from here."

"So, home is?"

The question threw Augie. Home was here, wasn't it? It didn't always feel that way.

"I'm from Maine. But we moved when I was thirteen, so I don't know."

Typically, Augie avoided sharing details about Maine, afraid of having to explain the reasons for their move. It all led back to her dad, memories of the restaurant and the waitress, how she hadn't spoken to him since she was ten. These were things she didn't share.

"Ah, Maine. That's one of my favorite states, at least of the ones I've been to. A few years ago, during spring break, I hiked part of the Appalachian trail with some hockey guys. Ended at Mount Katahdin. It was amazing. I'm really glad we went when we did." An air of sadness hovered around his words.

"Why's that? Pandemic?"

Chat went quiet as he grabbed a pitcher from the counter and turned the faucet on, rinsing the pitcher by tipping it up and down, up and down, as if it were an hourglass.

"I mean, yeah. I also got injured my sophomore year. I was in a coma for a few days, then couldn't play hockey anymore. Couldn't do anything, really. I don't usually mention it—I got so tired of everyone feeling bad for me, and it's difficult to explain."

Augie studied him. "That's awful." It was the first and truest thing that came to mind.

"Yeah." He set the pitcher down. "It *was* awful. But it worked out in the end. Like I said, I was going through the motions before. I didn't like how intense hockey was becoming. It was just the only way I thought I could get to Europe. I have an uncle out there, and a friend from college. I've been sick of St. Cloud for years. I didn't want to end up like my dad, who has never even been to Canada. Can you believe that? It's so insane. It's only like three hours away. He was too lazy to get a passport."

Augie didn't know how to respond. She'd been so snappy with him before, judging him for his take on college, for everything. It made more sense now. She, of everyone, understood feeling stuck. She, of everyone, understood not wanting to be like one's father. She'd never seen Chat so solemn. It felt jarring and intimate.

"Of course, I couldn't feel too sorry for myself," he continued, talking faster. "COVID hit not long after my concussion, and everyone was knocked off course. No one could play hockey—or travel. I had to do PT on my own, couldn't get into the right hospitals. Anyway"—his voice swung an octave higher—"that's my little sob story. Things are looking up. Now that I've graduated, I can finally make plans. And hey, I'm finally out of St. Cloud, too. Can you believe this is the first summer I've lived somewhere else? Not exactly Germany, but I'm going to book my flight this week. So that's something."

"That's great." Augie sucked in a breath. "Really. I'm glad it's working out."

On instinct, she reached out and put her hand on top of his. Then he put his other hand on top of hers, and she felt lightheaded, like sunlight was shooting from their stacked palms. Her hand burned with electricity, her whole body buzzing like it had on the boat.

Everything felt different after that—like they'd moved past some hurdle. They talked easily as they finished cleaning. They discussed what they had studied in college (Augie: communications, Chat: business); how they usually spent summers (Augie: the Club, Chat: a landscaping company, though it didn't pay well and the noise hurt his head after the injury); how many siblings and pets they had (Augie: zero, Chat: two younger sisters and a bunny named Mr. Bun Bun). Augie was so wrapped up in his presence, she was disappointed when Zami and Teuta reappeared, arms filled with covered trays. She felt Chat's mood fall, too.

"Egg bake tomorrow." Zami nudged Chat with his shoulder as he slid a tray into the fridge. "With za'atar and feta. You'll love it."

Augie didn't like to imagine Chat being there all week. She also wished she had asked him more about Mrs. Crawley, what it was like living with them—why she was so horrible to Augie—but they'd been so caught up in their own world, she hadn't thought of it.

It wasn't until the last dish had been stored, the last surface wiped, the last cutting board packed away, that they heard the screams from outside—and all froze in unison. Even the boys looked up from their screens.

Before anyone could register what was happening, Zami was off and running. For a large man, he was quick on his feet, and he raced to the deck and back again, lunging for the fire extinguisher. Chat rushed to follow, pausing down the hall as he remembered the boys. He whipped around to Augie. "Max, Cooper, can you?" he yelled as he chased after Zami.

Things moved in a whirlwind from there. Zami hosed down the table, turning it to a mess of white dust; the guests and Crawleys were equally disheveled, and eventually they all split off to their rooms to regroup.

Augie also wanted to scream when she went to the porch and saw all they were now responsible for cleaning. It took a whole extra hour to get rid of the fire extinguisher residue—to sweep and vacuum and strip the table, to run the dishwasher again and again. Zami tried to keep them in good spirits as they worked—he said they were lucky the fire hadn't caught the table, that these things happened, that the Crawleys would pay them extra—but Augie was tired. When they were finally finished, the clock was pushing nine and all she wanted was her bed.

Of course, she still wanted one more moment with Chat. She wanted to say goodbye. So as they packed the last of the bags and began running everything back to the car, Augie lingered by the stairs, listening for him. She hovered against the banister until she finally heard his laugh echoing from somewhere nearby. She listened closer as Teuta and Zami walked past.

"Coming?" Teuta held open the front door.

"One second. I think I forgot my water bottle. I'll be right out."

As they left, Augie heard Chat more clearly from down the hall. She walked toward the sound, arriving at the front sitting room where they'd started the evening. She'd thought he was alone with the boys, but now she heard another voice.

Mrs. Crawley.

"Don't worry about it," Chat said, his tone light. "It's all good. People love a story. Everyone still had a good time."

Augie stood outside the door. Mrs. Crawley sighed—and was that a sniffle? Was she crying? Augie desperately wanted to inch forward and look inside, but she was afraid.

"So chaotic," Mrs. Crawley said.

A rumpling of movement—were they sitting on the couch together?

"Did you know Abby wasn't even invited?" Mrs. Crawley continued, her voice muffled, as if she were talking into a napkin. "Incredibly rude. And I just, I don't know what has gotten into Bill. I can't believe he even invited everyone up here. Especially, you know, *him*."

"Josh Mike." Chat's voice had an unfamiliar harshness. "Such a fucking dick."

Augie straightened. She had never heard Chat swear before. He and Mrs. Crawley were speaking their own language—their own practiced back-and-forth.

"I loathe him," Mrs. Crawley agreed.

There was another muffled sound. Augie imagined them on the couch, Chat's arm around her for comfort. She felt ill.

"Hey, they'll be gone tomorrow. And the weather's gonna be good. We'll relax. Whatever you want to do."

"I can't believe I was mostly worried about the weather before," Mrs. Crawley scoffed. "This is such a disaster. I'm so glad you're here."

It went quiet. Augie pictured his hand on top of Mrs. Crawley's, as he'd done with Augie an hour earlier.

"Augie?" Augie suddenly heard from down the hall.

She staggered against the wall.

"Hey, Aug?" Teuta called louder as Augie pushed away, her feet clapping the hardwood as she rushed toward the foyer, her face hot.

In her wake, she felt the room go silent.

"What?" she whispered as she moved forward.

"Your water bottle's in the van." Teuta pointed behind her, confused.

"Oh. Thanks, let's go." She ushered Teuta back toward the door, desperate to leave before anyone caught her spying.

Still, as Teuta stepped outside and the cool air rushed over them, Augie heard footsteps, and she stopped. Part of her knew she should leave right then—that she should race outside and disappear—but another part of her held out hope that Chat wanted to find her.

She made the mistake of turning around.

Mrs. Crawley's eyes turned to slits, her mouth a straight line. Her whole demeanor was disheveled yet restrained, her clothes wrinkled, her hair tangled, but her expression and stance were stone. She didn't flinch until finally, she pursed her lips and spat the words that would haunt Augie the rest of the night:

"Get the hell out of my house."

13

New York, January

Augie's memories of New York felt at once crystal clear and like a black hole. Still, in the weeks after dinner at Julia and Micah's, there was a catalog of moments that stuck out. It made her crazy, how she felt energy and attraction radiating off him, but everything inside her brain told her it couldn't be. That he was just being friendly.

The dinner itself had been innocuous. Once Julia had joined them and the Greek takeout arrived, they sat together and talked about the agency, about Augie's lottery project. They'd joked about how the team was too old to understand their target audience, and Micah said Augie would soon be running the place. Julia was kind and supportive, telling Augie not to take any bullshit, to hold her own. Augie liked Julia. She reminded Augie of Robin and Leah.

It wasn't until after dinner that she felt another jolt of attraction to Micah. He had been helping her put on her coat, holding it out as she slipped her arms in one at a time, when she turned back to him while zipping it up, their faces now closer. "See you Monday," he'd said quietly, before reaching for her zipper and tugging it higher.

"Stay warm." He'd let go of the zipper, moved his hand upward, and nudged the bottom of her chin with his thumb, holding it there for two full seconds. Augie had stood, stunned, before turning to the door.

As she walked home in the cold, she'd touched her own chin, trying to make sense of the gesture. Was it meant to be playful? Parental? Or was it meant to make her feel as it had—drowned with want?

She next saw him at the office. The agency was housed in a Midtown skyscraper. Augie felt like she was in *The Devil Wears Prada* as she swiped her badge for the elevator and made her way to the seventeenth floor. She was wearing her new pencil skirt, holding folders of preliminary lottery research. Despite the nerves drumming inside her, Augie was proud of herself for becoming the competent young professional she had envisioned for so long.

It was Tuesday when he first sidled up to her cubicle. "Knock, knock," he'd said as he sat on the side of her desk, scanning her workspace. She'd decorated it with an old ceramic penguin pencil holder; a framed picture of her, her mom, and Leah from her eighteenth birthday; and brand-new floral sticky notes. As Micah looked at everything, she felt childish and dumb. He'd picked up the frame, paused. "Is this the Greenes' pool?"

Augie had stuttered, thrown to remember that he was related to Leah, a second-cousin-in-law or whatever. It was too strange to imagine him at the pool where she'd spent so much time.

"Yeah, she—they—threw me a birthday party that year."

"Cute." He set the frame down gently, and Augie wondered if he meant the party, or the picture—or her. He rubbed his hands along his jeans, which scrunched the shoulders of his blazer. He looked exactly like a creative director should. And incredibly handsome.

He seemed to be genuinely checking on her, though, because he continued to ask if her payroll was set up, if she'd figured out the internal communication system—if her recycling center apartment was treating her well. The fact that he remembered their past conversation sent a surge of energy through Augie's body.

Augie tried to remain casual yet confident as she told him she was starting to find the junk inspiring, actually. "I made a bouquet of flowers out of pipe cleaners."

He laughed. "That's the spirit. Maybe you should join us creatives. But really, if you need anything"—he leaned over her to the computer—"feel free to ping me anytime." He was inches from her now, but he didn't have room to type as he hunched down, so he grabbed the back of her swivel chair and rolled her to the side. "See? Just here." He opened the internal messaging box, found his name, and sent an emoji of a cat saying, "You're cool!"

"You are cool," Augie heard herself say.

He smirked. "I'll take it." And with that, he tapped her desk and left.

Micah never said goodbye. When he came by her desk, soon a routine, they'd have some flirty exchange, then he'd disappear. No "See you" or "Have a good day." Another week in, she called him out on it.

Why do you do that, she typed in the messenger right after he'd left, her heart pounding.

Do what? he'd replied a second later, surely just having gotten back to his desk.

Why don't you ever say goodbye? Or like, ciao? Have a good one? A common pleasantry? You always disappear.

Well, I'm never really saying bye. We're only three floors apart.

I guess.

Do you want me to say bye?

I guess.

Does that mean you want me to stop talking to you?

Augie's hands hovered over the keyboard. No.

Okay, then.

Augie had laughed silently, secretively, as she started to sweat. BYE, she wrote, before signing off.

Things took on a new tone from there. Even as Augie worked hard, conducting focus groups and compiling insights, preparing briefs for the creative team, Micah was always on her mind. It was fun to have a crush—someone to think about while running or waiting in line. Even if it couldn't go anywhere, it thrilled her to think of him.

He was often in her physical space, too. At lunches or agency meetings, he'd catch her eye, engage in light conversation. Their interactions always felt more surface level when around others, which made Augie wonder if he was suppressing feelings, too. But Micah was one of the top directors. He met with the president and VP every Wednesday. There was no way he'd be interested in a clueless twenty-two-year-old.

But then, the last Friday in January, a snowstorm hit the city. It had come out of nowhere. Augie had always thought New Yorkers were accustomed to snow, but with only a few inches, the city seemed to shut down. People were freaking out about getting home. It made Augie feel proud. Having grown up in Maine and Minnesota, a few inches of snow didn't scare her. When Micah messaged and asked if she needed a ride to her apartment, explaining the streets and subways would be crazy, she joked that this was nothing.

Back in my day, she typed, I walked 3 miles in a snowstorm. But really, I'm okay. Thanks.

But you live on 72nd and Amsterdam? Right?

Yes.

I'm heading to Columbia anyway. Televised panel somehow not canceled. The 123 is fucked. I already ordered a car. I'll drop you.

Augie said okay.

When they finally got to her street, the snow was fully coming down. The driver got out to clean the wipers, and for a moment, it was only the two of them inside the car. The snow covering the windows made them feel even more alone, drawn curtains of white, the back seat now shadowed. Micah wore a blue sweater that matched both their eyes. As Augie gathered her bags and scooted to the door, they both hesitated.

"Hey," he said as she reached for the handle. "You're doing a really good job, you know. Cheryl told me. They're all really impressed. Keep it up and we'll get you a new title in no time. I'll keep an eye out for you, put in a good word."

Augie felt warmed by the flattery. She missed the recognition that came with school grades and test scores, those routine validations.

"Thanks." She nodded into her shoulder. "I appreciate that."

"You're so formal." He sighed and adjusted his knees.

"I'm being professional," she teased.

He paused, staring at her as the snow fell faster. "You make me bad at that."

"What?"

"Being professional." He tugged once at her scarf.

She scooted closer.

And before she knew what was happening, he was kissing her, her whole body melting into his, the snow and cold and reality as distant as the moon.

* * *

When Augie had requested the Fourth off, Aida had given her a whole week, citing a slow schedule, small wedding, and the fact the newbies were finally getting the hang of things. Augie hadn't realized then how relieved she'd be to avoid everyone at the Club.

She had barely slept the night after the cabin. The whole drive back, she'd replayed Mrs. Crawley's words, the moment she'd overheard between her and Chat. None of it made sense. Why did Mrs. Crawley hate her so deeply? It's not like she knew Augie and Chat had slept together. There was no way he had told her. At least, she hoped not.

Even if Mrs. Crawley *did* know, why would she care? Chat and Augie weren't dating. She wasn't around the boys, breaking the "rules." Was Mrs. Crawley just—jealous?

It was impossible the two didn't find each other attractive. It was equally impossible they weren't growing closer, given how much time they spent together. Augie hated to recognize that she felt jealous of Mrs. Crawley. She wanted to be the *opposite* of her: to be kind and humble and hardworking. She didn't want to sink to her shallow level, to feel envious of some bored, mean housewife. In thinking that, Augie knew she'd already faltered.

When Augie had finally fallen asleep, she'd dreamed of Chat. They were in the middle of her New York apartment. He'd been on top of her, kissing her, when the whole room began to sway like a boat. His face had morphed into Micah's then—that sharp, sly smile. And finally, as she pushed him away, Danika had appeared in the doorway, screaming to *Get the hell out*.

Augie had woken sweating. It had felt like a warning. She needed to be careful. There was no denying she was involved now, though: She liked Chat too much. She hated Danika too much. She was too eager to know what was going on. Could they really be hooking up? The thought made her feel crazy.

Augie had told Leah everything that had happened at the cabin, of course. She'd also asked for help looking them all up online—she knew Leah was always game for stalking—but Leah had said she was sorry to report she'd already tried.

"When this whole thing kicked off, I creeped on Danika and couldn't find anything," she'd explained. "It's kind of weird, actually. Usually people that hot like to show off. But Danika is wiped clean. All I could find online was a mention of her from some design school in California, a link to their cabin, a quote from her about a PTA fundraiser."

"What about Chat?" Augie had said.

"He won't accept my friend request! Rude, if you ask me. I saw he only has twelve posts, though, so maybe he just hasn't seen the request. That's kind of hot, honestly. Danny, on the other hand, won't stop posting screenshots of NHL scores. It's giving me the ick."

Augie told Leah not to worry about it, trying to downplay her disappointment and the way her curiosity was killing her. It just felt like there was more to the story, that there was something she was missing—something to explain Mrs. Crawley and Chat's closeness, why she despised Augie, why Chat seemed indebted to her. The Crawleys had always been sketchy and closed off, but this was next level. It didn't add up. Augie asked Leah to keep her ears open, to see if anything else popped up. Augie herself refused to get back on social media. It would be too hard to face all her old messages and photos, all her New York musings—all her failure.

Augie used her time off to start on her "Get Your Life Together" checklist—the three-pronged agenda she'd come up with after New York. She knew only progress would make her feel better.

The agenda was straightforward: First, she would complete a wealth of personality tests to illuminate her true self; second, she'd research cities all over the country and determine where she was meant to live; and third, she'd make a list of entry-level, in-house marketing positions. Even though all the contacts she'd built through professors and informational interviews in college were linked to traditional agencies, she knew the ad world was small; given all that had happened, she had to avoid them. She didn't want to risk talking to someone who would reach out to her old agency, ask for a referral. It would be too mortifying. No one would want her.

Augie sat at her old high school desk, staring into her three glowing, empty spreadsheets. It was hard for her to focus in her room. When they'd moved in, Augie had spent months decorating. As an insecure thirteen-year-old, she had wanted all her new friends to step inside and know exactly who she was—to love her. She'd painted her walls her favorite aqua blue, pinned up paper crane mobiles across her ceiling, covered her walls in posters of *Sex and the City* and *Monsters, Inc.* and the Killers. Now, it was distracting; it all felt so earnest and immature.

Still, Augie was proud that, by the following Monday, a full week after the Fourth, she was about to start on her fifth personality test—the Enneagram. Leah swore by it, and as soon as Augie scrolled to the first question, Leah burst into her room, as if the test alone had conjured her. Augie had shut her phone in her closet—no distractions!—and was shocked to see her.

"Do you have me on mute or what?" Leah kicked off her sandals, dropped her purse, and climbed onto Augie's bed with her iced Caribou Coffee. She crossed her legs and shimmied out of her blazer, her hair wild around her shoulders. She must have come right from work.

"You and the rest of the world." Augie danced her hands over her keyboard and read from the screen. "Do I usually welcome or avoid confrontations?"

Leah leaned back, fluffing a pillow behind her, sipping her drink. "Enneagrams! You're gonna be a five. And I think we both know the answer to that."

Augie reached for a hair clip on her desk and threw it at her. Despite the distraction, it was nice to see Leah. She had been working at the hotel nonstop, and while they'd texted and chatted on the phone, they hadn't caught up properly. All their latest conversations had also revolved around Chat and Mrs. Crawley—though they hadn't discovered anything new.

"Okay, well, I will get out of your hair"—Leah opened and closed the clip like a mouth—"but I wanted to see if you could come to El Verde tonight. My mom's friend is in town, and we're going to the tasting menu. It'll be fun. My dad is coming, too."

Augie slumped down, resting her arm and chin along the back of her chair. She didn't have it in her to face Robin or Wyatt tonight—to lie about New York while they treated her to an expensive meal. She felt guilty—relieved to have an excuse.

"I wish I could, but I have the men's golf tourney tomorrow. I have to be up at five."

Leah groaned. She set her coffee on Augie's nightstand. "We really need to get you on a nine-to-five so we can make the most of this summer. At least have some fun."

Augie turned back to her screen. "I feel like it'd be worse to have two short-lived jobs on my résumé."

"I'm only saying, it's not like you have to work all these random Club shifts. I could ask Mallory about a job for you. They need a lot of help with the new restaurant. Marketing and everything. I bet they'd hire you. And . . ." She grinned. "Well, there's one more reason we're going out tonight."

Augie twisted around.

"The big news is . . . Mallory finally hired me!" Leah raised her arms in a mock-cheerleader pose, but the moment felt so forced, a second later, she let them fall to her sides. "From unpaid intern to director of operations. Vague AF because let's be real, I do everything."

Augie hated how her heart sank. She hated what that said about her: that she was so caught up in her own shortcomings, she couldn't be happy for her friend.

"That's amazing, Lee." She jumped up to hug her. "Seriously, that's great. Congrats!"

"Thanks," Leah sighed.

Augie slowly sat back at her desk.

"It was a long time coming, obviously. But it's a good night to celebrate." She fiddled with the edge of Augie's duvet, a new sincerity seeping into her face, which made Augie feel worse. "Are you sure you can't come?"

"I really wish I could, but it's going to be such a long day tomorrow. Let's celebrate again soon, though, okay? Whatever you want."

"Okay, yeah. Hannah suggested we go to Eleven for sushi."

Augie tensed. Leah had told Hannah first? Eleven was one of the most expensive rooftop restaurants downtown.

"Definitely. Let's do it."

It went quiet before Leah spoke again, hesitating, like she was about to walk out onto a thawing lake.

"I am serious, Aug. The Harrisons really do need help with the restaurant. They're shooting to open in a few weeks, and they're super behind. I'm sure Mallory would hire you, even part-time. It could be *good* for your résumé."

"I appreciate it. But, I'm good." Augie didn't want a different job. She wanted to get out of Minnesota entirely.

It was a difficult thing to explain to locals. Of course, Minnesota wasn't all bad; there were beautiful lakes and bike trails, a cool downtown art scene, lots of sports teams to cheer for, but to Augie, it felt claustrophobic. Suffocating. It seemed everyone had lived there for generations—if you weren't from the area, it was hard to break in. Aldon Lakes was especially cliquey and insulated. As much money as people had, they never left. They liked being big fish in a small pond. Augie had always felt like an outsider, like if she stayed there, she'd never grow into someone new; she'd become frozen in time, forever the same version of herself.

"You know, Aug, it's not like this is the worst place to start out. You could still get experience while you keep applying. I don't get it. I don't think you have anything to prove."

Augie tried to ignore the pressure building at her temples. "I do, though. To myself. Seriously, I'm happy for you . . . but this isn't where I want to be. This isn't what I want to do. I don't want to get sucked into the Hotel Harrison. It's basically the same place as the Club."

"Right. Okay." Leah stood, scuffing on her sandals.

"I don't mean it in a bad way. I'm sorry. I really am happy for you."

"I know," Leah repeated, picking up her purse. "I just think *you* could be happy, too. If you'd stop getting in your own way. You need to get over New York, okay? Ad agencies merge, people get fired. Guys turn out to be Fuckboys. It's not the end of the world."

"Leah, I—" Her conscience was spiraling, her lies tangling inside her.

"Look, I'm tired, okay? Work is stressful right now. It's all fine. We'll get together later. I'll call you."

She left before Augie could respond.

Augie knew she would see Chat at the men's guest charity tournament. She felt it in her bones, a rare visceral instinct. Though, at one point, she had also heard Mr. Dryer say Bill's latest partner in crime was insanely good. Part of Augie was eager to see him, but she still felt clouded by her conversation with Leah. All around, she felt a thrumming drumline of nerves.

Augie spent all of the breakfast shift watching for him. She wasn't surprised they didn't show. That's what made the pretournament breakfast so annoying: Despite the staff waking at dawn to set up, most players went straight to the course. It was only the first event of the day, too; the real party was the end-of-tournament happy hour. This meant the servers had to kill four to five hours while the men played eighteen holes. It wasn't like they got to hang around, either—they had a whole list of back-of-house chores to complete: fill salt and pepper shakers, clean the ice and coffee machines, prep for future events.

Augie didn't mind the chance to hang out with TC. Together, they went to the ballroom to fold napkins for a wedding shower the following evening. The theme was *Swan Lake*, and naturally, they'd requested napkins as birds.

"Is it weird that I enjoy this? It's like origami," Augie said as she and TC stood at a round, linen-less banquet table, the bare wood ugly and exposed.

"Not at all. You're giving us life!" TC said in a cartoonish voice as he dipped the head of his recent fold.

Augie pressed a swan to her cheek, stroking it like a pet.

"So, who do you think will take it all this year?" TC glanced out the west windows toward the eleventh hole.

"I don't care so long as the happy hour ends at a decent time. They always stay so late. It's, like, because it's for charity, they feel good about drinking all night long."

"Jägerbombs in the name of a good cause." TC pulled the last stack of laundered napkins from the plastic wrap. "I think my money's on Bill and the manny."

Augie creased a fold with her thumb, sliding it back and forth until the friction hurt.

"They've been playing together nonstop. It seems kind of weird to bring your nanny as a guest, but whatever. As always, the royals do as they shall."

Augie grabbed another napkin, silent.

"Not that I'm being sexist," TC continued. "I love the idea of a male nanny. Kid is nice, too. Polite. Maybe I should have been a manny. You've met him, right?"

Augie set her finished swan in the plastic bin, squishing it against the others. "Yeah, here and there with the boys. The swim meet."

"He plays hockey, too, you know. Athletic little asshole," TC joked. Augie knew TC was a big hockey fan, that he even taught skating lessons in the winter.

"We were shooting the shit the other day at that kids' golf night, too. I got caught with him and Danika at the bar while Bill was out there on the Putt-Putt greens, trying and failing to get Cooper to practice. Hate to tell the guy, but I don't think they're gonna be future partners. Maybe that's why he likes playing with the manny."

Augie kept her face down but cleared her throat. "You talked to him and Mrs. Crawley?"

"Yeah, it was so funny, the three of us were all talking hockey. Mrs. Crawley was getting kind of drunk, she kept ordering mojitos, but she was so into it. She knew all about it. All the positions, the different leagues. Even the European rankings. Wouldn't have guessed it."

"European rankings?" Augie looked up.

"Yeah, we were talking about how Chat—that's his name, right? Weird name. Anyways, we were talking about how he'd hoped to go pro, play for France Two or Belgium, but he got hurt or whatever. That's a bummer. That would have been so cool. I wish I had been even close to good enough to play in Europe."

"What did Mrs. Crawley say?"

"She was so into it. She was slurring, sure, but all the same. She was telling me all about the import rules, the Optibet Baltic league, how she'd gone to games in Sweden and Estonia and Norway. I was surprised. Impressed."

Augie stopped folding. Mrs. Crawley had gone to hockey games in Europe? Wasn't that where Chat had been trying to play? Maybe this was why they were so close—was it as simple as bonding over a sport?

"Did she say anything else?"

"Not really. She was pretty out of it by the end. Ah, alas, we're out." He crumpled the plastic wrap that had held the clean napkins into a ball. "We need sixty total, right? Did Aida say there were more in her office?"

"Oh, yeah. I think so. I can go check," Augie said, suddenly eager to be alone.

As Augie walked down the hall, she imagined Mrs. Crawley and Chat talking about hockey, traveling. She wondered how Mrs. Crawley had gone from design school in California to gallivanting across Europe. But with money, Augie supposed anything was possible. Maybe it was a long vacation. Maybe she'd grown up with some hockey-obsessed dad. Augie felt another swirl of jealousy. She'd never been to Europe. She didn't know the first thing about hockey. She didn't know which sports her dad liked.

The office was always a mess, and Augie shoved the door open, fighting a pile of boxes. It wasn't Aida's fault. It was the only place they had within a stone's throw of the ballroom to store extra place settings and uniforms and votives and the like. Luckily, Augie spotted the napkins right away. She stepped over a bushel of fake flowers to grab another plastic-wrapped stack before noticing that Aida's computer was logged on.

Aida had always told them if they ever noticed she forgot to log off, to please do so immediately. Mr. Dryer was a stickler about privacy; he'd scolded her for breaching protocol before.

Augie adjusted the napkins under her arm and stepped to the computer, moving the mouse to the bottom left to exit. She paused before she clicked. Discovering the open computer at this exact moment felt too destined to ignore. And while she looked over her shoulder, hesitating just so, she sat down.

Augie opened the master file and scrolled to the singular number blaring in her mind: 9119. The Crawleys' member number.

At first, the spreadsheet of contact information and invoices looked standard, and Augie felt a little regretful as she studied the columns of numbers, but a second later, she saw something strange—in the notes column were the red capitalized words: "PAST DUE." And as she scrolled all the way to the current billing cycle, she saw it was in the negative.

$59,989.43 in the negative.

Augie sat back, blinking, when she heard someone at the door. She rushed to close the page and log off.

As Aida pushed into the office, cursing the mess at her feet, Augie stood up, raised the napkins, and yelled, "Found them!"

It was difficult for Augie to focus after that. She knew she shouldn't be this obsessed with the Crawleys, but she couldn't help it. On top of everything, they were in debt to the Club? More and more, Augie sensed something was awry. More and more, she wondered how much Chat really knew about them.

Augie wished she could text Leah about what she'd seen, but it felt tone deaf after their previous conversation. Augie needed to apologize first, needed to call her. So, for now, she told herself not to overthink—just lie low and get through the day.

Yet as she and TC finished the swans and returned to the kitchen, Aida raised a set of golf cart keys from her pocket and instantly, Augie cringed.

"It's your lucky day. The golf staff is falling way behind." Aida handed Augie the keys. Usually, everyone coveted the chance to help drive the snack carts and escape into fresh air, but today, Augie dreaded the thought of running into Chat and Bill out on the course. As much as she wanted to see Chat, she didn't want to be cornered with him and his foursome. How awkward.

"Are you sure no one else wants a turn? If Liss wants to drive, I'm fine to stay. Really."

"What? You love this. And Liss is already out there working the midway station. I swear the pros did a horrible job organizing this year. Though to be fair, it is record numbers. I don't trust any of these new kids to drive, either. It's all you! Have fun. Start on eleven, please."

Augie grew increasingly anxious as she made her way to the lower patio, checked that her cart was stocked with beer and Gatorade (it was impressive and unsettling how plastered these guys could get while still scoring under par), and started the engine. All she could hope now was that the other carts would hit the Crawley group on their rotation, that they wouldn't fall to her. She said a silent plea as she finally pressed the gas.

The first two holes were fine. The men were tipsy already, their colorful polos vibrant in the sun, but they were harmless. Augie handed out Leinenkugel's and waters and took down numbers with no fanfare.

Augie relaxed a little as she drove. It was gorgeous out there. The breeze pulled at the wisps of her ponytail, the blankets of grass spread out around her like an alien planet, and light danced off the lake in the distance like sprinkled salt. Still, everywhere, she searched for Chat.

Another three holes later, Augie thought she might be in the clear when, as she rounded the putting green of hole fifteen, which practically skimmed Crystal Bay, she spotted Mr. Crawley. Then, to make matters worse, she heard the unmistakable cackle of Joshua Mike—finally spotting him leaning on his putter dressed head to toe in lime green. Augie held her breath as she scanned for the rest of their group, confused as she suddenly noticed Wyatt Greene, Leah's dad. While he and Mr. Crawley were golf rivals and often paired in the same group, it didn't make sense he was partnered with Joshua Mike.

Mr. Crawley, Joshua Mike, and Wyatt were gathered on the edge of the green now, peering into the valley between them and the water, their silhouettes framed by the blue beyond. They had fallen silent, and Augie braked the cart as she heard the light, hollow clip of a chip, then saw a speck of white arching up across the sky like a spotlight. She focused on the ball as it landed on the green, rolled to the left, right, and straight into the hole.

Joshua Mike screamed in agony. He fell to his knees, his head tilted back as he raised his hands to the sky.

"How!" he yelled.

"That's my boy." Mr. Crawley clenched his fist in an excited uppercut. "Excellent shot." His hand unfolded into a high five as Chat appeared from the other side. He was smiling and wearing a monogrammed white Club hat, tufts of dark hair fighting out above his ears. He pressed his hand to Mr. Crawley's.

Augie's heart smacked against her ribs as she waited for the men to notice her. She didn't want to see any of them—even Wyatt. While she and Wyatt were close (they always teamed up against Leah and Robin, teasing them on trips about being picky eaters or jet lagged), it was strange running into him at the Club. He and Robin were always polite, as were the rest of her peers' parents, but it humiliated Augie all the same.

"You bastard! You're too good." Joshua Mike shoved Chat as they walked off the green.

"Lucky shot." Chat took off his hat and wiped his forehead with his shoulder.

"Lucky shot my ass; you're a goddamn prodigy. Next time, I get him as my duo." He noticed Augie and rushed toward her. "Oh, thank god. I'm parched as hell. You've been sleeping on us. What gives?"

Wyatt Greene waved as he put away his putter and headed toward her.

"Our apologies." Augie hopped out of the cart and headed around back to the cooler, smoothing her shorts. In the moment, even her cutest uniform felt hideous. "We're a little behind."

She didn't look at Chat, but she felt his attention all the same. Her heart pounded even harder; she felt her pulse in her neck, in her wrists, in the soft backs of her knees.

"Afternoon, Aug." Wyatt pulled off his golf gloves. "How's it going?"

Despite herself, Augie was relieved by his presence. Wyatt Greene had a gentle, steady demeanor. Like Leah, he was a good listener, though Lyle was the one who had been a carbon copy of their dad.

"Going fine." Augie forced a smile.

"Let's hope we can wrap this thing up soon, huh? It's a hot one." Wyatt moved closer to Augie as everyone grabbed beers from the cooler. "My guest canceled last minute, as did Josh Mike's," he whispered to Augie. "Which leaves me . . ."

Augie mouthed, "Sorry."

"Well *we* were sorry you couldn't join us last night. That really is a fantastic restaurant. And as I told Leah, it was only fitting we got to celebrate her new job on Lyle's birthday. It's all the more proof he's watching out for her. And that lobster bisque. Incredible. We'll all go back."

Augie's whole body clenched. Lyle's birthday? It had been Lyle's birthday celebration, too? July eleventh. She usually went out with them every year. It was the one time they spoke of Lyle openly. How could she forget? Her mouth went dry.

"I'm, I'm so sorry I wasn't there. I didn't realize . . . I'm sorry."

Wyatt studied her, seemingly surprised by the intensity of her remorse. "No, Aug, don't worry." He reached out and squeezed her shoulder. "Really. I wasn't trying to make you feel bad. It's okay. We'll celebrate again soon. Like I said, I want to go back to that spot."

Augie nodded and was about to apologize again when Mr. Crawley and Joshua Mike joined them.

"Ugh, no IPAs?" Josh Mike whined as he opened both coolers.

"Oh, sorry, no, not today," Augie said.

Joshua Mike booed, grabbed a Summer Shandy, and, to Augie's relief, walked to his cart.

Mr. Crawley reached for a water and smiled at Wyatt. "I can't believe you agreed to play with him."

Wyatt rubbed his forehead underneath the brim of his hat. "You're telling me."

"If you'd agree to be my partner for once and let us clobber everyone . . ." Mr. Crawley trailed off. "Let me know."

"Oh, hey now. You know that wouldn't be fair. It's an unwritten rule, right? The best of the best can't play together."

Augie closed the cooler as the sun fell over the ice, and the men jolted when the clasp snapped into place.

"Oh well. I guess I should stick with the youth while I can, old man." Mr. Crawley gave Wyatt's arm a light punch as he moved past him toward his cart.

"I am an old man," Wyatt sighed to Augie. "But, all right, I should go. Hang in there, kiddo." He dipped his hat to her as he headed toward Joshua Mike.

Augie looked out to the lake, blinking away a gust of wind, but a second later, she felt the air shift in a new way—Chat. They were alone now. Still, she was no longer excited to see him; she was too consumed with guilt about Leah. All she wanted to do was call her and apologize for everything. She was such a bad friend these days, forcing all her petty drama on Leah when Leah was the one with real problems—a real job. Once again, a guy was taking over Augie's focus.

"Hi," Chat finally said, clearly thrilled to see her.

Augie studied his blue Lacoste polo, white pants, golf gloves—Club hat. He pinched the collar of his shirt and reached out to touch hers.

"We match." He laughed, grinning manically. "I haven't worn a polo in years."

"What a coincidence." Her voice was harsher than intended, but she couldn't help it. She looked away, watching the men drinking by their carts, updating their scorecards.

"Okay, another random run-in means you're thinking it again."

Chat leaned closer. "I was never supposed to . . ." he began, prompting her to finish the sentence.

Augie opened a cooler and grabbed a piece of ice, squeezing it in her fist until the water melted through the cracks of her fingers.

"See you again." She looked straight up at him.

"I'm sorry I didn't get to say goodbye at the cabin, by the way. That was all . . . a lot."

"It was something."

Chat pulled back.

"At least people love a story," Augie said before he could respond—echoing what she'd heard him say to Mrs. Crawley. She hadn't planned to do it, but her frustration was growing. Chat and Mrs. Crawley shouldn't be consuming so much of her energy; she just needed to know once and for all what was really going on between them. Did he actually *like* her?

Chat scrunched his eyebrows. Augie wasn't sure he remembered saying those words, but he was registering her attitude all the same; the previous ease of their back-and-forth was gone.

"Do you want a water?" she suddenly asked, exasperated. She'd always been like this: the first to break a spell of uncomfortable silence. To feel bad.

He took the water without saying anything.

On reflex, she rolled back her shoulders, and in her moment of weakness, she asked what she really wanted to know. "How was the rest of the week?"

"It was fine. The weather was good. I can't complain. But I was still working, so. It was still work."

This wasn't the answer Augie had wanted. She wanted to hear it was awful—that Mrs. Crawley was horrible, a pain in the ass to be around.

"I've been working a lot, too." She latched the coolers. "I was glad to have some time off."

"Yeah, I could use a break. I've been with them nonstop. At this point, I feel like I'm a thirtysomething dad."

"That cabin is pretty special, though." Augie gave him a challenging look. "Not exactly a bad place to work."

Chat stepped closer, moving his head toward her ear as if he was about to whisper—but at that moment, Mr. Crawley and Joshua Mike returned for more drinks, and Augie realized she needed to write down their orders.

"Uh, gentlemen"—she backed away from Chat—"if you could let me know your drink totals and what number you'd like to use, that'd be great."

Joshua Mike guzzled the last of his beer before crushing it in his hands. "I think we should get at least one free drink. Since it took you so long to get out here."

"I understand. I can ask Aida when I get back, but for now, I need to write them down. For inventory's sake."

Mr. Crawley gave his order while Joshua Mike scoffed.

"Oh, come on. How about I play you for it?" He burped. She wished Wyatt would come back, but he was still at his cart.

"I'm sorry, I can't."

"Come on, I know we're way ahead of those other guys. We should be killing time, right? Come on, one shot, one putt. One beer. We'll make it easy. Here." Joshua Mike held his putter out like a sword. He shook the head of the club at her, and she imagined swinging it into his shins. Its silver rod reflected in the sun.

"I can't. I'm working."

"Consider it part of the job. Wait a second." He moved closer to her. "Aren't you that girl from the cabin? With Zami?"

He glanced to Mr. Crawley and Chat for recognition.

"How about I play you for a beer?" Chat stepped between them, grabbing the head of the putter, swinging it upside down until it was pressed to the ground. "She's busy."

"Not *that* busy," Joshua Mike sang as he reopened a cooler. He took another beer. It didn't matter, Augie thought. She'd charge him for five. She knew his number, too.

"She's basically one of us! An old friend." He popped the top of his beer. "She's been to the elusive cabin! She's been through the life-threatening fire! You might as well join our foursome."

"Hey, are you hungry?" Mr. Crawley turned to Chat, ignoring Joshua Mike. "Gotta keep you fueled up if we're gonna take this thing."

He rubbed Chat's shoulders with two hands. Everything about this moment was making Augie uncomfortable.

"Oh fine," Joshua Mike whined and glanced at her name tag. "But next time, Augie, you owe me."

They all moved toward their carts, and for the last time, Augie slammed the coolers shut.

Augie would have paid to leave the happy hour if she could—the ultimate sign of a bad shift. It was a cacophony of a shit show: Beer glasses crashed from tables; metal chafers clanged back and forth as men piled chicken fingers and French fries and mini Reubens onto plates; everyone was jeering and guffawing, throwing around handshakes and *fuck yous*. Trophies adorned every table. "Participation awards," TC joked, and the whole room was cast in a dizzying glow from the rainbow of colorful, sweat-soaked polos.

The entire staff was struggling. The players had all arrived in waves, which threw off the timing of food, the lighting of Sternos, the stocking of the bar. The newbies looked like they might cry as they raced food back and forth, hands stinging from hot metal trays.

A few hours in, things finally started to relax. While most men were officially drunk—the valet would have to drive at least a handful home, or call a wash of cabs—they were manageable. Tired. Most were standing around the tables or mingling on the patio, everyone congratulating Mr. Wright and his guest, who had taken first place.

Mr. Crawley and Chat came in second. Augie avoided watching the ceremony, tuning out the golf pros' congratulations and Mr. Crawley's acceptance speech—"Couldn't have done it without my bud here"—as he took the silver. In fact, Augie had avoided watching Chat the entire event. Even when she spotted him from her periphery, even when she felt his attention land on her like a gavel, she focused elsewhere. She was tired, too. Tired and fed up with them all.

So, she was all the more surprised when, as she went to the lower level and unlocked the door to the storage room—they needed more IPAs, Joshua Mike was on a roll—Augie felt a hand on her back. She jumped.

"Sorry," Chat said, stepping away.

"What are you doing down here?" Shock vibrated through her.

"I didn't mean to scare you."

"Then what are you doing?"

Before he could respond, they heard a group yelling and laughing down the hall, likely headed to the men's locker room directly to their left. They both went still.

Augie filled her lungs and sighed in annoyance. "Fine, come on."

The contrast of the storage room to the Club was drastic: It was a huge, cement room, all exposed pipes and locked chain-link gates and endless boxes of booze. It was chilly, too, and as such, they all called the room "the cave." Augie shivered as she stepped inside, unlocked a gate, and slid it to the side—the sound of grating metal filling the room. She looked down at the boxes and searched for the IPAs, trying to concentrate on the task at hand.

"Now, this is where they should throw parties." Chat stared up at the ceiling, his fingers clasping the chain-link metal. "A warehouse party? Isn't that a thing?" He paused when Augie didn't respond. "Okay, look. I really don't mean to bother you. I know you're working."

"What do you want, then?" She was exhausted.

Chat looked boyish and disappointed as he adjusted his hat.

"I wanted to say I was sorry for Joshua Mike, for earlier. He is a complete fucking jerk."

Augie didn't move. "You don't have to be sorry for Joshua Mike. It's not on you."

"I know. But I was with them, and they were being assholes, and—"

"It's nothing new." She crouched over a box, scanning the labels, not looking at him.

"You know," Chat said after a second of silence, "I don't love hanging out with them, if that's what you think." His tone was impatient now, similar to her own. "I didn't even want to play today. I'd rather have stayed home with the boys."

He seemed upset, and it made Augie more irritated.

"Yeah, well it doesn't exactly suck to get paid to play golf all day. Or to go on vacation to a cabin-mansion, for that matter. It seems like you're all buddies." She wished she could ask him everything point-blank: What was his relationship with Mrs. Crawley like? Did he know they owed the Club money? How well did he know the Crawleys in general? She didn't know how to bring it up without seeming insane.

They searched each other, locked in surprise and challenge.

"Okay, but it's not exactly perfect, either. I wouldn't say we're *buddies*. I'm just stuck with them all the time. I don't know anyone else here besides you. And I know you don't exactly love seeing me. I'm not asking you to feel bad for me, I'm only saying—don't think I'm basking in it. At least you work with cool people. And you don't have to sleep at your job."

"You're right," she snapped. "I do not sleep at the Club, despite what some may think. And I do work with cool people. But you know what else I have to do? Carry up boxes of IPAs for the Joshua Mikes of the world. I wasn't even supposed to be here this summer." Augie's voice cracked, and she was glad to notice the box of IPAs to her side. She bent down to pick it up as Chat pulled off his hat, sticking it in his back pocket.

"This is coming out all wrong. Augie." He ran a hand through his hair. "I know we joke about it, but I really don't want to bother you. I really like being around you, talking to you . . . I haven't met anyone I liked this much in a long time . . . but if you want me to stop, I will. Just say the word."

Augie strained to lift the box, glad for the physical distraction, though her whole body felt weak. She hadn't met anyone she liked this much in a long time, either. She wished they'd met at a different time and place. She did like hearing that his life at the Crawleys' wasn't perfect, though. She hoped he didn't like Mrs. Crawley as much as she thought.

"You don't have to stop talking to me."

The connection between them pulled tighter.

"And you do have friends." She paused. "What about Max and Cooper?"

Chat smiled, relief radiating off him. "Well, yes. Cooper is my ride or die."

"See." Augie's muscles flexed as she adjusted the box. "I'm sure it'll work out. You don't need to be sorry. About Joshua Mike or anything."

Chat pivoted as he watched her go. He pointed to the box. "Do you need—"

"I don't need help."

"Okay."

Augie reached for the door and felt her body nearing his, only the box between them.

"So, I might be pushing it here, but does this mean I can see you again? Maybe on purpose next time?" Chat put his hands in his pockets, twisting his forearms forward.

Augie studied his hopeful expression.

"I thought you weren't allowed to hang out with people at the Club? Didn't you say that at the swim meet? When Mrs. Crawley"—she hated saying her name, the way it soured the space between them—"came to the pool? You basically ran away."

"Oh no, it's cool. She just worries about the boys, and other mothers, at the Club. Especially around the pool . . . Cooper wanders, and he's not a good swimmer. I just didn't want her to worry. I probably overreacted." Chat pointed out his thumbs from where his hands were still in his pockets. "But when the boys are at activities or in bed, I'm off duty. A free man." He lifted and widened his arms as if taking in the world.

Augie didn't buy it. There was no way Mrs. Crawley would be okay with them spending time together, "off duty" or not. She so clearly despised Augie, wanted a tight grip on Chat. Still, Augie was flattered by his words. In a weird way, she also felt like she was winning.

"Look, Chat," she sighed, "this summer is crazy, okay? I lost my real job, and I'm looking for another, so I need to focus. I don't know if I can make plans or whatever." In her mind, she added, *As much as I want to.*

The box was straining her arms now, and as her grip suddenly gave out, Chat reached forward and caught the bottom of it, crossing their forearms. Augie felt the hot intersection of their skin. Her gaze flicked from their arms up to his mouth. His face was just a foot away now. For a second, she thought he might lean across and kiss her—but then they heard banging at the door.

"Augie?" TC called. "Any luck with those IPAs? You-know-who is pitching a fit."

"Be right there," she yelled back. "One sec."

Chat stood still as TC said thanks.

A second later, the silence felt louder than ever. Chat's presence felt louder than ever.

"You can't be down here," Augie whispered, though to her surprise, she was almost laughing now. What did it matter, really? Who the hell really cared?

"This is kind of the holy grail."

Augie twisted her mouth to hide her smile.

"Okay, I'll let you go. Be careful with that precious cargo."

Augie readjusted the weight of the box in her arms and moved toward the door.

"Augie, one last question. How about instead I just get your number?"

Augie leaned into the door's horizontal handle until it clicked.

"Well, I am trying to stay off my phone. But"—she paused, knowing this was a bad idea, yet continuing all the same—"if you really want to get in touch, my last name is Elling. You can find me on LinkedIn. That's the only social media I'm using these days."

Chat beamed. "That makes sense. I couldn't find your profiles. Though, again, I was only *lightly* stalking. I appreciate the invitation to connect."

Augie thought of Leah's comment then, how he hadn't accepted her friend request. It seemed surprising given he had tried to find Augie online, although Leah had said he didn't post often. He didn't seem like the kind of guy who would be social media savvy; he was too down to earth.

"All right, I gotta go. *We* have to go." Augie pushed the door open and glanced down the hall to make sure they were in the clear. "You leave first. I don't want you to get locked in here or something . . . You know they'd *all* be missing you."

"And I'd be missing *you*." Chat stepped out the door, cocked his head, and spun back toward her. "All right, was that too far? Too cheesy? A little cringe?" He smiled wider as he walked backward down the hall, holding eye contact as he pulled his hat from his pocket and put it on.

Finally, despite herself, Augie laughed.

Chat Efhart • 9:37 PM
This is really you right
Not Allie Von Something
Augie Elling • 10:14 PM
That's just my boat persona.
But yes, it's just me now.
Unfortunately.
Chat Efhart • 10:15 PM
Definitely not unfortunate
Although I liked the boat persona too
How was the rest of your night?
Augie Elling • 10:16 PM
It was fine, long.
Mr. Quaglia's group would not leave.
Had to get the valet to kick them out.
Chat Efhart • 10:16 PM
Oh yeah they were slamming those moscow mules
Weird drink of choice
At least it wasn't IPAs
Augie Elling • 10:17 PM
That's true.
Couldn't have handled another trip to the cage.
Chat Efhart • 10:17 PM
My new favorite spot
Augie Elling • 10:18 PM
You're cut off from the cage.

Chat Efhart • 10:19 PM
Fair enough
Boundaries drawn
Augie Elling • 10:19 PM
Apparently not, since I'm talking to you right now.
Chat Efhart • 10:20 PM
Well I feel honored
Do you have a day off soon?
Augie Elling • 10:22 PM
Thursday.
What about you?
Chat Efhart • 10:24 PM
Well Mr. C is gone this week and Mrs. C is working a lot
So it's going to be a little crazy
Plus we have 3 birthday parties
On top of taekwondo and art class
One party is a rave
Augie Elling • 10:30 PM
She works?
Chat Efhart • 10:30 PM
She's a designer
Decorator?
Or whatever you call it
That's why their houses are so cool
Augie Elling • 10:35 PM
Got it.
Well sounds like a week for all of you.
Chat Efhart • 10:35 PM
Taekwondo is especially rough/hilarious

Cooper hates it
He's a lover, not a fighter
Secretly excited for the rave tho
Apparently there's going to be a DJ?
And we're supposed to wear neon?
Will report back

Augie Elling • 10:47 PM

Insane.
Good luck.

Chat Efhart • 10:48 PM

Thanks
But hey
Next week will be less busy
And both boys have a new spanish class that starts at 11
So no pressure
I don't want to push the boundaries
But if you ever wanna meet at hyla
I'm there all the time
Or we could go to noelle's for ice cream
The sundaes are amazing

Augie Elling • 10:50 PM

If you're not getting malts at Noelle's, you're doing it wrong.

Chat Efhart • 10:52 PM

Malts?
Definitely doing it wrong
Need you to show me your ways

Augie Elling • 11:02 PM

Yes. They're iconic.

But okay.

Maybe.

Chat Efhart • 11:05 PM

I'll take maybe

I should probably go to bed

I'm on a 5 yr old's schedule

Augie Elling • 11:07 PM

Gnight

Congrats on second place.

Chat Efhart • 11:08 PM

I'll take that, too

Good night, Augie

14

Danika was glad when Bill left town after the golf tournament. He had a business trip in Chicago Wednesday through Friday, and he'd been tense lately. The house felt better without him. They didn't even sit down for dinner. Rather, she and Chat stood around the kitchen island next to the boys and picked at containers of olives and slices of Gruyère, or whatever casserole Zami had left in the freezer. Danika always had an extra glass of wine, standing against the counter with one leg bent, pressed to the other like a flamingo. Sometimes, at her encouragement, Chat had a beer.

Though this week, she would admit, they could have used Bill's help. On top of regular activities, Cooper had three birthday parties, each competing to be the best: One was a rave complete with a DJ; the next was ranch-themed, with an entire farm of animals dumped on the front lawn; and the last was a monster tea party, featuring endless cookies and cakes. Danika already feared what Cooper would expect for his sixth birthday come fall.

Danika felt bad watching Chat rush from one place to the next. She thought about canceling plans to help, but she reminded herself that's why they'd hired a nanny in the first place. She had a job now—she had work to do. She was also glad to have an excuse to avoid the other parents. It was a win-win. She'd even asked Chat to remind them she was busy working the Briar Ridge project. If it came up.

She knew she would come up. Word about the drama at the cabin had spread, and people were more intrigued than ever. A fire was excellent gossip. Under normal circumstances, Danika would be horrified, but she was glad it overshadowed the other passive-aggressive plays—the "Would You Rather" game and the crude remarks. Plus, the fire had been Bill's fault, not hers. That was another pillar of marriage, Danika reasoned later: a constant exchange of blame.

Once everyone had gone downstairs after the fire, Bill had asked to talk to her in the garage. He had been desperate, red-faced. "Do you not understand," he'd finally snapped, "that I invited them here for a reason? I need them to have a good time. Please, Danika. I need you to get it together." Still, Danika had been drunk and indignant. She slurred that he was the one who needed to get it together, then left to go to the bathroom—and find Chat.

Now, Danika felt purely confused. It didn't make sense why he needed those men in particular to have so much damn fun. It felt off, like he was hiding something. For the first time, Danika wondered if Bill was having an affair. She'd be surprised—while a flirt, he held himself to high moral (and religious) standards—but it'd be an explanation for his strange behavior.

Infidelity had always been a confusing topic for Danika. Her mother had been so proud she'd never cheated on her father while he was deployed, unlike so many others. "Do you see those broomsticks on the porches with the lights on?" she'd explained to Danika one evening as they drove around base at dusk. "That means they're open for business. It's an invitation."

Danika sometimes wondered if her mother should have left her father. Her parents had fought hard and often. Maybe a divorce would have made them all happier. She'd said this to her mother once after a particularly bad fight, but she'd only scoffed, said, "And then what? What do you suppose I do?" Danika hadn't known how to respond. Her mother always said she'd drained her potential by marrying her father—that her ship had sailed as soon as she signed up for army life, became a dependent. "Really, Danika, tell me. How do you suppose I start over?"

But she and Bill were different, Danika reminded herself. They hardly ever had blowout fights. They respected each other, viewed each other as someone, or something, to be proud of. Their family was picture perfect; their life was a dream come true.

No one had overheard them in the garage and she'd successfully hidden her other, deeper grievance of the night: how much she despised Augie.

Danika had tried to broach the subject with Chat over the week. First, after the fireworks. She'd told herself to wait until morning when she was sober and calm, but she couldn't help it. As they helped the boys brush their teeth that evening, she'd looked at him in the mirror and asked if he was friends with that waiter. Augie. He had looked away, said they'd talked at the Club a few times, but he didn't know her well, not really.

The next time, they were sitting on the dock, dangling their feet in the water, catching minnows with the boys, and she—after asking which days he planned to go to Hyla that week, claiming she wanted extra ajvar—mentioned it was nice Teuta and Zami worked so closely with the Club. Then she asked if he ever saw any members, or staff, at the bakery. He had once again averted his eyes. He said no, he never saw anyone he knew. "But I don't know anyone," he'd added, laughing, before jumping in the water.

Danika wasn't sure how to feel. He was clearly uncomfortable, but she truly did not think he would lie to her. They were too close. He also hadn't done anything wrong. Augie was the one chasing him around, up to the cabin. She was the problem.

The week had been so lovely, too. Danika didn't want to ruin the memories of swimming and fishing and roasting marshmallows by harping on her. She'd have to trust him, Danika reasoned. Trust him, and keep him busy.

That week, indeed, was busy. Danika spent hours finalizing her trade account before receiving her vendor ID—the golden ticket to buying with a designer discount. It had been a long process; she'd had to issue her LLC, set up a separate business bank account, provide proof of accreditation, and more. But here she was, finally a true professional. She couldn't wait to start buying for the model home. That was her plan for Saturday: Once Bill was back to take the boys, she'd head to Oval at the Galleria. Hopefully with Chat.

Danika was aware that furniture shopping wasn't everyone's idea of fun, but she figured Chat would want to get out of the house. While Chat was an extrovert—if she was going to indulge in Jackie's little theories—he didn't venture out often. She had made it clear he was off duty once the boys were in bed, wanting to downplay how much she liked having him around, but he rarely left. She got the feeling he didn't like going out by himself, and he claimed he didn't have any friends in the Cities. This made her feel better about the Augie situation—and, even more, she basked in the idea that he might simply enjoy her company. Once, they'd watched six reruns of *Friends* after the boys fell asleep. Another time, they'd killed hours on the deck of the Walleye, eating nachos, sipping Blue Moons.

"So what exactly makes it a Galleria and not just a mall?" Chat said. They stood in the cedar mudroom, putting on their shoes. "You sure you don't want to go to the Mall of America? Ride the roller coasters?"

Danika laughed and slipped one arm into her Sandro sweater. There was nowhere grosser than the Mall of America.

"Well, the stores are nicer. More artistic. So, it's more of a gallery than your average JCPenney. No roller coasters."

"Am I underdressed?" Chat wore a green Wild T-shirt and his standard gym shorts.

"You're fine," Danika assured him, although he was.

Beyond them, from the living room, they heard Max begin to cry, Bill begin to groan. They rushed to the car.

If it was possible, Bill was even more on edge since he had gotten home from his business trip. Danika had tried to ask him what was wrong, but he brushed her off, poured another drink. She knew for certain Bill was hiding something now, and she had a growing sense it was something wrong with work. But if Bill wasn't ready to share, it was pointless to force him. She had to wait—and double down on her job. Making Briar Ridge a success could only help.

"The design store can be a little over the top," Danika explained as they parked at the Galleria, "but I think the buyers will love it. I'll need your honest opinion on some pieces, too."

This was true. Chat had already visited Briar Ridge with them several times, and Danika liked to think he could help balance out her choices.

"Oh, and the Grazing Globe is an amazing restaurant. If we have time, we'll grab lunch." Danika knew they'd have time. She'd already made a reservation.

"All for it," Chat said as they started across the lot. "Just as long as I don't have to eat any more birthday cake."

"Chat, sick of cake? I never thought I'd see the day."

The Galleria was gorgeous. It had two sprawling levels, an arched glass ceiling, a baby grand piano surrounded by flowers, and low fountains running down the center of each corridor. The air smelled clean and expensive.

"Think they'd mind if I played 'Chopsticks'?" Chat pointed as they passed the empty piano. "Or do you know 'Heart and Soul'? We could duet. Those are, unfortunately, the only songs in my repertoire."

"'Heart and Soul'? My god," Danika said earnestly, "that brings me back."

Danika's pace slowed as her mind plunged back to North Carolina. Her mother had signed her up for piano lessons one summer on one of her "we're going to be better" kicks, but after only two weeks, she said it wasn't worth the money. Now that old tune plinked through Danika's mind, and she wondered what her mother was doing at that very moment. She'd moved to Idaho for some new guy she'd met online the year Danika left St. Cloud, and they'd only seen each other once since, right after Cooper was born. Danika was too scared to combine her then-world and now-world. Her mother had never even met Bill. And while Danika could not tell Bill the primary reason she kept their distance, there were plenty. He didn't fight it. No man begged for a mother-in-law.

"Personally, I think it'd be a hit. I'm pretty bad, though. My mom is the piano prodigy."

Of course Katie was, Danika thought.

"Ah, I forgot to call her back." Chat tipped his head as if talking to himself. He looked surprised and guilty as he glanced to Danika, who was pretending not to have heard.

Danika hoped he didn't notice how anytime he mentioned his family, she shut down. Originally, she thought she'd actually pry into the subject—she was so eager to hear what they were up to, how they were—but in reality, each time the subject surfaced, she went quiet. She didn't want to risk revealing herself. For better or worse, Chat also didn't mention his family often.

Danika was still relieved that the few times she had heard him on the phone with his mom, he'd continued to refer to Danika as Mrs. Crawley, never using her first name. Surely if Katie heard "Danika," it would make her pause.

After running a few errands, they headed toward the lower level, where Oval encompassed half floor. They stepped onto the escalator behind a woman in a tweed dress and a man in a checked sports coat, and as they floated downward, Chat leaned up to Danika.

"Hey, I think you lied to me," he whispered.

Danika heartbeat grew in her ears. "What?"

"I think I am underdressed." He nodded toward the regal-looking couple.

Relief folded over her. "Absolutely not. You look great."

Time slipped by as Danika explored the showroom, soaking in natural woods and crisp fabrics, all the low-lit lamps. She circled the latest collections, the dining tables she'd been coveting. Danika was a regular by now, and salespeople flocked to her. Danika grew lost in thought as she worked, imagining each piece in Briar Ridge. She was so entranced that she had no idea how much time had passed when she heard her phone ding—their reservation reminder.

"Oh, shoot." She sat up fast from a sectional. She searched for Chat, who sat at a nearby desk, looking at his phone. "Hungry?" she called out.

Danika said her goodbyes and promised to call in orders that evening. Part of her was disappointed to leave, but she was excited for lunch. She didn't want to go home yet.

"I really don't know how you do that," Chat said.

"What?" She shifted her purse on her shoulder as they started up the escalator.

"Design stuff, decorate. How you make it all look like it does. Those Briar Ridge houses are so empty. I wouldn't know where to start. I'd put a bed and a chair in each room and be like, that's the best I got. You would have died if you saw my dorm room."

Danika smoothed her hair, ignoring the butterflies in her stomach. She wasn't sure Chat had ever complimented her before—not like this.

"Oh, everyone has talents. I could never play hockey."

"Oh, I think you'd be pretty good."

She felt flattered once again. She didn't want to reveal any more knowledge about her history with hockey, though. She'd already slipped that day at the Club, talking with that bartender. She'd regretted that immediately. "Who knows. Maybe in another life."

"Maybe."

As predicted, Chat was taken with the restaurant. It was beautiful—dark blue wallpaper and long gold mirrors, ceilings covered in vines—and the menu was exceptional, a taste of the world. It had everything from Chinese shu mai to Scottish herring to the cheesy Georgian bread she knew Chat would love. Though he rarely brought up his travel plans, she hoped this would be a natural way to talk about them; she was finally ready.

As requested, they were seated in her favorite booth in the back. Above, a brass monkey chandelier offered low, warm light that reflected in the speckled mirrors at their sides.

"Okay, so, I think we need to get the shashlik," Danika said to Chat as the waiter brought her wine and Chat's Coke. The menu was huge, and Chat kept flipping it back and forth.

"I don't want to panic order." He hunched forward. "Ah, I love Peking duck."

"Me too," Danika lied.

Danika felt like she was floating as they ordered and began to eat. Everything was perfect. Together, they rolled slices of duck in thin, floury pancakes, pulled apart buttery khachapuri, made fun of each other's chopstick skills. Normally, Danika wouldn't eat so much, but she felt as if she were experiencing a parallel world—a life that could have been. Bill and the boys seemed impossibly far away.

"I think I overdid it," Chat said as the waiter brought yet another dish. He'd just been telling her about how he wanted to visit Spain after Germany. Danika tensed, waiting for him to discuss visiting the Baltics—but there was no mention of Latvia.

"Okay." He put his hands on the table as the waiter left. "I'm going to run to the bathroom. On top of everything, I shouldn't have had three of these." He twisted his Coke glass.

Danika reached for the last of her second glass of wine. She wanted another, but she was driving home. Chat rose and she pointed him toward the back.

Alone, Danika breathed deeply, rolled the Riesling around on her tongue. She felt more peaceful than she had in a while. She'd needed this, she realized—she'd needed to escape the house and whatever was going on with Bill.

Thoughts of Bill brought her back to reality, and she pulled out her phone. She was happy to see no new calls or messages. She put it back in her purse and studied the table, wondering if they should pack up the leftovers. She was organizing the dishes when she saw a flash of light, heard a ding. Chat had left his phone on the table. It had a big crack in it—she'd told him she'd help replace it by summer's end, though he kept refusing—yet, despite the shattered glass, and despite the fact she was viewing it upside down, she could still read the words on the screen. It was the LinkedIn app. Accompanied by the words You have one new message from Augie Elling.

Danika froze, her neck straining in place as the world seemed to grow louder around her. She swallowed. Then, before she could stop herself, she grabbed the phone.

Danika's fingers moved on reflex as she glanced from the cracked screen to the back of the restaurant, and quickly, she typed in Chat's passcode: "1-2-3-4." She had learned it once when they needed driving directions. It was so Chat. So direct. As soon as the home screen flashed before her, she opened the LinkedIn app, clicked the inbox, and just like that, as she glided her finger upward as if raising the volume of her pain, she felt all the ease and joy of the day snatched away.

There were so many messages. Not one or two—but whole conversations, lines of texts. Danika felt physically ill as she scrolled, pressing her finger to the glass to find the beginning. Finally, she found the first message he'd sent, the night after the golf tournament. Danika held her hand to her abdomen, all the food she'd eaten threatening to rise. They were flirting. Joking. Referencing a boat? When had they been on a boat? Danika felt her esophagus burn as suddenly, the phone started to vibrate, and she dropped it on the table. *Mom* flashed on the screen alongside Katie's picture.

"Hey, are you okay?" Chat appeared next to her, standing at the table.

Danika blinked, her mouth dropping open. "Your, here." She felt faint as she held his phone out to him, shoving it away.

"Oh, damn, thanks." He reached out, his ears blushing. Had he seen her? Did he know what she'd seen? "I should probably take this. Do you mind?"

Danika forced a weak smile. As soon as he left, she flagged the waiter and asked for another glass of wine—a half carafe, actually. Chat always wanted to drive her car. This time, she would let him.

By the time they got home, the boys were watching a movie. *Of course*, Danika thought, incensed as she stared into the TV's snowy Arendelle. Bill always sought the easy way out. She didn't have it in her to say something, though. Her mind was too pickled with Riesling and consumed with thoughts of Chat and Augie, all those words. She felt incredibly off—incredibly *hurt*. She was simultaneously angry at Chat for blatantly lying yet also wanted him closer to her than ever.

On the drive home, Chat had asked what was wrong. She'd swatted it away, but now, as she went to the fridge and poured another glass of wine, she had to face it. If that girl was going to try to seduce him, Danika needed to at least know he'd stay loyal to her. That he cared about her. That their friendship and bond were real. She wouldn't be able to handle it otherwise. She'd be, once more, alone.

"Ah, this is the best part." Chat nudged Cooper over on the couch as Olaf started in on his song about summer. Danika sensed that Chat was about to snuggle up with the boys, and then her chance would be over. She stepped forward.

"Hey, Chat," she said as he leaned back. "Can we talk for a second?"

Chat paused, sat up. "Sure."

"Let's go to the patio." She held her wine tight and turned on her heels.

Danika didn't know what she was going to say as they headed toward the enclosed patio, settling into the low armchairs, the sun streaming through the glass around them, lighting up the pale blue cushions and rounded glass coffee table. She stared at the arrangement of white tulips in the center. She bit a piece of chapped skin from her lips.

"Look, Chat." Danika's mind sputtered. She focused on a single tulip. She truly did not know where she was going with this, but she plowed forward anyway, some subconscious, desperate part of her taking control. "I wanted to thank you for coming with me today. I know furniture shopping is not your most favorite activity."

"No, it was great, I—"

"No, I know, I'm not crazy," she cut him off. "So really, I appreciate it. I also appreciate your driving home. I'm sorry that I drank, am drinking, a bit more than usual today." She winced as she sloshed the wine in her glass, feeling raw and exposed but maniacally thrilled by it all.

"Don't be sorry." Chat jiggled his legs. "It's a Saturday. You can do whatever you want. No judgment. Have fun."

Danika took a more confident sip, happy to be a passenger in her own mind.

"I especially appreciate it because, well, I don't want to put you in a weird spot, or overshare," she said, knowing on some level that was exactly what she was doing, "but today is a tough day for me. Today is sixteen years since my father killed himself."

Chat's legs slowed to a stop.

"And it's so bizarre, because I was sixteen at the time, and it's been another sixteen years since, which means that day is now the exact midpoint of my life. I feel so strange, like from now on, I'll be further away from him than ever." This was the first time Danika had put these feelings together, the first time she'd found the right words. Even if the anniversary of his death wasn't until the following Tuesday, July eighteenth, everything else was true and newly clear in her mind.

"Mrs. Crawley." Chat scooted forward and rested his elbows on his knees. "Danika." His eye contact was so heavy, she had to blink. "I'm so sorry."

Danika felt blood rush to her face. She'd never heard him say her first name before—his voice sounded just the same, an echo of the past. Danika picked up her glass, her arm shaking.

"Thank you. It was a long time ago, obviously, but it's still a tough day. Even more so because—you won't believe it; I still can't—but it's also the same date that I officially got divorced from my first husband, signed the papers." She raised her eyebrows and took another sip. This was true of the real anniversary, but not today. "Ironic, right? Not exactly my best day." She almost told him this was why she hated the number eighteen but caught herself at the last minute, remembering today was only the fifteenth.

Danika went quiet. Then, she laughed out loud, shaking her head—at her heartbreak, at her reckless admission. *What am I doing?* she suddenly thought, sobering. She hadn't meant to share this. She really had not. She was fully out of control now, some inner demon reaching out its arms to pull Chat closer—closer to her secrets and truest self.

"It's a lot of loss. A tough day, week, month, really." She slipped out a breath and batted her hand in the air, trying to backtrack.

"Danika," Chat repeated. He reached one hand out to her knee. She stared down at his fingers. It turned silent as a low heat settled in the base of her stomach.

"I don't know why I'm telling you all this," Danika whispered.

She continued clutching her glass as she stared at Chat's hand on her leg. She felt the pressure of each of his individual fingers, as if his fingerprints were burning through her jeans into her skin, making her his.

"It's okay." He squeezed her knee with his whole hand as he looked up at her, his head tilted to the side as if she were a hurt child.

"But, Chat, you have to promise me," she said slowly, "not to tell Bill."

"What?" To Danika's dismay, Chat dropped his hand.

"Bill," she repeated, talking faster. "He cannot know about the divorce, that I was married before. It's a long story, but he'd loathe me if he knew." Her panic was peaking now—because it was true. This was why she had not mentioned her divorce to a soul in Aldon Lakes. "I'm sorry. I don't know what's come over me." She smoothed her hair solemnly. "I shouldn't be putting this on you. It's just, *this day.* But I do need you to promise me. You know how religious Bill is. I know it seems dramatic, but it would be a mess."

"Don't worry." Chat's expression grew more focused. "I'm here for you. Really. I can keep a secret."

Danika stared at him.

"Don't worry," Chat repeated. He scooted closer to the edge of his chair, and Danika couldn't help but find comfort in his concern. He *did* care about her; his sympathy felt genuine—their connection real. It made her feel worthy and loved.

Danika didn't know what to say next, but before she could speak, Chat stood. For a second, she was terrified he was turning to leave, but as he rose and opened his arms, she understood, clarity washing over her like sunlight. She set down her glass. Stood to meet him. Embraced him. She thought she might cry as she rested her cheek against his chest. And as she clung to him, turning her face inward, clenching her arms around his strong, curved back, she became fully lost in the memory of touch—fully transported in time. She could almost smell her old high school house, that beat-up pickup truck, the T-shirts she'd steal to sleep in. As another beat passed, she felt so disconnected from her body that, without hesitating, she suddenly leaned up and pressed her lips to the space below his jawline, the tip of her tongue meeting the salt of his skin.

It took a few seconds before he spoke. But more than her name, what finally snapped Danika back to reality was the feeling of his throat tensing under her mouth. She jumped back.

"Oh my god, Chat, I'm so sorry." She pressed her hand to her forehead, turning toward the windows. "I must be losing my mind. I didn't mean to—"

"It's fine, it's fine." Chat stepped forward until they were inches apart again. "Seriously. This is a tough day. Don't think twice about it." His expression was so assured and steady that, to Danika's surprise, she let her shoulders relax.

"I promise I'm not coming on to you." Her eyes filled as she tried to laugh.

Quickly, Chat pulled her into another hug—but this time, her arms were at her sides, so as he wrapped his arms around her body, it was as if she were in a straitjacket, forced to calm down. It worked. He rocked them side to side, shifting their weight from one foot to the other.

"I know, I know," he said over the top of her head. She held her breath until he pulled away. Still, he kept his hands on her shoulders as he leaned down to look straight at her. "It's really okay." He shook her shoulders once, teasing, dissolving any last awkwardness.

Danika rubbed her nose.

"Though, you know, anyone would be flattered if you *were* coming on to them." Chat dropped his hands, smiling. "You know you're beautiful. That anyone would be an idiot . . . any guy would be an idiot . . . to let you go. Your ex"—he studied her—"it's his loss. I mean it. You're amazing."

Danika's breath shuddered as she suppressed her emotions.

"And look"—he glanced to his watch—"there's only six hours left in the day. It will be over soon. Why don't you go finish *Frozen* with the boys? You'll never guess what happens."

Danika laughed for real. They'd all seen *Frozen* too many times to count.

"Okay. I hope it's a happy ending."

Chat was the one laughing now. "Me too."

15

"This half is cheese, and this half is meat," Teuta said.

Augie sat at a communal table by Hyla's front window. It was a few minutes before open, and she'd brought her laptop to job search while her mom helped Teuta. Zami was visiting his brother in Iowa, and Augie's mom liked to support Teuta whenever she could. Augie usually did, too, but after their conversations about Augie's job search on the drive to the Crawleys' cabin, Teuta insisted she just come hang out and work on her applications.

Augie was glad that now that she was messaging Chat, she had a better idea of his schedule; she knew he was too busy to be at Hyla today. She wasn't ready to see him yet, let alone around her mom.

She was enjoying talking to him on LinkedIn, though. It didn't feel as intimate or all-encompassing as texting—and the reward of conversation helped her get things done throughout the day. She'd tell herself she could not check her inbox until she completed X or Y or Z. This additionally helped space out her messages to him. She liked to keep him waiting, to imagine him checking his phone again and again, growing more eager to hear from her. In a twisted way, each message felt like a dig against Mrs. Crawley.

Messaging Chat directly also made Augie feel like she was taking control of the situation. Especially after deciding not to bug Leah about him anymore. Augie had felt so awful about missing Lyle's birthday dinner. While she had apologized profusely, and Leah had said it wasn't a big deal, that she didn't expect her to remember, Augie still felt distressed. She promised to make it up to her—though Leah reminded her she'd be busy up until the Hotel Harrison's restaurant opening. But at least they were back to texting as normal.

Even now, Augie took a photo of the fresh platter of mantia Teuta had set in front of her and sent it to Leah. Mantia was their favorite. Augie breathed in the fried, egg roll–like squares.

"Watch out, they're hot," her mom called from behind the counter as Augie lifted one to her mouth. Her mom wore a purple Hyla apron with the logo Augie had designed years ago.

Teuta adjusted a few chairs as she made her way toward the kitchen. The whole bakery was a mash-up of colorful furniture and art, sunflower paintings alongside framed cartoons, one lime green wall, one blue, an L-shaped bookshelf in the corner that served as a Little Free Library.

"You sure you're good?" Augie said as her mom and Teuta shuffled in the kitchen.

"We're good, girl. You keep up those applications." Teuta returned carrying creamer and sugar for the coffee stand. "We've gotta get you out of that Club. I don't know how you can stand it anymore. The Fourth of July about did me in."

Augie pulled apart the mantia, watching the steam rise.

"At least we got to hang out with the cute manny, right?" Teuta lowered her voice so Augie's mom couldn't hear, knowing it would embarrass Augie.

Augie forced a laugh, looked at her computer. Even on the ride back from the cabin, Teuta had been after Augie to ask him out, citing how cute and nice he was. How often he came into Hyla, raving about all the food, asking about Kosovo and those early days in Minnesota.

Augie felt bad about lying to Teuta. Maybe, if she told her everything, it would bring them closer, but it felt too difficult now. There was no way to honestly explain the situation without admitting how much she'd withheld at the Fourth of July, how scarred she was from New York, and how weird everything was with Mrs. Crawley. It all seemed too messy, and she didn't want to lose Teuta's respect.

"Do you guys have any more parties coming up?" Augie asked, changing the subject.

"Let's hope not." Teuta swirled a stack of napkins with her fist. "I keep telling Dad to cool it on the catering, we're so busy, but you know how he is. He can never say no. Especially to our regular clients. That's how we ended up doing the Crawley party so last minute. He can't say no to dear old Danika."

Augie twisted her mouth, unsure whether she'd meant this endearingly or condescendingly. "Do they have parties often?"

"No, not really. They are some of our oldest clients—she doesn't cook—but they don't usually host. I was shocked they even had people to the cabin. Especially Joshua Mike." She shook her head, her dark braid swinging. "It's no wonder it turned into such a disaster." She sighed and glanced out the window, frowning.

"Why do you think they don't have parties?"

"Oh, I don't know. I get the feeling Danika is kinda a homebody. I like that about her."

Augie clenched her jaw, suddenly curious how well Teuta knew her. Maybe she, of all people, had a sense of their money troubles.

"Those private parties are expensive, right? I mean, you guys are definitely worth it. I'm only saying, maybe that's why they don't have them often?"

"Yeah. I suppose. I don't think that's really a factor. You saw that cabin. Maybe I'm too old and tired for *any* party now. Maybe you should help me apply for new jobs." She laughed as she turned and began cleaning the windows.

"What do you mean Danika is kinda a homebody? I feel like she's always at the Club."

Teuta wrung her rag between her hands as if searching for the right words. "It feels like she's always playing along, if that makes sense. She acts different—nicer—when it's only you and her, one-on-one. She's smart, too. She was one of few people who knew where Kosovo was right off the bat. She used to live in Europe."

Augie felt frustrated to hear more good things about Mrs. Crawley. Mrs. Crawley had definitely not been nicer to her when it had been only the two of them, *one-on-one*, lighting those candles on the porch.

"I'm sure everyone acts a certain way at the Club, though. *Extra* extra. I applaud you for sticking with it, I really do." Teuta sat next to Augie and patted her arm, reading yet misplacing her distress. "I know it's not the job you want, but don't sell yourself short. There are two types of people in this world: People who have worked in the service industry, and those who have not. Never be embarrassed about it. Put that shit on your résumé." She tapped her computer.

Augie scanned her résumé, where she had definitely not listed her job at the Club. It didn't fit with all her college clubs and competitions and DECA work. Augie suddenly wondered if Teuta viewed her as spoiled.

"Yeah. I should. The Club's not that bad, though. At least it's not the The Manor. Thanks to you." Augie wanted Teuta to know she admired her—wanted to feel close to her again.

"Thank god for that." Another shadow moved over Teuta's face.

This was true. If not for her, Augie likely *would have* applied to The Manor. It was the default summer job for most high school kids—especially girls who wanted to show off in the jean shorts and tank top uniform—but Teuta had forbidden it.

"Try to keep your spirits up, Aug. You never know what good thing is just around the corner."

Augie sucked one side of her cheek, pausing. "I don't know if there will be some good thing around the corner. I kind of feel like I'm being punished."

"What makes you say that? You're the best of the best."

Augie looked out to the bakery, instinctively studying the bulletin board on the far wall—the pinned-up scratch card Teuta had won all those years ago. That money had come at the exact right time, Teuta had explained. She'd been twenty-one and struggling at The Manor. She and Zami could barely make ends meet, but then, *boom*, and $50,000 later, they had enough to open the bakery. Look at them now. It was a fairy tale, really, Augie had always thought, even if it made her uneasy. What if they *hadn't* won? Where would they be? To Augie, it was anxiety-inducing to believe fate was stronger than self-determination. She hated any lack of control.

Augie had often thought of Teuta when she was working on the lottery campaign at the ad agency. It was amazing Teuta had even thought to play. Maybe she had felt it inside her—that she was lucky. Maybe on some level, she knew the universe would reward her for being a good person. Maybe fate and karma *were* most powerful. If that was true, there was no good thing coming Augie's way.

Augie leaned back and tightened her ponytail, batted her hand in the air. "It's okay. It's nothing. I'm too in my head right now. I've taken too many personality tests." She adjusted her wrists on her laptop. "It's all good. Really. No worries."

Whether she believed her or not, Teuta stood up, kissed Augie's head, and flipped the door's sign to "Open."

On the eighteenth, Augie had to work a baby shower at the Club, and things were already off to a bad start. The host, Mrs. Harrison, arrived late to set up. She explained she'd had to go to three party stores to find gold and pink napkins. Augie tried to hide her annoyance as they unpacked bags of ribbon and sequins and taffeta. Augie found it infuriating when people were particular yet disorganized. This shower also seemed to be held to higher standards because it was for Miriam Silver, a news anchor on KARE 11—a local celebrity.

To make matters worse, one of the newbies called in sick, so it was only Augie, Aida, and another new girl working. They were all overwhelmed as they sorted the decor, the mess of pink.

"So do we think it's a girl or a boy?" Augie said, irritated.

Aida stifled a laugh.

Now, ten minutes to start, Augie was worried for different reasons. She had a feeling Robin would be there. She had forgotten to ask Leah outright, but she knew Robin and Miriam were friends. It would be the first time she'd seen Robin since New York.

She was also stressed about seeing Mrs. Crawley, though she was trying to feel more apathetic than afraid.

Augie still braced herself as the women began to arrive, each wearing a dress fit for Easter brunch. First, there was Mrs. Anderson, then Schmidt, Fravel, and Cline. Augie always found the women worse as a group. Even if they were fine individually, together, there was an air of competition, a passive-aggressive politeness. It was most obvious at the women's golf or tennis tournaments—everyone silently undercutting one another. At least the men didn't hide their outbursts and insults. It was almost a relief when people were openly volatile.

Then suddenly, there was Mrs. Crawley, drawing everyone's attention as she entered the room. She looked stunning in a light blue dress, nude heels, natural yet refined makeup. Augie fingered her bowtie.

"Thank you," Mrs. Crawley said to the new girl as she took a Bellini from her tray, tucking her straw clutch under her arm. She surveyed the room, and Augie felt her pause as she saw her—betraying the briefest blip of recognition and scorn—before turning to Miriam and Mrs. Harrison. She gave them each light hugs, congratulating Miriam.

Augie kept her head down as she refilled drinks and reminded Mrs. Harrison of the timeline. But as the shower continued and women shuffled, she became overly aware of Mrs. Crawley. Out of the corner of her eye, she watched her every move. It didn't help that Mrs. Crawley was seated in her section, which meant Augie would be serving her. So be it. At least they were on a more equal field at the Club. This wasn't the cabin. The Club belonged to them both.

Nonetheless, as lunch service started, Augie tensed each time she approached her table.

She couldn't help but notice every detail about Mrs. Crawley: how she barely ate, how she kept touching her pendant necklace, how she smelled of patchouli and Riesling. She seemed more talkative than usual, too, discussing some design project, the boys' Spanish classes, Hilton Head. She was acting strangely outgoing and chatty, her words sliding into one another like a sentence with no spaces.

The only time she stopped speaking was when Mrs. Cline complimented her necklace. Mrs. Crawley froze, mid-sentence, as Mrs. Cline leaned down to study the pendant, asking if it was amber.

"Is it from the Baltics? Latvia? Poland?" Mrs. Cline asked, using it as an excuse to dive into her own story about purchasing gemstones during her Viking Baltic cruise. Mrs. Crawley held the stone firmly between her thumb and forefinger, silent. Everyone eyed one another awkwardly until, finally, Mrs. Crawley came to and said, "Yes, amber, from Latvia. Yes. It was a gift. From an ex." She laughed loudly, hiccupped—and Augie was sure then: She was drunk.

Of course she had the freedom to get drunk on a random Tuesday afternoon, of course she had endless men buying her jewelry, of course she'd been to Latvia—a place Augie could not place. She didn't even know if it was a city or a country.

Augie focused on clearing the room from then on, eager to stay out of Mrs. Crawley's sight. She knew it was a mean thought, but she hoped Mrs. Crawley would make a fool of herself. She also wondered if she always drank this much and Augie simply hadn't noticed before, or if it was something about today. As always, she wondered what Chat thought.

"Augie, my girl!" Robin appeared out of nowhere, arms outstretched despite balancing a silver gift bag.

"Robin!" Augie fixed her face.

"I was hoping I'd catch you! I've missed you." Robin pulled Augie into a hug. Augie typically made sure not to be overly friendly with members while working, but Robin didn't play by the rules. Augie wouldn't get in trouble, either. Robin was more or less royalty.

"I missed you, too." Augie realized it was true. Robin had always been so supportive of her, so enthused that, unlike Leah, she wanted to move out of state.

Miriam and Mrs. Harrison approached.

"I'm so sorry I'm late." They all hugged, and Augie noticed everyone watching. Robin was a true force: She had the same long, lean body as Leah, same inviting smile, and even more radiating confidence. Plus, everyone knew she was brilliant, successful. In a twisted way, their family's tragedy also gave her power. People couldn't imagine her grief. They respected her strength. The fact that she had maintained Lyle's innocence all this time, yet never blamed anyone else, put her on an even higher pedestal. She was a class act.

"I wrapped a meeting at the Carlson Towers, and I raced here," Robin explained to Miriam. "I'm thrilled to see you. Look at you!"

Augie went to the kitchen. Robin always drank spiked Arnold Palmers, and she rushed to make one. Robin was busy talking when she returned, but as Augie handed her the drink, she focused on Augie once more.

"I really cannot believe I'm just seeing you now, here, Aug." Robin grabbed her hand. "I'm sorry the agency turned out to be a bust. Who could have predicted that merger? I know Julia and Micah were shocked. I'm still so proud of you. I know something better will come along."

"Yeah, yes. I was over the other day. The pool—it's freezing."

"Polar plunge! And can you believe it? Leah! Officially at the Hotel Harrison." She clucked her tongue. "It is good experience, but, I really do wish she'd explore."

Despite everything, Augie felt a tinge of solidarity.

"We'll see how it goes. We have to catch up properly. Come over this week. We'll order Thai, like old times."

"Robin," Mrs. Cline interrupted. "Can I steal you for a moment? I wanted to talk to you about the South Loop fundraiser, if you have time."

"I'll see you this week, okay, Augie? Don't work too hard."

As Robin backed away and Augie resumed cleaning, she was unsure how to feel. Anytime she talked to Robin at the Club, she felt both proud and pitiful.

"Augie," she heard then. She couldn't place the voice at first, but as she looked around, she stopped. There in the corner, Mrs. Crawley was waving her over.

"Can you come here for a moment, please?" She smiled in a straight line.

Augie went numb, still—then started toward her. She didn't know why she moved so willingly. It was instinct, maybe. Maybe it was simple: She was in serving mode. Obedient.

As Augie approached, she made sure to look directly at Mrs. Crawley; she was not going to back down. But Mrs. Crawley's eyes were red and dead, revealing nothing except that she was drunk. For a second, despite everything, Augie felt bad for her.

"Augie," Mrs. Crawley repeated, chewing on her name in a way that felt mocking. "We were talking about how lovely this event is, and how hard you all work." She set her Bellini on the bookshelf behind her as she reached into her purse, swaying slightly. "And we know we don't do this often, but we thought we should do better. So, a little something for you. For your friend, too." Her eyes skated to the new girl across the room, who was struggling to carry a stack of plates. She took two bills from her clutch, slicing them through the air.

Augie focused on the crisp twenties between her French manicured fingers. She felt too confused to respond. What was this? A bribe? A show of power?

"That's very kind, but there's no need. We're happy to do our jobs." Augie took a small step backward. Outside of golf caddies, staff rarely received tips. While it technically was allowed, members knew better than to make a habit of it. Part of the Club's appeal was that it was cashless, as if real money did not exist.

Mrs. Crawley's mouth twitched as she held her smile taut. Around them, Mrs. Adams and Schmidt sipped their wine, picking up on the tension.

"Oh, come on, hun," Mrs. Adams interjected. She grabbed the twenties and folded them into Augie's apron pocket. "It's just a little something. You all work so hard."

Mrs. Adams had a son in Augie's class at school, and she'd been to several parties at their house. Last summer when Mr. and Mrs. Adams were at a wedding in Italy, Garrett had even held a three-day beer Olympics in their basement. Augie could clearly picture their black felt pool table, their wine fridge, the massive blue-tiled bathroom where Leah had spent hours puking.

"It's nice to see you, dear." Mrs. Adams leaned in. "I was telling Danika here how you and Garrett went to high school together. And the U. Go Gophers!" She raised her fists. "He's working at Wells Fargo down in Milwaukee, if you heard. It all goes by so fast. You must have just graduated too?"

Augie felt hot and stuck. "I did, uh, yes, I'm only here for the summer."

Mrs. Crawley stared at her, her pupils shrinking to dots.

"Yes," Mrs. Crawley said. "Advertising can be tough. Especially in New York." Her voice oozed with alcohol and arrogance. She turned to pick up her drink as Augie felt faint.

"Ah, the Big Apple! That's so exciting," Mrs. Adam continued, unfazed. "I'll have to tell Garrett you're back. He comes home a lot these days. I'm sure he'd want me to say hi."

Augie took another step backward.

"Yes, tell him hi," she stammered, turning as she heard Mrs. Adams say what a nice girl Augie had always been, that it was too bad the job market was so tough right now. Augie closed her eyes. She jammed her hand into her apron, grabbing for the slippery bills.

She whipped around, walking straight up to Mrs. Crawley.

"I can't accept this." She held the bills out to her, her arm hanging in the air.

Mrs. Crawley didn't move. Augie felt Mrs. Adams and Schmidt look at her, each other, back to Augie, but Augie didn't break eye contact with Mrs. Crawley.

Then, without thinking, Augie let go of the bills. Slowly, each fluttered to the ground like a drifting autumn leaf. The women all looked on, their chins dipping one degree at a time.

"Ope, well," Mrs. Adams finally said.

Augie left before she could register Mrs. Crawley's reaction, beelining for the kitchen. She didn't care if the whole room was watching now, if Aida would question her later. Who did Mrs. Crawley think she was? Where did she get the gall? She could have offered Augie a thousand dollars and Augie would have left it at her feet.

She would not give her the satisfaction.

Augie Elling • 4:05 PM
Hey sorry I've been MIA.
It's already been a long week.
And a weird day.
Chat Efhart • 4:29 PM
Hey!
Was starting to worry you were ghosting me
How are you?
What's up?
You okay?
Augie Elling • 4:34 PM
Yeah I'm fine.
I know this is kind of random.
But has Mrs. Crawley said anything about me?
She was at the baby shower I worked today.
And was acting weird.
Chat Efhart • 4:36 PM
That is weird . . . she hasn't said anything
I think she's having a bad day tho
What did she do?
Augie Elling • 4:38 PM
She gave me a tip.
And said something about me in New York.
No idea how she'd know about that.
Chat Efhart • 4:39 PM
That's nice about the tip I guess?
Was she just trying to be nice?

That is weird about new york
I didn't say anything, ofc
I have nothing to tell!

Augie Elling • 4:40 PM

Not a big deal, just curious.
We can talk more later.
Hey, we should do ice cream.
Thursday?

Chat Efhart • 4:43 PM

Yes!
Perfect
Let's definitely talk in person
Malts on me

If they met after dark, they'd go to 89 Elm. It was easier to park inconspicuously there; two main roads paralleled each side of the house. They'd arrive at different times, slip in through the back porch. They couldn't turn the lights on and risk illuminating their bodies, calling attention to the place, but this only heightened the moment. They'd set their phones on the floor, flashlights facing up—small fires on the ground. It felt fun and romantic, like they were camping. The light illuminated the ceiling, and after, lying together, chests heaving, they held their hands up to the light, casting shadows above as if they were kids again. They made a wolf, a rabbit, a clown. They laughed in unison. They pressed their palms together like a prayer, going silent.

They did not speak their wishes out loud.

One night, they made the mistake of falling asleep—which ended in panic. They'd woken up frantic, scrambling, desperately grabbing their phones.

From then on, no matter the time, they set multiple alarms.

There was always a limit. There was always an end.

16

The dress arrived just in time. Danika stood in the center of her sprawling closet to admire the garment. She'd ordered it months ago without an occasion in mind, knowing one would arise. Now, it had.

The piece was silky and stunning—a made-to-order Siriano gown described as golden green, like the color of a Fabergé kiwi. It absorbed light at all angles: its rouching up on one hip, its twist at the halter, its delicate plunging back. Danika had sent in her measurements, and it fit her perfectly. All night, she'd be fielding compliments. Admiration. The thought sent a tingle down her spine. She needed this. She touched the dress once more, the fabric falling through her fingers like cool water.

The event didn't start for another two hours, and her hair and makeup girl wouldn't arrive for another half hour, but it was time for a cocktail. She flicked off the closet lights and headed downstairs.

"So, should we pop this?" Danika said as she moved into the white marbled kitchen. Chat sat at the counter, elbows up, eating a sandwich. She moved to the fridge and pulled out the massive bottle of champagne that had arrived with the invitation to the Harrisons' restaurant opening. She held the bottle by the neck and placed it on the counter.

"That some capital-C?" Chat eyed the bottle.

"Exactly," Danika said, proud he remembered what she'd taught him about sparkling wine: how only bottles from the Champagne region of France were real champagne.

The pitter-patter of rain grew above them, and Danika looked up at the skylights, hoping it would stop. She didn't want any spots on her dress.

"Might as well pop it." Bill walked into the room, holding a glass of bourbon.

"Well if you're drinking *that*, then I won't," Danika said. "This won't keep."

"Oh, rope Chat in for a glass. I believe in the three of us."

Danika studied Bill, noticing his fresh shave and good mood. He had even picked his suit for the night already; it seemed they were both eager for the event, which had come as a surprise. Mallory and Malcolm had delayed the opening of Alondra several times, citing issues with the chef and zoning and the deck revamp, and the invitation had caught everyone off guard. "Nothing like the element of surprise," Bill had joked. The invitation had also included a comped room at the hotel for VIPs, to which Bill replied, "Why not? This is why we have Chat."

"Okay, so can we 'rope you in,' Chat?" She reached for three glasses, glad the boys were already in bed.

"At your service. Seems like this is going to be a real party." Chat reached for the invitation on the counter. He flipped over the heavy card stock. "What time are you leaving?"

Danika told him eight as she used both hands to pour the bottle.

"We'll have to go back with you, Chat." Bill leaned against the counter. "The food is supposed to be amazing. The rib eye especially."

"Sounds good to me. And thank you," he said as Danika handed him a glass. "I hope you have a good time. It's a good way to end the week, right?"

Danika smiled at him, intimacy passing between them. Since their conversation after the Galleria, their dynamic had shifted for the better. Their connection was deeper. Now, she knew they were true partners and confidants.

While Danika *was* a little embarrassed about the whole hug-kiss moment, she didn't regret where it had brought them. She was also glad to know they would never cross that line. While it had truly never been her intention, it made her trust Chat all the more. Plus, she'd still gotten what she'd really wanted: confirmation she was beautiful—even to him.

In a strange way, she no longer felt weird flaunting herself in front of him. She knew nothing would come of it—nothing except the thrill of attention, a heightened sense of being alive. Even now, as she moved about the kitchen, she let her sweater fall open, revealing her black tank top and braless chest.

"Okay, I've gotta go shower, but I'll check on Max after." Chat rounded the counter toward Danika and put his plate in the dishwasher. "You gave him that Tylenol at five thirty, right?" Max had been fighting a summer cold.

"Oh, yup. Five thirty." Danika was disappointed to see him go.

Danika couldn't help but wonder if he was leaving to talk to her—Augie. She wanted that girl as far away as possible. In the week since seeing their messages, she'd kept Chat extra busy. She'd asked him to run additional errands, swing by the post office, grab last-minute items at Lunds & Byerlys. "I'll pay you overtime, of course," she'd remind him. She knew he'd never tell her no.

She didn't understand why Augie had to go after Chat. She could have anyone—anything. Why waste her time chasing someone who was so clearly unavailable? Danika felt that on some level it was personal. She remembered the way Augie had reacted at that happy hour; she'd glared at Danika as if everything wrong in the world was Danika's fault. And god, the baby shower. That day was the real anniversary of her dad's death and her divorce, and while Danika had been a little out of control, she hadn't done anything bad. The "tip" hadn't even been her idea—it was Mrs. Adams who brought it up. But Augie had humiliated her, throwing that money at her feet. Yes, Augie—with her alien blue eyes, her basic U of M degree, her five little months in New York (Danika had found her LinkedIn)—was bad news.

"I'm going to steam a few shirts, then I'll need your opinion," Bill said, dragging Danika back to the present. He picked up his glass.

"The stripes." She'd already noticed the shirts he'd pulled earlier.

Bill smiled at her, and for the first time in what felt like forever, he stared right at her. They hadn't had a real conversation in weeks. He had seemed happier in the past few days, though, which Danika took as a good sign.

She was about to take advantage of the moment and ask how he was, or tell him details about the model home—anything to bring them closer—but as she opened her mouth, Bill's phone rang. He picked it up off the counter and studied the number.

"I gotta take this." He tapped the counter. "But, Danika." He studied her as if he too wanted to break the surface. "There's something I need to tell you. Let's talk in the car, okay?"

Danika felt a flash of adrenaline. Yet she kept her face calm as she told him, "Of course."

Finally, she thought.

17

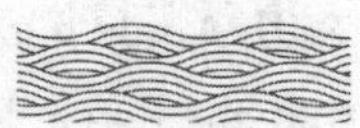

The wedding that Saturday was canceled. While Augie's first reaction was excitement—like learning about a snow day—when Aida explained it was because the groom found out only days before that the bride was cheating on him with a groomsman, the feeling dissolved.

It is pretty depressing, Aida had texted. There's no reimbursing at this point. Can you imagine? All that money. If I were him, I'd come stuff myself on hors d'oeuvres.

Augie didn't know what to do with herself. She almost never had Saturday nights off, and her mom had a dinner with colleagues, while Leah was working the Hotel Harrison's restaurant opening. Augie had made a point of asking about it, and Leah was happy to describe it all: the various food stations, the fire juggler, the acoustic band. It sounded more extravagant than any Club event, and Augie imagined the Crawleys amid the partygoers. As Leah said, it was A-list and adults only. Surely, they would be there. Surely, Chat would not.

She and Chat were reaching a pinnacle. They'd been messaging so much, she decided they needed to either see each other or stop. If she was being honest with herself, she also wanted to know where she stood—on top of simply wanting to see him. Since the baby shower, Augie felt she and Mrs. Crawley were silently at war. Especially after Chat had to cancel their ice cream date last minute, citing some "dire" errand he had to run for her. Augie had the feeling she knew exactly what she was doing: keeping them apart.

Augie didn't want to say anything about it to Chat yet. She worried she'd sound paranoid. Still, Augie felt certain Mrs. Crawley had some way of tracking her, that she had at least looked her up online. How else would she have known about New York? It infuriated Augie to imagine how Mrs. Crawley saw her: some pathetic, desperate cater waiter.

Underpinning it all was the infuriating question of *why*. Augie could not understand the reason Mrs. Crawley would care so much about Augie and Chat being friends—not unless she and Chat really were having some sordid affair. All around, Augie needed answers.

So, finally, it was time.

Feigning ignorance, she messaged Chat to ask what he was doing that night. Augie explained she had a surprise Saturday night free, then paced her room as she waited. She wouldn't admit it outright, but this was a test—did he want to see her badly enough to break Mrs. Crawley's rules? Her pulse doubled as she checked her phone again and again.

Thirty minutes later, her phone dinged, and she lunged for it.

Chat Efhart • 7:18 PM

Hey my bad I was in the shower

But damn!

I'm usually off saturday nights

But tonight they're staying at the harrison hotel for some restaurant opening

So I have the boys all night

This sucks
I really want to see you

Augie felt a sinking disappointment as she sat in her desk chair, swiveling back and forth while watching the sky fill with the salmon-orange of sunset. She couldn't deny something about this night still felt inevitable: the broken wedding, her mom spending a rare evening out, everyone from the Greenes to the Crawleys gathered at the hotel. She started typing.

Augie Elling • 7:24 PM
How insane would it be if I came there?

Augie watched the dots appear and disappear. Appear and disappear. And then:

Chat Efhart • 7:18 PM
You know
It's been a while since I did anything insane
Can you be here at 9?

18

Danika hadn't been to the Hotel Harrison in months, despite passing it almost every day. It flanked the end of Aldon Lakes Boulevard, nestled along the east side of Lake Minnetonka. It was pretty from the outside; she would give them that. It had a large deck that faced the water, light-bulbed lettering that glowed like an old-time movie theater, endless balconies.

The lobby was also pretty. It had custom built-in sculptures and herringbone floors, a long brassy counter with a mirrored top. But that's where Danika's compliments ended. The whole space needed more texture, more light. It did not give the impressive first impression one would expect. Again: Mallory should have let her help.

Danika and Bill had never stayed at the hotel, and Danika was surprised when the bellhop greeted them by name as he called the elevator. They headed to the fifth floor.

Alone in the elevator, Danika and Bill studied each other's reflections in the mirror. She looked exquisite: her eyes charcoaled and vivid, her hair shining and coiffed to one side, falling over her bronzed, bare shoulder. Bill winked at her in the mirror. It was like when they'd met. Danika reached for Bill's hand. On nights when she was this confident, she carried her beauty around like a piece of jewelry, a gemstone she held up to the light.

Danika was also on a high from the Uber ride over—from Bill finally telling her what had been going on. He'd started by saying that while he knew it was not ideal, and he was sorry to have to ask, he needed her to be amiable toward Joshua Mike.

"Look," he started, talking with his hands, "I know you hate him—trust me, I do too." He'd grabbed both his knees. "And I know the Fourth was a lot to ask, but the truth of it is, he's the biggest shareholder in Briar Ridge, and he's been a real pain in the ass. He's making it difficult for all of us. The way he wants to do the dividends—well, it's confusing, but he wants to reinvest the money into the development, and I need my payout now. We just need to appease him. We need him to follow our lead.

"I need your help." He pulled a flask from his pocket. "We all know how much he likes you. He wants to know more about the interior design. To talk to you about it. So, if you could schmooze him a little." Bill rubbed his forehead. "I really hate to ask. But I'm stuck. We have a vote coming up about financing in a few days, and while he *said* he's agreed to our terms, you know how hotheaded he is. I need to keep him happy until then. So tonight, please play along. Be nice. I'm sorry I didn't tell you earlier. I hoped I could fix it on my own."

Danika looked from Bill to outside, watching the highway lights stream by in blurry, disorienting lines of light. "Should I be worried about this?"

Bill took a sip from the flask. "No, no. I think—we're good." He wiped his mouth. "We're good. I just need Josh to stay in his lane. Then, we'll be all set. We'll be back."

Danika tensed. "Back?"

"No, I mean we'll be great." Bill reached out for Danika's knee. "I'm really glad to have your help. That you're working with us." He pressed his shoulder into hers.

Danika took his flask, took a sip. *That's right*, she thought. No matter what, she would always be his greatest asset, his most reliable partner—his oldest soul. He would always need her. "Okay," Danika agreed. "I'll play nice. You know, I can usually get men to do what I want."

Bill laughed. Then, for the first time in months, he leaned forward and kissed her.

Danika and Bill unlocked their room, dropped their bags, grabbed a drink from the minibar, and touched up their outfits as they prepared to return downstairs. Danika paused and studied herself in the mirror, pretending to speak. She liked to watch her mouth move, wanting to see how she appeared to others while talking. Silently, she told herself, "You look perfect."

For a moment, she considered the white bed frame—too boring and stark—and debated whether she and Bill should have sex. But she didn't want to mess up her hair. Instead, she stepped to the window and stared out at the darkening water of Lake Minnetonka. The sun would set in an hour or so, and after, the lake would disappear completely—turn into a flat expanse of black.

The moment before every party felt like gearing up for a performance, and Danika focused as they made their way back to the elevator.

Danika and Bill walked toward the back of the first floor, and finally, they stepped inside Alondra. Danika sucked in a breath, realizing, suddenly, that she had not been prepared for the design to be so impressive. She had allowed herself to believe it would be tacky—that as a result, she'd feel better about herself.

This was not the case. Despite the theme, the decor was perfect—full of clean lines yet intense character. Danika felt a pang of insecurity as she scanned each detail: the gold-and-white-tiled floors, the jade green tables, the low bamboo chairs, the incredible braided vines and macramé adorning the walls. The ceilings were retractable glass, and another equally impressive flower and wire installation cascaded from the center to the floor.

It was all so gorgeous and alive, Danika barely registered the guests. But, to her dismay, she noticed the Greenes nearby. They looked attractive as always, Robin, Wyatt, and their daughter—that young, pretty blond—all dressed in black. Danika squinted as she saw the girl talking into a headset. Was she working this event? *Of course*, Danika thought, indignant. They were all so incestuous.

Out of nowhere, Holly Fravel grabbed her arm.

"I'm not sure I'd call it *magical realism*, per se"—she handed Danika a martini—"but it is something, huh?"

Danika took a bitter sip. She knew Holly also felt bad for making fun of it all.

"Look at you," Holly crooned. "Stunning as always." She paused. "You good?"

"What? Yes, of course." She gave Holly a quick side hug.

At least the rain was going strong. Danika was glad for the storm now; she didn't want the party to be perfect. And as the crowd continued to grow, she moved toward the windows, which were huge and pressed right up against the water. Danika imagined that if they were only a few feet lower, it'd be as if they were in an aquarium.

The rain was calming, and Danika felt a bit better until she felt a hand on her—a hand that went straight to her lower back. Instantly, she knew who it was.

"As usual, you're the most gorgeous woman in the room." Joshua Mike moved next to her, facing outside. The rain slid in thin lines down the glass like roads on a map.

Danika readied herself. She dipped her head in thanks. "I like your tie. Hermès?" It was easier to play along now that she had context, a reason. Regardless, they both seemed taken aback by her compliment. Joshua Mike slid the tie through his hand, grinning.

"So, what do you think of the place? What's your expert opinion? A bit too *kitschy*? A bit too *Jungle Book*? I do love that bar."

"I have to say, it's lovely. Though not exactly my personal style."

Joshua Mike lifted his tumbler. "For what it's worth, I prefer your personal style. I love that cabin. Can't get enough of it. I can't wait to see the model home. I'll tell you, this little Briar Ridge project, it's been a trip."

Danika took another sip of her martini, buying time.

"It's going to be great. I trust Bill's vision."

Joshua Mike curled his mouth in a half smile. Danika couldn't help but wonder if he was trying to play her too—it felt like he was hiding something, or after something.

"I trust *your* vision more than Bill's, if I'm being honest." A new, playful look crossed his face. Danika couldn't place it. "And let me know"—he smacked his lips—"if you ever need a second opinion. On the model home, your design business, mortgages—hell, anything. I'm here for you. I know you're working now, and, I have to say, it'd be smart to get your personal finances in order. I'm happy to help. Just say the word."

Danika's brow furrowed. She looked out to the water, the rain now pummeling the top of the lake.

"Thank you. Cheers." She raised her glass, hoping it would end the conversation and the bad feeling pitted in her stomach.

"You have my number, don't you?"

Danika didn't think she'd ever saved it, but she told him yes.

"Okay. I'll text you now in case. Really, feel free to reach out anytime. For anything. I'm at your service." He gave a small bow.

Danika didn't know what to say—and was relieved when Mallory and Malcolm appeared beside them. She gathered herself, thanking them, congratulating them.

As the night continued, Danika replayed Joshua Mike's words in her mind. Something about his offer, his mention of their finances, *mortgages*, made her feel nauseous. For the first time, she wondered if Bill was the one lying. She told herself not to be crazy. Why would she trust Joshua Mike over her own husband? Yet, there was something she could not shake.

Time moved slowly from there. As the clock ticked to ten, everyone paused to listen to Mallory and Malcolm's speech. They stood at the center of the bar and rambled on about how Alondra was their dream come true. Danika hadn't seen Bill since dinner, but as they spoke, she spotted him across the room with Wyatt Greene, laughing and drinking. He seemed too relaxed. Or maybe her anxiety was unfounded—maybe she'd simply had too much to drink. She needed to clear her head. She slipped away to the bathroom before the speech had wrapped.

As Danika stepped inside, she set her purse on the counter and checked her phone for the first time that evening—and saw Joshua Mike's text.

Here for you. X, JM.

Danika twisted her face in disgust. He just wanted to sleep with her. That was it, she decided. She snapped her purse shut.

As Danika turned to leave, the bathroom door swung open, and to her dismay, Jackie walked in, shimmying in her bedazzled seafoam dress. It hugged her frame so tightly, pushed her breasts up so far, she looked like a mermaid. Without speaking, she sidled up next to Danika at the sink.

Danika washed her hands, waiting.

Jackie leaned closer to the mirror and turned her head from side to side, but eventually, she blew out a long breath and faced Danika, propping her hip against the sink.

"Okay, so, D." She wobbled her head. "I need to be straight with you. Woman to woman."

Danika pulled her shoulders back.

"I know Josh has a thing for you," Jackie said, her gold earrings jingling. "And I know you and Bill are having some financial hiccups. I just want you to know, even if Bill goes bust and Josh helps *you* out, he is not going to leave me for you. No matter what."

Danika couldn't help it—despite everything, she laughed.

Jackie's face turned colder. "I mean it."

"*I* mean, I don't know what you're talking about. We don't have *financial hiccups*," Danika scoffed, defensive, desperate. "I would never be with Josh. He's repulsive. He loves to make trouble."

Jackie tightened her mouth. She leaned closer to the mirror, touching her top lip, her tone growing to match Danika's. "You women think you have everything and everyone all sorted, all wrapped around your finger. Maybe you do have some sort of hold on Joshy . . . I know he's obsessed with you, always saves photos of you . . . but he will *not* leave me. I want you to know that for certain."

Danika's whole body felt off balance. She had the sudden urge to shove Jackie—along with everything she was saying—away.

"I get it, okay, you're hot," Jackie continued, gesturing to her body. "That dress is—" She kissed the air. "So, if you want to join us sometime, say the word. If he does give you that loan, and you feel like you owe him, we could all get together. We'd all get what we wanted."

Danika pivoted away, pressing her hand to her stomach, sick.

"Just as long as you remember: I'm not going anywhere."

A loan? A *threesome*? Danika felt violated, horrified. And, worse, she had no idea what was truly going on—or how to fix it. Danika hated feeling trapped. All she knew for certain was that she had to get out of that party.

She had to get home.

19

The rain picked up as Augie drove toward the Crawley house, her windshield wipers pumping, mist coming off the road like smoke. She blared her music loud, so she couldn't think; she wanted to keep running on the energy and emotions dragging her forward.

Chat had explained it would be best to park on the side street. Cooper's room faced the front, and he had a habit of waking to cars coming up the driveway.

I'm sorry, Chat had messaged, I know it's raining, but I'll be watching for you.

Augie had asked if there were cameras, hoping the question wouldn't scare either of them away from their plans, but he assured her the Crawleys never checked them.

So, at exactly nine o'clock, Augie parked on the street and looked into the rearview mirror, inspecting her face as the rain pummeled her car, the sound like static. She felt good—she was wearing her best-fitting jeans and a tight black T-shirt. She reached for the U of M umbrella from her back seat.

The driveway was long and winding—the house was truly hidden—and Augie kept her head down against the rain. She didn't look up until the Crawley mansion flashed into view. Chat stood in the glass doorway, framed by a yellow rectangle of light.

Augie couldn't ignore her rising nerves as she stood before the house, registering its massive cement angles and all its darkened, shining glass. She pummeled forward, moving faster as Chat opened the door wide and she ducked inside, shaking water from her hair while placing her umbrella on the stoop.

Augie had worried it'd be awkward at first, but as Chat grinned, she realized he was wearing the same black band T-shirt and silver gym shorts he had the night she ran into him at the Club. Her nerves were displaced by excitement, a strange comfort. She leaned into him, and as he hugged her, a ripple of want and memory coursed through her. She felt the skin of his neck against her closed eyelids.

"Welcome to my humble abode." He pulled away and extended his arms, still smiling.

Augie had been in her share of nice houses, but this instantly felt different. Like she'd stepped into some modern, cozy, otherworldly planet. The floor was white marble, and it flowed into the kitchen, out to a floating staircase to their left, and down a wide hallway to their right. The ceilings were high, and as she followed Chat to the kitchen, Augie stared up into the wooden beams similar to those at the Crawleys' cabin. The whole house felt like a lighter, sharper version of that space. Mrs. Crawley obviously had a signature style.

Augie continued to gawk as they entered the kitchen and she took in the living room, the fireplace with its low orange flames and spread of couches adorned with soft pillows and throws. Next to her, flanking the wall, large geometric prints hung under individual lights like in a museum. Augie stared at each print. She loved them. She loved the whole house. She hated that Mrs. Crawley was talented. She felt a flame of anger inside her.

Augie knew it was an ugly thought, but it helped to remember their debt. To be reminded that not everything was as perfect as it seemed. Though for the first time, Augie wondered if the number on the computer had been a mistake. Nothing seemed wrong here. It felt like paradise.

"Not too shabby, right?" Chat moved to one of three silver fridges. "Do you want a drink?" He opened the door as Augie imagined Zami cooking there, leaning over the gas range. The flame inside her grew.

"This is a special occasion." He pulled out a magnum bottle of champagne, lifting a spoon from its neck. "She always says this keeps it fresh, but I don't buy it."

Everything about this moment felt bizarre, and Augie ran her hands along the cool stone counter.

"I can't believe you live here." She hoped she sounded casual as she studied Chat's face, though she felt slightly better as she took in how excited he looked. He wanted her there.

"Right? I literally got lost that first week. These okay?" He grabbed two gray mugs. "She once told me those champagne glasses were like a hundred dollars. I don't trust myself."

"Sure." Once again, Augie wondered how Chat could live with such a snob.

They talked and drank as Augie walked around the living room, touching the pillows and studying the bookshelves while Chat rambled on about the boys. She examined everything as if searching for criminal evidence, and was startled by the book collection; she'd assumed it was simply for show and would be filled with classics and fake spines, but there was a range of contemporary titles: Ann Beattie, Lorrie Moore, Joan Didion.

"Does she read a lot?" Augie asked.

"Kind of. When it's nice out, she'll read on the patio. We watch TV more, though. In the movie theater room. Do you want to see it?"

Augie turned to him, a realization blooming: This house was probably the nicest house Chat had ever visited. While it ranked high on Augie's list, and while it was probably one of the more unique, well-designed homes she'd been in, movie theater rooms no longer impressed her. She didn't care to see the Crawleys'. It was odd to think that although she'd never be a true Aldon Lakes person, the town had become part of her. She hoped this didn't make her a snob, too.

She told him she'd love to see the theater room.

"This way." Chat grabbed her hand, surprising her—and energy singed between their palms.

The basement was as massive as the main floor. A slick, see-through black fireplace divided the space, with a pool table on one side and a bar on the other. Chat dropped her hand as he walked toward a wall of bookshelves, pushing it open, a secret door.

"Wild, right?" He held it open like an overly enthusiastic tour guide.

The movie room was typical: reclining love seats, stadium seating, framed movie posters. Leah's was nicer. Augie told him it was awesome.

"Do you want another drink? Anything to eat?" He leaned against the edge of the pool table, something vulnerable seeping into his voice. He finished the last of his drink and set his mug on the table's edge. "Sorry. I'm not used to having houseguests. I hope I'm not being a bad host."

Augie leaned against the table next to him, matching his pose. She turned to him and had another realization: Chat might be more nervous than she was.

"Are the boys okay? They're asleep, right? They won't hear us?"

"Oh, no, don't worry." Chat raised his wrist, his Apple watch. "I have this connected to Max's monitor. They're way, way up there. On the third floor." He pointed to the ceiling. "They're so far away, it's like we're not even breaking the rules."

Augie studied his blush. Now, she wasn't sure if he was more flustered about breaking rules or by his feelings for her.

"Let's have another." Augie nodded toward the bar.

Chat stood up and reached for her mug, and his fingers brushed hers in another zap of electricity.

He walked to the counter and pulled out a barstool for her before going behind the bar. Then, as Augie settled at the counter, he leaned forward on two hands and asked for her ID.

Augie laughed, and the joke—along with being settled at the bar—made their dynamic feel more natural. Augie could tell they both felt better as they talked and Chat mixed drinks. They reminisced about high school parties, college memories, about the time Chat refilled an entire bottle of his parents' Jack Daniel's with apple juice and his sister called him out. He also told Augie about the time half his senior class got busted drinking at a back-to-school party, and aside from the guy who hid in the washing machine for six hours, Chat was the only one who got off scot-free. It had been hockey season, he explained, and because he was the captain, he had only been pretending to drink.

"I felt so bad when the cops did the Breathalyzer and it blew zero. My friends were like, what the hell!" Chat scooped ice from the freezer. "I'd already locked in a hockey scholarship, though. I couldn't risk losing it. My dad would've killed me." He held a drink out to Augie. "Here, the house special."

"Also known as a vodka cran?" Augie took a sip.

"I can't say I'm the most skilled bartender." He smiled and sat next to her on a stool. For the first time, Augie tried to pretend they were on a real date. Still, she couldn't stop thinking about the Crawleys. She was more curious than ever.

"Do you miss hockey?" she said, steering the conversation. "Do the boys like hockey?"

"Nah, I wish. Bill's pushing golf instead. Not that it's really sticking . . ."

"And Mrs. Crawley?" Augie paused, lifting her drink to her lips. "Does she like hockey?"

Chat studied her, hesitating. "Um, yeah, actually." He wiped the side of his mug. "But I mostly miss playing as a kid, as sad as that sounds. I loved playing out on the pond every winter. It was more fun when it wasn't so serious, you know? In college, there was a lot of pressure, and then between my injury and COVID, I don't know." He paused, cracked his thumb knuckles.

"But like I said, it all turned out okay. Getting hurt was both the worst and best thing that's happened to me. And here, see this?" He pulled up his T-shirt sleeve, revealing a tattoo of a bubble-letter number thirteen. "I got hurt on Friday the thirteenth, and my jersey number was also thirteen. Ironic, right?"

He held his sleeve up, and slowly, Augie reached out to touch his arm. With one finger, she traced the outline of each digit, then rested her whole palm against his bicep, covering the art completely. She watched goose bumps rise over his skin.

Their faces were closer now.

"So"—he cleared his throat—"when I see this number, I can either think about it negatively, like that was the day my life plan went up in smoke, or I can see it and think, 'That was one chapter. It's all part of the story.'" He exhaled, and Augie slid her hand down his bicep to the crook above his elbow.

"I know it's kind of dumb"—he shifted in his seat; her touch had stirred something in both of them, she felt it—"but it reminds me of the power of perception. Taking control of your own mind."

"I get it." Augie was certain that later, she'd replay this moment. She still held his arm.

"The whole thing was pretty unremarkable, too, if you can believe it. It was only this other guy and me. We were at center ice, and his shoulder clipped my jaw, and that was it. I collapsed. It wasn't some bloody mess, some big dramatic event. I don't even think he got a penalty. It was just unlucky. Friday the thirteenth."

Augie felt upset thinking about it. "Do you feel okay now?" She dropped her hand.

"I do." Chat swiveled on his stool. "It was a long road. Honestly, the worst part was not being able to listen to music because it made me dizzy. I finally found the right doctor, and he basically rebuilt my brain. No joke, by like having me play Ping-Pong while balancing on a skateboard. And then I started thinking about other ways I could get to Europe *instead* of hockey, and I was talking to my uncle Trey a lot when I was depressed—he lives in Latvia, played hockey there—and he helped me plan everything." Chat suddenly froze, his face white.

For a second, Augie wondered if he was self-conscious about admitting he'd been depressed, but before she could reassure him, he started talking faster.

"I also have a friend in Germany, so that also got me excited, gave me something to look forward to. Like I said, it all worked out. Though I do still kind of regret college." He held a smile, teasing. "But I really am glad I'm here this summer. That I met you."

Augie felt flattered and tipsy as she tried to process everything—his injury, his outlook, his compliment.

"So what about you?" He shifted tones. "What's your story? You still haven't told me about New York. We can pretend this is a real networking event if you want, Ms. LinkedIn."

"Oh, yeah. I'm sick of thinking about that."

Augie turned out to the room, staring out the glass doors, noticing the outdoor fire circle, the rain pummeling the covered outdoor furniture.

"Wait a second, is that a pool?" she said, incredulous as she noticed another darkened, tarped expanse.

Chat nodded.

"Why go to the Club if you already have a pool?"

"These are answers we don't have, my friend."

Augie recoiled at the word *friend*.

"That's insane. What a waste of money." Augie tried to detect any flinch at the mention of their money, but he didn't react.

"I know. This house is nuts. Even the boys' rooms are crazy."

Augie finished her drink and set it down hard. "I think I need the rest of the tour."

Chat hopped off the stool. He extended his palm to her like Aladdin.

Augie knew, as they continued up to the second and third levels, that they were touching more and more. Despite the word *friend*, this flirting was not one-sided, nor in her mind. It was undeniable. When Chat showed her the gigantic, greenhouse-style playroom, he pulled her hips into him; when they sauntered into the formal dining room, they sat next to each other, feet skimming beneath the table; and when they walked up the last set of stairs, Augie stopped to look at a family photo, and while she was staring into Mrs. Crawley's smile, Chat bumped into the back of her, his whole body cradling hers from behind, his breath on her neck.

When they got to his room, Augie stopped. It wasn't a room—it was a whole apartment. There was a functional, single-walled kitchen, a high-top table with more barstools, a sitting room with a tan leather sofa and two fancy blue armchairs, a TV bigger than the one she had at home. She felt stunned.

"Where is your actual bedroom?"

He pointed to one of two doors.

Augie pictured her own room, her junk-filled studio in New York. Her face burned. Here he was, living like them. Living like a king.

"Trust me, I know this is a lot," Chat said, as if reading her mind. "It's definitely not what I'm used to. This is like half the size of my whole house back home."

Augie ran her hand over the soft, leather couch.

"I'd ask if you wanted to *see* my room"—he reached out, hooked his finger in one of her belt loops, and turned her around to face him—"but I don't want to sound like I'm implying something . . ." His words were a contrast to the way he suddenly stepped toward her, closing the space between them, his legs on either side of hers.

Augie's breath hitched as she looked up at him.

Chat leaned forward, lifted her chin, and as Augie closed her eyes and could practically feel his lips on hers—out of nowhere, his wrist chimed.

"Oh, shit." He pulled away as Augie blinked. He studied his watch. "Damnit. The monitor. Max. He's getting over a cold and—one second." Chat sighed and backed away, turning fast as he adjusted his shorts. "Make yourself at home. I'll be right back."

Alone, Augie felt rejected. She tried not to overthink the abrupt departure as she stood still, the silence ringing metallic in her mind. She felt strange being there by herself, as if the house knew she was an intruder. She didn't move at all until she noticed the bookcases around the TV and squinted, recognizing two spines—two of her all-time favorites: *The Curious Incident of the Dog in the Night-Time* and *Bel Canto.* It made her lightheaded.

Augie sat down on the couch, staring out at the room and feeling more and more unsettled. Nothing seemed to make sense anymore: Chat living in a place like this, Mrs. Crawley reading her most cherished novels. Augie felt antsy then, and as she looked to the door, willing Chat to come back, she stood up.

She told herself she was looking for Chat, yet as she moved down the hall, she acknowledged a pull she couldn't explain—as if there were answers and clues out in this mansion that could unlock something inside her, make sense of everything that hurt.

Intuitively, she knew where to go.

When Augie pushed through the double doors to the main suite, she felt momentarily weak, her knees buckling slightly, like when you're dreaming and you fall. The room felt like a penthouse. The bed was huge and white with fluffy yet crisp pillows. The headboard was not a headboard but rather a pale blue expanse of wall that reached the high ceiling, an intricate chandelier hanging above like a web of Christmas lights. Low white tables anchored each side of the bed, and more delicate lights adorned the walls. There was also a sitting room with luxe cream couches and a glass table with lilies, a glowing vanity with rounded mirrors, and finally, an arched entryway to the bathroom, which reflected more glass and light.

Augie walked around the room in a somnambulistic state, touching vases of perfume, velvety throws, skimming her fingertips along the smooth white dressers. When she reached the bed, she sat down and fanned her arms out, stroking the impossibly soft duvet. As she lay back and stared up at the chandelier—a galaxy all its own—she felt Chat appear at the door.

He called her name, but she didn't respond. Then he asked what she was doing.

Augie waited a few more seconds before she dragged herself to sitting. She looked at him as the lights above twinkled, refracting out around them.

"Sorry. I wanted to see everything."

"This room is pretty cool. She showed me once on our first tour." His tone was casual but forced as he stepped farther inside.

Sitting on the bed, staring out at him, the smooth white carpet between them, Augie couldn't stop herself. "Do you like her?"

Chat moved forward. "What do you mean?"

"Do you like her? Mrs. Crawley. Do you think she's a good person?"

"I don't think she's a bad person."

Augie glanced to her side, catching her reflection in the mirror. She imagined Mrs. Crawley's reflection in the exact same light.

"I don't think she is. A good person."

Chat ran his hand through his hair. He walked to Augie and sat down next to her.

"I know she can be cold at times." He gripped the edge of the bed. "I get why you'd think that. She's been through a lot." He hesitated. "Her dad died when she was young, and she's been divorced . . . and I get the feeling she's just been hurt a lot. I think that's why she acts like she does sometimes. Why she's not overly friendly. Why she's kind of anxious at the Club."

Augie focused on her lap, tensing. She didn't want to know any of this; she didn't want to feel bad for Mrs. Crawley. And Chat was wrong: There was no way she was *anxious at the Club.*

"I really shouldn't be saying anything. Bill doesn't know about the divorce, he's religious, so please don't say anything."

Augie was, again, bothered by his concern.

"I trust you," he added as if this was some big compliment.

Augie felt her mind and heart all tangled up, like the light fixture hanging above, and she followed the one instinct that felt crystal clear. She leaned forward and kissed him.

It felt like everything unlocked in that moment, the room disappearing around them. Their mouths were all over each other, their hands were all over each other—and soon both their shirts were off, Augie rolling on top of Chat as he lay back on the bed, his hands climbing over her jeans and up her spine. They moved in tandem as they kissed more intensely, inhaling each other.

But at the very moment she reached for the waist of his shorts—deciding she needed to be as physically close to him as possible—Chat's wrist buzzed once more. They paused, still pressed together, before Augie pulled her hand away and they searched each other's faces, waiting, listening. In their panting silence, they heard not Max's, but Cooper's voice from the hall. And, a second later, they heard what he was saying.

"Mommy! Mommy! You're home!"

Chat stared up at Augie, his face blank, before suddenly, he scrambled out from under her, racing off the bed. Augie reached for her shirt from the floor as she stood, swiveling her head as Chat tugged on his shirt and rushed toward the door.

"Shit, shit, shit." He raced back to the bed and used two hands to smooth the duvet, studying it with intense focus, before he finally looked to Augie, who'd realized her shirt was on inside out. She crossed her arms. Outside, they heard Mrs. Crawley tell Cooper she was sorry for waking him. Her voice was distinct—the door to the room was half open.

"Oh, fuck," Chat whispered before inhaling a stifled breath.

"Okay, it's fine, come here." He seemed to shift to flight mode as he grabbed Augie's hand. "Okay, here's what we do: You stay in the closet, and I'll go talk to her. I'll tell her to take Cooper to bed while I check on Max."

Augie sensed he was talking to himself more than to her.

"Then when she's gone, I'll come back for you, okay? We'll go down the back stairs." Quietly, he opened a door to their side.

Augie could barely think as he guided her into the closet. She usually responded well to a crisis—once, when Augie and her friends were caught in a storm out on Lake Minnetonka, Augie had been the one to keep everyone calm and direct them to the closest dock; another time, when they were carving pumpkins and Fiona Palmer sliced her finger, Augie had been the one to wrap it up and drive them to the ER. But this was different. This time, it was her fault.

Slowly, she stepped farther inside the closet, taking in her surroundings. Of course, it was nothing like a regular closet. The lights had been left on, and she could see everything clearly: the twinkling glass island that housed Mrs. Crawley's jewelry, the symmetrical walls of built-in drawers and hangers and shoes. The open space didn't offer much for hiding, but she needed to hide. What if Mrs. Crawley came in here? What if—her thoughts were interrupted as she heard voices growing louder, and she realized she had jinxed herself.

"I need to get out of this dress," she heard Mrs. Crawley say as Chat protested, as he rambled on about how Cooper really needed to go back to bed, how he really needed to check on Max, whose cough was getting worse. Mrs. Crawley kept repeating herself, her voice desperate and slurred, as she told him that she "had, had, *had* to get out of it."

Just as Augie sensed Mrs. Crawley moving toward the closet, she rushed to a wall of clothes and shimmied in behind a row of long, thick coats. She pressed her back flat against the wall, willing herself not to sneeze as a fur collar swayed in front of her. She clutched her abdomen and stared out through the gaps of light between the hangers as Mrs. Crawley burst inside.

There was no way not to watch. And no way not to notice: Mrs. Crawley was drunk. Or deranged. Her eye makeup was smudged, her hair all over. She moved fast, clawing at a zipper at her lower back, grasping at the halter's knot around her neck. She struggled for a moment, cursed to herself, before finally she tugged the right strand, and the dress fell away, the whole piece slipping off and landing in a shining green puddle on the floor. Augie glanced away, ashamed. Mrs. Crawley wasn't wearing a bra, only a thin nude thong. Still, a second later, Augie couldn't deny the draw to study her, tracing her lean, defined muscles all the way from her calves to her triceps to her neck. And that's when she saw it—that's when it finally clicked: that silver chain around her neck, that necklace, that amber pendant she always wore. The one she'd told Mrs. Cline at the baby shower she had gotten in Latvia. As a gift. From an ex.

Latvia. Latvia. *Latvia.*

The place Chat's uncle lived. The place he played hockey. Trey? Uncle Trey?

Augie's mind was on overdrive, and she wished she had more time to think—but as Mrs. Crawley pulled on a black nightgown, flicked off the lights, and left—only seconds later, the lights flashed back on and there was Chat, looking back and forth inside the closet, panicked.

Augie pushed an arm through the coats, and instantly, he was there. He pulled her out.

"Okay, she's with Cooper now," he said as Augie stumbled forward. "Come on." He grabbed her hand, dragging her toward the door. "We gotta move."

20

In her lowest moments, Danika's mind turned against her. It doubled down. Whenever she needed to pull herself up and think positively—to save herself—her subconscious did the opposite. It was like that game when someone said, "Don't think about a horse! Don't think about a basketball!" and images of horses and basketballs flooded in. She was her own worst enemy.

This was a pattern Danika recognized, but one she could not stop. Once she reached a certain point of despair or lack of control, the devil on her shoulder took over, conjuring bad thought after bad thought, bad memory after bad memory, each served one at a time as if from a conveyer belt. It was harder to stop when she was drunk.

So that night, after tearing off her dress and changing into pajamas, as she stumbled back into the brightly lit hall—makeup still a mess, head still spinning—and went to tuck Cooper in, her mind was already working against her. Memories began to flash on overdrive.

There was her mother, painting her fingernails at the kitchen table only to piss off her dad, who hated the smell—the fight that ensued. There was her father, building a bonfire one night for her at eight years old, joking the whole time, until she realized he was drunk, and then he passed out on the grass. There was the halter top she'd worn to a middle school dance, the one a girl had called cheap, *Because your dad's only an E-7.* Always, there was the smell of bacon, BLTs, the last thing she saw him eat—bringing her back to the day the military police showed up on their porch, explaining he'd shot himself out on the running trail.

The next set of memories came from St. Cloud. Dark at first, then illuminated with love. She remembered the day she first saw him mowing the lawn across the street, the way he'd pushed up his sunglasses, pulled off his orange work gloves, and yelled, "Hey, are you the new girl? I'm Trey."

More flashbacks cut in and out from there. Searing snapshots of sounds, sights, smells, and tastes: the freezer-burn cold of hockey rinks, the harsh vowels of the Latvian language, the fresh, piney sting of Riga Black Balsam. The cold lights of a taxi in the night.

"Mom?" she heard Cooper say as she stepped inside his room, steadying herself. She went to his bed, where he sat upright. His night-light glowed with swimming images of fish, reflected across the walls of his room in swirling, neon circles. Cooper's face was heavy with sleep. She sobered, softened.

"It's late, hun." She pulled his covers higher. Moved his elephant closer.

"I heard you come home."

"I know. I'm sorry." She touched his forehead.

He yawned. "Love you a lilac."

Danika swallowed. Cooper used to have a habit of saying "I love you like a lot" before bed, and sometimes he'd say it so fast, it sounded like "I love you a lilac." It had become their inside joke. It was the first thing to comfort her all night. Here, despite everything, Danika was reminded that she had what she'd always wanted: unconditional love.

"Love you a lilac," she whispered. She kissed her hand and pressed it to his cheek, worried her mouth still reeked of booze.

Cooper nestled into his pillow, and Danika sat in the dark, the carousel of night-light fish still dancing around her. She watched them for a moment, their colorful striped bodies, until she grew dizzy and stood up, going to the window. Cooper always insisted on sleeping with the curtains open, but she tugged them shut now, hoping he'd sleep in. It had been a long night.

As she soaked in the steady pour of rain, she froze. Because spinning down the driveway below was a pinwheel of color—a hideous mash-up of maroon and yellow. The U of M.

It was shocking how bright the umbrella looked in the dark. Danika could not peel her eyes away, even as she felt everything drain from her body—as she became a shell of herself. She seemed to fill with a whole new feeling, a new substance pouring inside of her, all the way up to her skull: a thick, growing lava of rage.

How could he.

The stinging, sour hurt came after.

She knew that from then on, whenever she saw those colors—umbrellas in general—they would bring her back to this night, to this moment, this pain. This thought, of everything, broke her. All she could do was watch and hope the girl would see her, too. That she would turn, look up, and catch sight of her silhouette in the glow of the window. But, of course, she didn't. It was a memory missed, a haunting averted. Danika hated her for it.

21

New York, March

Augie and Micah first had sex in the middle of her living room. She hadn't planned for things to go that far. But of course, she hadn't planned any of it.

Immediately following their kiss in the cab, they'd had a more innocuous routine: Each morning at six a.m., they'd meet at the coffee bar before their coworkers arrived and make out against the fridge. It was easy to hear when someone was coming, yet the risk of getting caught made it all the more thrilling.

After a week or so, they began meeting at dive bars and restaurants. They only went to places Micah said Julia would never go. "She's an elitist," he joked once as they slid into a bar's booth. Augie didn't respond. She didn't like to think about Julia, how she was Robin's cousin—how they attended each other's weddings and ski vacations and held family reunions at the Greenes' cabin. It was easier to stay in the present, to keep kissing Micah and not think at all.

It was only natural that after a few weeks of making out all over Manhattan, one Saturday night, Micah showed up at her apartment.

Augie was home, unsurprisingly. She hadn't made many friends yet, which she tried not to dwell on. But between work and the affair, even simple tasks like grocery shopping felt tiring, and Augie didn't have the energy for a social life. She never texted back the girl from work who'd invited her to karaoke, never reached out to Leah's friend of a friend.

So when Micah called that night, she answered. She could tell he was a little drunk, and she went down to the street to tell him to go home—but as he explained he'd had a bad night, they lost a major account, Julia was out of town, and all he wanted to do was see Augie and this funky little apartment she kept talking about, she caved. She let him up.

Micah was enthralled. She realized later he came from a long line of family money—New York money—and had never lived in a place as crappy as hers. While the living room was large, with high ceilings and windows, and her room was off to the side, the main space was filled with boxes of junk and art supplies: Styrofoam, clothes hangers, felt, glitter, dried-out clay.

"I feel like Willy Wonka," he said, laughing and stumbling around, shaking a bag of googly eyes at her.

Augie stood back, uneasy and excited. She knew what was about to happen. She had a brief thought, one she'd always remember, as he twisted a pink pipe cleaner into a flower: she could stop this. She could be the better, bigger person. She didn't. For the first time in her life, Augie felt grossly alive. Grossly alive, mature, and a little cruel. Finally, she was someone new.

Later, her perspective would shift. The affair would become a source of regret and shame that she could barely stand to touch. But right then, she had no thought of the future. No idea of right or wrong. No thought of anything but Micah, pulling her closer, telling her how he would split her in two.

* * *

Augie hadn't gone running since New York, but the Sunday after she'd nearly been caught in Mrs. Crawley's closet, she pulled on shorts and tied her sneakers tight. It was dawn, the air was cool, and she'd been up for hours, anyway.

She blasted an old playlist as she ran her high school route. She felt relief in the nostalgia as she sprinted down Brown Road, up and over the bridge, looping onto the Luce Line, the wood-chipped trail that snaked through the trees; it was as if, however briefly, she could fool herself into thinking she was seventeen again. It had been so simple to know the real world was out in front of you, waiting. That you weren't there yet. It'd been so much easier to feel hopeful.

The nostalgia was only a Band-Aid. As Augie reached mile three and rounded the edge of Long Lake, flashes of the previous night came back to her: the smell of fur coats; the struggle to hold her breath; the glow of Mrs. Crawley's skin; that amber necklace. The word *Latvia* blaring in her mind. The end of the night had been a blur, but she still remembered how Chat had rushed her down the hall and back stairs and straight out the door. He hadn't even said goodbye.

Augie sat down on one of the benches on the side of the lake, glad no one was around. Above, blackbirds swam through the sky and the sun slowly started to rise. She stared at the calm gray water and, again, back to her phone. Nothing. She still hadn't heard from him.

Augie felt as if her whole body was a concoction of bad feelings: embarrassment from sneaking into Mrs. Crawley's bedroom and being so forward with Chat; confusion about how Danika and Chat's uncle and Latvia all fit together; worry about whether Chat was keeping something from her; and mostly, hurt from the way he had basically shoved her out the door. It felt like a sign of his allegiance:

He cared more about Mrs. Crawley. Augie knew he was also worried about his job, but still. Mrs. Crawley had won. Women like her always came out on top.

At the same time, Augie knew she was to blame. She had screwed up. She never should have gone there in the first place. What was she thinking? Here was yet another rash, ridiculous decision. Augie didn't recognize herself anymore—this pattern of failure. But maybe all her previous years had been the farce. Maybe this was who she really was.

Augie's breath hitched, and she stood up. She walked around the water with her head down and searched for a thin, flat rock. She found one and held it like a boomerang the way her father had taught her. *If this skips, everything will be fine,* she bargained with herself, feeling desperate as she approached the shallow, lapping water. She pulled back her hand and whipped the rock forward, cringing as she watched—yet physically relieved as it skidded three times across the surface. She needed something, anything, to believe in.

As the day continued and Augie didn't hear from Chat, she told herself this was it. It was time to be done. She deleted the LinkedIn app. She turned her phone off. She didn't want to keep waiting for his messages. He had Mrs. Crawley. He didn't get Augie, too.

Augie showered and sat at her desk. While she planned to call Leah to tell her the latest revelations, she knew she was probably exhausted after the restaurant opening. Augie had to give her a minute. Augie was eager to talk to her, though. Even if she'd been trying not to rope Leah into her drama, she knew Leah would want to hear about all this—sneaking over, the Latvia connection. Because it was too strange not to mean something, right? Augie couldn't stop thinking about it: Was Chat's uncle the ex who gave Mrs. Crawley that necklace? Had they been in Latvia together? Were the hockey games she'd bragged about to TC *his*? Nonetheless, Augie promised herself that that morning, she simply needed to work. To focus on her own future. Chat had already been enough of a distraction.

But as Augie settled at her computer and opened her spreadsheets, her mom knocked and cracked open the door, raising a basket of laundry like an offering.

"Oh, thanks." Augie leaned back as Lilly set the basket on top of her bed. Augie noticed her work shirt for the Club on top. She didn't want to go back.

"How was your night out? Did you have fun?"

Augie focused on her computer. She had lied to her mom and said she was seeing friends.

"I should have stayed home." She moved her wet hair to her other shoulder, the water bleeding into her shirt, making her shiver. "How was your work dinner?"

Her mom began putting away the clothes, pulling a hanger from her closet.

"I can do that."

"I don't mind." She untangled the straps of a dress. "Dinner was fun," she said brightly. "A perk of summer session is new adjunct professors. They were nice. And . . . there's this guy."

"No way—who?" Augie scooted back her chair. Her mother rarely mentioned men—let alone dated. In the twelve years since her dad left, Augie could remember only two guys who made it past a first night out and into conversation. Even the mention of someone was a big deal.

Her mother smiled, holding a shirt with her chin as she folded its arms. His name was Peter. He was from Wisconsin and a mechanical engineering professor at the University of Madison, but he was moving to Minnesota to be closer to his aging parents. He was teaching three sections of math this summer at the U, trying to get an in. He had a pug named Pug. He was divorced with no kids.

"He loves to make pizza, apparently. Although I have yet to try it."

Augie stood. "He sounds so *nice*, Mom." She hugged her. They stood in silence until, finally, Augie turned away. The comfort of her mother always made her choke up, and now the morning's melodrama was catching up with her.

"Hey." Her mom slid her hand down the ends of Augie's wet hair, flicking the water away. "Are you okay? I know this summer hasn't been easy."

Augie felt her stress expanding inside her. She sat down on her bed. "I just feel so pathetic. I keep messing everything up. I feel like I deserve all the bad stuff happening to me this summer. Like it's karma. Like everything I worked for was for nothing. . . . in the end."

"Oh, come on, now." Her mom shook her shoulder. "I know losing the job was tough, but it's only one job. Even if you messed up"—she paused, and for the first time, Augie wondered if her mom knew there was more to the story than the merger, if she sensed, in their closeness, something worse had happened—"there's no point in beating yourself up about it. Regret is a wasted emotion, dear. You can't change the past. Karma isn't so black and white."

Augie scrunched her forehead. She had never wanted to ask her mom about all her own regrets. Augie wondered if these mantras were how she coped.

"Do you really believe that?"

"What?"

"You really don't have any regrets?"

Her mom pulled back. "Well, it's impossible to not have *any* regrets. I regret not calling my dad the night before he died. I regret not going to my friend Allison's wedding. I regret not keeping in touch with a few people. But it's not worth ruminating over. You learn, do better."

Augie pushed her tongue against her bottom teeth.

"You don't regret Dad, Minnesota, never working in publishing? All this?" She gestured to her room.

To her surprise, her mom let out her real laugh, that perfect scale.

"I do kind of regret letting you paint the walls such a bright blue." She squinted, holding her hand to her forehead as if blocking the sun. "But no, Aug. Of course not. You'd go crazy trying to compare paths not taken—playing the endless game of *what if.* And believe it or not, I love my life." She hugged Augie's shoulders with one arm. "I love you. I loved your dad. I loved Maine. The restaurant. I love it here, too. I told you, karma isn't so clear-cut. Things often work out in the end, despite the hardships. You have to give yourself some grace."

Augie took a slow, shaky breath. She was surprised, but she felt a valve turning inside her, a pressure releasing from her center—one she hadn't known was wound so tight. It had been years since she and her mom were vulnerable with each other. She'd always assumed she knew how her mom felt about everything—hadn't wanted to challenge their perfect ecosystem.

"It's going to be okay, Aug." Her mom broke the silence as she stood and folded the last of Augie's T-shirts. "You *have* to get messy in life. No other way to become as wise and wonderful as your own mother." She batted her lashes.

Augie shifted her weight on the bed, growing so fully sick of thinking about herself, she couldn't stand it. "Okay, so"—she hit her thighs—"when do we do a pizza party with Pug and Peter? And all the pickled peppers Peter Piper picked?"

Her mom laughed again with her head back. "Touché, darling. Soon, soon. Let's plan a party promptly."

22

The boys were screaming, and Danika had a headache. She sat alone on the steps of the Big Room, watching them attempt to play mini golf. They'd gotten the set last year for Christmas: a nine-hole felt course complete with plastic flags and clubs and rainbow-colored balls. It was one more attempt by Bill to make them love golf. They typically paid it no mind, but Chat had motivated them to use it this summer.

Cooper still preferred to arrange the balls in patterns and hit them apart. He liked how it sounded, like a firework, he said. Max liked the golf aspect at least a little. He'd swing and miss, swing and miss, pick up the ball and plop it in the hole.

Even now, Cooper kept taking breaks to tell Danika about his latest picture book. Since art camp, he'd been drawing fervently. He'd completed his fairy-tale series, another about squirrels living above a neighborhood, and now, he was plotting a story about a magic stingray that gives a boy superpowers. "The whole thing takes place underwater," he'd explained.

Danika thought it was charming, but she didn't want to hear about it today. Her head was pounding. She'd slept like hell. She'd told Bill she'd left the party because she felt sick. *Too much wine.* He hadn't pried, hadn't come home until eight a.m.

Danika couldn't stomach the thought now, that both Chat and Bill were lying to her. Betraying her. She felt confused and hurt—but she knew she needed to harness her anger. She knew, from experience, it was better to feel mad than heartbroken.

Danika was glad they were gone today. They were playing an invitational in Apple Valley and wouldn't be back until late. Even so, that morning, she'd waited until the last minute to go downstairs. She'd barely looked at them as she ushered the boys to the playroom. She sensed their paranoia, all their lies and half-truths pulling them under.

Danika let out a breath when they finally left the house. She needed time to think.

"Mom, look at this." Cooper squatted near the fake sand trap, a patch of tan felt. Inside, he'd lined up the balls in a spiral.

Max stumbled over and grabbed the blue ball at the center, and Cooper screamed.

"Boys." Danika rubbed her temples.

"You can't have that one." Cooper pried the ball from Max's fist while Max wailed.

Danika went to them, again explained the concept of sharing, and told Max he could have the green ball instead. She felt queasy as she settled back onto the stairs. Yet as she watched Cooper help Max set his ball at a new hole and practice his swing, her heart constricted.

How *dare* they put the boys at risk? Everything they did—herself, Bill, Chat—was supposed to be for them. Max and Cooper were the center of their lives. Who did Chat think he was, bringing a stranger into their house? And how was Bill being so reckless, risking their family's finances, security?

Danika needed answers. She needed to fix this. She owed it to the boys. She owed it to *herself.* She had worked so hard to build this life—to build the stability she never had. She wasn't going to let anyone throw their lives into turmoil. Finally, her fury was eclipsing her pain.

Danika picked up her phone and scrolled through her messages.

She called Joshua Mike.

Joshua Mike had been surprised yet elated to hear from her. He said he had a party that evening, but he could meet her the next night, Monday. He said name the place, he'd be there.

As little patience as Danika had, she was glad to have time to prepare. Especially because there was another conversation demanding her attention—she needed to confront Chat. She was relieved they already had plans to meet at the model home that same Monday; he was going to pick up the framed art prints from the Galleria, then come help her arrange furniture. Alone in Briar Ridge, they'd be able to talk for real.

At least the model home was coming together, Danika thought. At least one thing was going right. Danika had leaned into the Japandi style: cozy yet minimal; refined yet natural. She'd anchored the living room with a long, low-slung tan couch, stunning suede pouffes, a circular wooden coffee table. The kitchen was also gorgeous, immaculate—all stones and blues and teak. The house had perfect balance. She'd love to see anyone else try to re-create such peace.

In fact, as soon as Danika stepped inside the model home that Monday afternoon, she instantly felt better. The house was light and pure and untainted. She knew people would be drawn to it, this fresh start. She was glad it could only get better from there, too; she hadn't even started on the accents. She couldn't wait to hang artwork, place vases and plants and lamps.

Chat arrived exactly on time. He knocked before pushing open the door, lifting the large frames wrapped in craft paper up and over the doorframe.

"Delivery," he called before spotting her. Being at Briar Ridge always felt more intimate, so far away from their Aldon Lakes life. Chat smiled softly as she stood up from the couch. They hadn't been alone since Saturday night—hadn't truly spoken since before the restaurant opening.

It was awkward between them, and Danika was glad they each had somewhere to focus as Chat moved farther inside: Danika went to the prints and started tearing away paper, and Chat, who hadn't been in the model home since the furniture arrived, began walking through the rooms. Danika felt unsettled as he walked around—it felt like watching someone read something you wrote—and Danika stared into the Hopper prints, distracting herself. She tended to go for more basic art, but buyers needed to feel something. And everyone was moved by Hopper's pieces. He was also famous enough for people to recognize the prints even if they couldn't name the artist, which made them feel smart. It was a winning combo. Danika studied *Summer Evening*, the melancholy couple on the porch.

Danika tried to ignore the tension peaking between them, but even as Chat went upstairs, she still felt it. She suspected he knew she'd learned about Augie, too—that Danika was aware she'd been in the house. He was acting more shy than normal. Even now, as he returned to the living room, he put his hands in his pockets, sheepish.

"Danika." He swung his head at the ground. "This is incredible. Really. It's amazing. I couldn't picture it all before . . . when you bought all this." He waved to the furniture. "But seriously. I'm so impressed. It looks perfect."

Danika allowed herself the praise, hiding her relief.

"Thank you. We still need the accent pieces, but those will come later. Did you know people *glue* down accessories for open houses? They literally superglue frames and candles and everything to the tables so people won't steal them." Danika hadn't realized she was this nervous. "I really hate to do that." She glided her hand over the end table, fingering knots of wood. "It's unfortunate, how impossible it is to trust people."

Energy swelled through her as Chat's ears went fully maroon. He pushed his hands deeper into his pockets.

The plan had not been to bombard him right off the bat, but the friction between them was too obvious. Danika took it as a sign of their closeness; they didn't know how to act fake with each other. Their bond was real.

"Chat," she sighed, suddenly exhausted and eager to get this over with, "I know she was there. In the house."

Chat looked at his feet. "I figured. I really don't know what to say." His voice was quiet. "I'm so sorry. It was a mistake. I never should have invited her over. Or I should have at least asked you first. I feel awful about it."

Danika tried to remain steady, not allowing herself to focus on the words: *invited her over.* It was easier to place the blame on Augie, her conniving plans.

"I only thought, because the boys were asleep, and it was so late . . ." Chat trailed off. "I didn't think you'd care, or that anyone would get hurt. I wasn't thinking. I really, *really* don't want to break your trust." His voice cracked, and Danika suddenly worried he might cry. It was strange how now, their roles felt reversed. Though hadn't she always been the one in charge?

"Here, come sit." Danika walked to the couch.

They sat on either end, and Danika curled her legs up under her, trying to find the right words—when Chat started talking. He held a white sample pillow in his lap and flung his hands around, explaining how it had all happened so fast, so last minute.

"I should have asked you, but I didn't want to bother you." He leaned into the couch. "You seemed so stressed that night. I've also been meaning to ask . . . are you okay? Did something happen? I'm sorry I didn't check in earlier."

Danika tucked her chin down. She didn't want to make this about her. Especially because she hadn't gained enough control of the situation to share anything—to be sure of anything. She wouldn't see Joshua Mike until later that night.

"Look, Chat, it comes down to this: I need to be able to trust you. With the boys, our house. You've been so fantastic this summer, but this was so out of line. You blatantly broke the contract. Bringing a . . . girlfriend around the boys. A stranger into our house."

Chat grabbed at the back of his neck. "I know, I know." He swallowed, and Danika watched his Adam's apple rise, click, fall. "I messed up. It won't happen again. I've really appreciated this summer. All you guys have done for me. It's been so amazing to be here, and I only ever want to help you, to make your life easier. I hope you can forgive me."

Danika adjusted her legs. Despite his apology, she could only focus on the fact he hadn't corrected her when she'd said *girlfriend*.

"I need you to do better." She was unable to broach the subject directly—to ask what she really wanted to know: *Do you love that girl?* She felt sick with nostalgia and jealousy.

Danika knew young love.

Chat continued apologizing as Danika studied the room, the flawless space and world she'd created. He scooted closer as he talked, and as she glanced to him and down to her lap—her jeans, her white tank top—she couldn't help but wonder: Did he still think she was beautiful? She felt suddenly aware of the space on the couch between them.

She just missed Trey so fiercely—missed being *young* so fiercely. All that freedom and possibility. She didn't let herself recognize the irony of how when she was young, all she'd really wanted was to be settled.

But you never got to mourn the previous versions of yourself—they simply disappeared. You never knew the last time a stranger would hit on you, the last time you'd kiss someone who was not your husband, the last day you were not a mom. It made Danika sick how quickly you could slip into a brand-new life, a brand-new self, even one you'd been chasing. It was like that poem she'd once read that said, "There is an age when you are most yourself." She'd always liked that idea—though the problem was, you'd never know at what age you were most yourself until it had passed.

Why was everything only clear at the end?

"Danika?" Chat said as she blinked.

She smoothed her hair with two hands as if coming up for air. "I don't know what to say, Chat. I don't know what to do. I don't trust that girl . . . and now . . . Can I trust you?"

Chat placed his hand between them, his palm up. "Danika. I promise. You can."

Chat opened his hand wider, and a second later, she slipped hers into his. He grabbed it so fast, it was as if his palm were a flytrap. He pulsed her hand before letting it go. "It won't happen again. We only have three weeks left together, and I really don't want to ruin it."

Danika didn't know how to feel. She didn't want to lose him, either—not to that girl, not to the end of summer.

"Well, four weeks," she corrected, "if you count Hilton Head. I already got your ticket." She smiled then; the ticket, after all, was a gift. Even if they hadn't talked details, Chat had said from the get-go he'd love to come—that he couldn't wait to see the ocean. Someplace new.

"Oh, yeah, right. Okay, I just, I wasn't sure about Hilton Head, with the timing. My Europe flight and all, but maybe. Maybe I can still make it work," he said, backtracking.

Danika's stomach churned. She immediately sensed he was staying behind for her. To spend more time with Augie.

Danika looked toward the windows, feeling disappointed—and even more, feeling *embarrassed* about feeling disappointed. Rejected. *Why* was she so desperate for his attention and approval? What did that say about her, how lonely she was?

Danika suddenly stood up, walked toward the windows, and crossed her arms tight. She stared out at the other empty houses, her back to Chat. Her breath caught in her throat. But a beat later, as practiced, she flipped her hurt to rage.

"Okay, well, Chat"—her voice went cold as she turned to face him—"let's focus on these last few weeks then, please? I know the boys will be sad when you're gone. So it'd be great if they—if we—could have your undivided attention. And I would appreciate it if there were no more uninvited guests inside my home."

Chat sucked in a breath, his face pale. "Yes, of course, Danika. I'm really—"

"No, Chat," she cut him off. "I'm the one who should be sorry. I should know better by now. I should know the only person I can count on is myself."

Chat closed his eyes.

"Though there is one thing I can't do alone: I can't move that dresser upstairs. So, let's go, please." Her voice shifted abruptly to fake and cheery; it felt manic. "Chop, chop. I'm meeting someone tonight, and I need to get the hell out of here by four."

She walked past him up the stairs.

DANIKA WAS GLAD she'd told Joshua Mike to meet her at the dive bar out in Mankato. Now more than ever, she needed a drink—and to get away.

The Drunken Moose was an hour south, known for its talking moose head and strong rail cocktails. She hadn't been in years, not since she and Bill went ironically, one night after they'd moved to Minnesota from Chicago. Danika felt another sense of longing as she sat on a cracked red barstool, neon signs flickering in the dark above her. She ordered a double vodka.

Joshua Mike arrived a few minutes after. He went in for a hug, but Danika recoiled.

"Fine, fine, fine." He pulled at the knot of his tie. His tan looked ashy in the low light. "I only thought since you invited me, I'd try my luck. But I get this isn't a date."

Danika looked beyond him, watching men in flannel shirts laugh and shoot pool. Joshua Mike was out of place in his suit. *Just get this over with*, she told herself.

"I always knew you had a dive bar side to you." Joshua ordered a whiskey, dropping a twenty on the bar. "Or you really don't want anyone to see us?"

"Thanks for meeting me."

He pulled out a stool, sat, and took off his suit jacket, draping it over one knee. "Okay. I think I know where this is going, but hit me with it. Jackie likes to talk, huh?"

"Josh." Danika turned toward him, her legs opening as she swiveled on the stool; she didn't stop them. At this point, who cared? She would use whatever power she had left. She was too far gone. "What in God's name is going on?"

Joshua Mike stared at her thighs, the space between them. He finished his whiskey in one gulp and knocked his glass against the bar. He shifted his weight to face her, leaning on his arm. "Are you sure you don't want to talk to your husband first? He said he was going to talk to you. Not that I'm not happy to help. The offer stands."

Danika tried not to react as the bartender refilled his glass. She gestured to hers, too.

"I have a feeling you'll find out soon enough, so fine. I'll get messy with ya. I'm only sorry this is what it took to spend time with you. As I've always said, you're the prettiest gal in Aldon Lakes."

Danika kept her face stone.

"All right, fine, fine, fine. Here goes."

Danika stayed quiet as he began to talk, drinking with an unsteady hand as she listened. He said that months ago, he'd overheard Bill talking to his lawyer—

"Frank," Danika interrupted.

"Yes, good ole Frank." Joshua continued to say they were discussing a few deals Bill had been involved in—a few bad deals. "Those St. Paul properties." Josh Mike swung his head. "Bill was being reckless, if you ask me. But hey, you know what they say, the bigger the risk, the bigger the reward. The problem was, he wasn't hitting that reward. He hasn't been for a while. Though no one could have predicted COVID.

"So, I approached him. I told him I knew he's going through it, and that he needed more investors for Briar Ridge. I knew he didn't want me involved . . . I've been blackballed lately, don't ask me why . . . but I have the cash, right? I told him I'll buy the last forty percent. Wyatt and Malcolm, they were being cheap, you know. But I love those houses. I said I'd bring the money, but I also wanted *you* involved. To help design, decorate. I knew you'd make it amazing. I like your style. I also thought it would be fun, you know, to be a team. I thought you'd enjoy it. I was looking out."

Danika's body went rigid.

"And I was right, of course! You're killing it."

Danika didn't know what to say. Behind them, pool balls cracked like gunshots.

"But I digress." He took a sip and smacked his lips. "Anyways, so there I am: I own the majority of Briar Ridge, and these guys are being so dumb about everything. It's not my first rodeo—I know we should reinvest the dividends rather than get a payout—but these guys are being shortsighted. Then, Bill finally admits to me alone that he needs the cash. He finally came clean. And, oh boy." Joshua Mike exhaled in a whistle. "He's in worse trouble than I thought. I hate the idea of y'all losing your houses."

Danika no longer felt tense now—only hollow.

"So, I tell Bill I'm happy to help. Nice guy I am. I tell him I'll give him a loan. Even more, I offer to buy the cabin. And Danika, if I'm being real with you, I'm only doing this because I care about you." He leaned in closer as she angled her body away.

"I know you're special, D." His voice was different. "I want you to have a good life. That's why, as I told Jackie, if Bill doesn't take me up on my offer, and you end up on your own, I'd still help you out. Whatever you need. A loan, a place to stay, you name it. You're a talent. It'd be an investment."

Danika didn't know how to make sense of anything, didn't know how to feel. While she'd suspected things were worse than Bill had let on—she'd never expected this. Losing their *houses*? Bill was supposed to be steady—they were supposed to be steady.

Josh studied her face. He waved for more drinks.

Yet as the bartender returned with the bottle, Danika stood. She hated him. She hated all of them. What she had said to Chat was true: She couldn't rely on anyone. She grabbed her purse.

"Oh, Danika, don't be like that." Joshua Mike slouched. "I feel bad, but it might be for the best, in the end, you know. I'm here for you."

She looked straight at him.

"I will never fuck you."

Joshua Mike laughed. "I'd never say no, but really, that's not what I'm after. I'm the one being honest here. Bill . . . he's the one lying. But, again, maybe it's all for the best. Money isn't everything, you know. Bill has his own demons."

Danika felt even more sick—and also like she could grab the knife the bartender was using to slice limes and sink it into his neck—but suddenly, she understood. She met Joshua Mike's eyes directly, an icy clarity falling over her.

"Who is he sleeping with?"

Joshua Mike glanced up at the moose head on the wall—the one all those years ago Danika and Bill had watched together, singing along to "Yellow Submarine"—and just like that, he told her.

It was becoming more difficult to meet. Their schedules were splintering. It made their texts more desperate—and risky. Tensions grew by the day.

Finally, they met one early morning at 63 Birch. They broke their own rules: They kissed in front of windows, in the wide-open kitchen. They could even see other houses from where they embraced, the model home just up the street. It was enough to remind them that soon, the community would be filling—people moving in and taking over all the rooms they'd considered, if only briefly, theirs.

Soon, the house would be sold. The summer would be over.

"I'm going to miss this," they whispered, soaking in each moment.

And, as if their words had summoned the end—that day, as they held each other—that's when they heard the knock on the door.

That's when someone rounded the corner.

Chat Efhart • 6:39 PM
Augie
Please talk to me
I should have messaged sooner
This was all my fault
I want to see you
Just tell me where to meet
Chat Efhart • 7:58 PM
I really don't want the summer to end like this

23

The end-of-summer luau used to be at the end of summer—the last week of August, right before Labor Day—but people complained it interfered with the state fair and the start of school. Now, it was a full month earlier, the last weekend of July. They colloquially called it The-Beginning-of-the-End-of-Summer Luau. It made Augie roll her eyes.

Augie hated working the luau. It was exhausting. Every member made a point to be there. Kids and nannies were included, and everyone dressed as if it were a competition. Women cryptically discussed their outfits all summer long, as if it were the Met Gala.

Of course, this year, Augie was dreading it more than normal. She'd asked Aida if there was any way she could take it off, but she knew the answer. Over two hundred people had RSVPed, and because last year people had complained about the crowded bar stations and bad DJ, Mr. Dryer was under extra pressure.

The only silver lining was that *everyone* would be working. Mr. Dryer had even called in Zami to help with the pig roast. Leah and Wyatt would be there, too. She joked she was her dad's date because Robin was again out of town.

Still, no one could distract from the fact that Augie would finally have to face Chat and the Crawleys. The luau would mark one week since she'd been to the Crawleys' house—one week since she'd spoken to Chat at all.

Leah and Augie were back to talking about them nonstop. Especially after Leah assured Augie she enjoyed it—that she lived for this type of gossip.

She'd even told Augie to come hash everything out in person. So one evening, they sat at the pool at dusk, dangling their feet in the water, going over the same pieces of information: how Mrs. Crawley had bragged about watching hockey in Europe, how she'd said her necklace was from Latvia—from an ex.

And then: how Chat had said his uncle lived in Latvia, played hockey there—that Danika had been divorced.

"It's all too coincidental not to be connected," Augie had repeated as she pushed her feet back and forth in the water, watching the ripples spread across the surface. "But it's also like, *who* is lying? Why? If Danika was with Chat's uncle, why not tell people they know each other? It would make the whole manny thing less weird." She stopped moving her feet. "Do you think they were actually married? That he was her ex-*husband*?"

"Well, if so, at least we know they're not hooking up. If she really was his uncle's ex-wife. Chat's ex-*aunt*?" Leah made a face.

It didn't feel right to Augie either; the chemistry between Danika and Chat seemed too strange to be simply familial.

Augie made sure to tell Leah how much she appreciated her help, knowing Leah was going to spend hours stalking Danika, Trey, Chat's family, even if they kept hitting dead ends. So far, the only people they could find online were his twin sisters.

"Hey, at least now we know they have a bunny," Leah had said, holding up her phone to show a photo of the girls cradling a black-and-white rabbit. *Mr. Bun Bun*, Augie remembered.

Augie craned back, looked up at the fading blue sky. Despite the dearth of information, and how depressed she felt about Chat, she still sensed they were on the cusp of something. She didn't understand it yet, but for once, her instincts felt right. They had to keep looking.

Still, they didn't have much luck over the week, and the day before the luau, Leah told Augie she was giving up. That Augie had to talk to him in person—to get answers from the source.

You know he's going to find you at the luau, Leah had texted. There's no way he'll pretend you're not there.

Augie disagreed. Even if she hadn't been on the LinkedIn app—and had no idea if he'd messaged—he'd clearly chosen sides.

Remember: I'm against "the rules."

Leah had sent back an eye-rolling emoji. He definitely wants to talk to you.

Augie was just glad she was successfully ignoring him. She'd even made progress on her checklists. With her new resolve, she had flagged five not-horrible jobs, and for the first time, she was genuinely excited about one of them: a nonprofit in DC that helped start-up companies with a focus on immigrant businesses. This aligned well with her previous work with Hyla. She'd love the chance to help people through advertising, rather than the New Jersey Lottery. Regardless, when she got to the part where she had to list references, she felt stuck. She couldn't include anyone from New York—and wouldn't it be strange not to? But she was so exasperated by everything, before she could stop herself, she wrote down Aida's name and contact info and hit send.

24

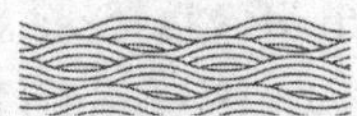

They were going to wear white. Bill, Chat, Cooper, Max, and herself. It would be a statement. It would be a vision. Danika needed to feel beautiful, to show off her family in flawless designer white. To appear as if everything was perfect. At least for tonight.

She hoped to fool herself.

Danika hadn't said anything to Bill about their finances, or the affair. She couldn't bring herself to face it yet. Still, he seemed to feel some shift in her.

"Are you okay?" he asked early that afternoon. Danika had been standing in her closet, picking out her jewelry for the evening and drinking from the bottle of wine she'd hidden behind her dresses—her emergency wine, she'd told herself. Though every day now felt like an emergency. As Bill entered, she pushed the bottle farther to the back.

"Are *you* okay?" She studied his workout clothes, his nonchalance. He'd been behaving as normal—not as if he was sending their whole lives into turmoil.

He nodded, perplexed.

Danika turned away. It was hard to look at him and not imagine him sleeping with someone else.

"Danika." He stepped closer. She was wearing her bathrobe, and he ran his hands over the white silk of her shoulders. "Thank you for whatever you said to Josh. He's been much more amiable lately. He didn't fight us on the last big vote, and he said you two had a good conversation about the model home. I appreciate it."

Danika tensed beneath Bill's hands.

"He seems to have turned a leaf, as they say." Bill chuckled. "We're all really excited about the model home, too. Everyone's so impressed. I knew what I was doing, hiring you."

Danika looked at him. She knew now that Joshua Mike had been the one to ask for her to be involved. That lie held a certain ache.

She walked toward the bathroom.

As Danika stood at the sink and stared into the mirror, she suddenly thought of her mother—suddenly saw her face in her own. Once again, she thought back to what she'd said that day Danika implied she should leave her father: "And then what? Just how do you suppose I start over? Just how do you supposed I get a new life?"

Danika felt sick with understanding.

She wanted to get to the end of summer unscathed, to finish the model home and soak in time with Chat before everything came tumbling down. Chat had been more attentive than ever, too—constantly asking how he could help, if she needed anything—and while things were different between them, it was still nice to be pampered. Even if his behavior was fueled by guilt, finally, she had him to herself.

Part of her wished she could open up to Chat and tell him everything about Bill, but they were no longer confidants. Like Trey, he had let her down.

But, now, the luau. This was one evening she could still control. One night where she could still feel like herself. Or at least the version of herself she had worked so hard to conceive. Because who knew who she'd be next. Her power was slipping away like the last light of day.

25

Every year, the staff wore colorful leis for the event, and as Augie slipped a ring of fake orange flowers around her neck, she was glad for the disguise, however small. Her heart beat so hard, she swore she could see the flowers fluttering against her shirt.

The setup had taken hours: They'd strung yards of string lights across the decks and twisted bamboo tiki torches into the ground. They'd also blown up the cartoonish plastic jungle animals—rhinos and gorillas and giraffes. Luau, jungle, Aida said not to ask questions.

Augie liked seeing the decorations come together. The whole space was transformed. The patio around the pool filled with tables with hot pink floral centerpieces, the grassy area beyond the pool housed all the elaborate food stations, and the wide stairs that led up to the Club's lower-level entrance had fake vines wrapped around the railings. Even the smaller, upper patio in front of the double doors had cocktail tables and extra speakers where people could look down on the party below. It became even more dazzling at night when the pool lights turned the water to an aqua lava lamp and the lights blinked brighter against the sky. Augie couldn't think about how far they were from sunset now. It was only five p.m. It was going to be a long night.

As they made their way to the break room for family meal, she tried to stay upbeat. Everyone seemed to be in a good mood, excited by the challenge of the night, the beginning-of-the-end of summer. She didn't want to be a downer. She was happy to see Zami, too. As he served summer orecchiette and told jokes about his beach bod, Augie laughed at all the right moments.

She didn't know what she would say to Chat. It would be too hard to explain her complicated feelings. Over the past week, she'd worked hard to explain them to herself. How could she admit that mostly, she was jealous of Mrs. Crawley? That Chat siding with Mrs. Crawley made her feel as though Chat had chosen everything Mrs. Crawley stood for: status, wealth, superficiality. It made Augie feel small and inferior, cementing her insecurities, how the Club members had always made her feel second rate.

Augie readied herself as they finished eating and Aida gave a toast saying how proud she was of how hard they'd worked that summer, how quickly the new staff had stepped up. It felt like an ending, but Augie wasn't sure of what exactly. She grew more anxious as they took their places outside.

No Club member wanted to arrive first to an event, so it wasn't until the clock hit six fifteen that people began swelling up the patio steps. As if on cue, the sky paled, the DJ switched to a cover of "Over the Rainbow," and the thick smell of charcoal and hickory began wafting through the air.

Augie saw the Clines first, sporting silky red summer-wear; then the Andersons in matching floral prints; then the Schmidts in boho chic; and so on. It didn't take long for the pool deck to fill with glowing tans and strappy sandals and screaming children. Augie was relieved when Mrs. Cline approached to ask for a mai tai. Work had begun.

Time moved quickly as Augie settled into the routine of the party. She kept an eye on the food as people began eating, ran drinks back and forth, helped TC with an especially large order of champagne. She was glad to be busy. It made it easier to avoid watching for Chat. She even forgot to check her phone, despite Leah promising she'd text when she and her dad were on their way.

In fact, Augie and Zami were so busy at the grill station that Augie didn't think about Leah until she was cleaning up their station, batting away smoke from the barbecue, and felt someone grab her arm. For a second, she imagined Chat. She was relieved to see it was Leah—until she took in her face.

Despite her bronzed makeup, gold hoops, and stunning orange halter dress, Leah looked wild. Immediately, she pulled Augie to the edge of the party, behind a blown-up palm tree.

"Why haven't you checked your phone?" she snapped.

Instinctively, Augie placed her hand over the front of her apron, the outline of her phone. "Sorry, the start is always crazy. I was just—"

"It doesn't matter." Leah looked at the crowd. She pulled them farther behind the palm tree. Her expression was one Augie hadn't seen before: eager and panicked and determined.

"What's going on?"

"This is crazy, but—listen."

Augie pushed away a palm tree leaf as it blew into them.

"I was looking up the Latvian hockey roster again, like we tried before. But this time, I went through the group photos from each year. And out of nowhere, I see this."

Leah shoved the phone toward Augie's face.

Augie went cross-eyed, studying the screen. It was a slightly pixelated picture of a hockey team, rows and rows of men in red jerseys.

A second later, Leah tapped the caption below the photo, pointing at a guy in the back row.

Trey Fortin, it read.

"That's Trey." Leah's eyes were so wide, Augie could see the pink lining of her eyeballs. "Once I saw his full name, I found more pictures." She pulled back her phone, scrolled, and pushed his Facebook toward Augie, impatient.

Augie couldn't deny it. While he had a longer face and lighter hair, his eyes and smile told her this was definitely him—Chat's uncle.

"So that's his last name? Fortin? Not Efhart like Chat's?"

"Exactly. He must be Chat's *mom's* brother." Leah was rushing, impatient. "Augie, there's more. This is crazy, but look. I didn't put it together right away, but the more I looked at his photos, the more it hit me. I'd seen him before. I knew I'd seen him before."

Leah reached into her bag. "He's the same T. Fortin as *here*." Her voice hitched as she pulled out the worn picture Augie had seen all those years ago—the one from Leah's shoebox.

It was the group photo from Lyle's summer training camp. His last summer alive.

"See." Leah tapped the left back row. "T. Fortin. Number thirteen. It's the same guy. The same Trey. He knew my brother, Augie. He knew Lyle."

Augie pulled both photos closer, looking back and forth, feeling dizzy.

"Augie?" Leah grabbed her wrist. "Trey could have been at The Manor that night, with Lyle. We need to find Chat, now. He has to know something." Leah scanned the crowd.

"I don't understand . . . so do you think Danika knew Lyle, too? That they all did?"

"I don't know anything for sure." Leah took a sharp breath. "But they *are* the same age, and this proves Trey knew Lyle. Something is definitely up." She folded the photo back into her bag, and Augie sensed the energy coursing through her.

"Okay." Augie tried to compose herself for Leah's sake—to finally be the one to be able to help. "Let's go. Let's find Chat."

26

Chat looked most like Trey when he dressed up. Danika always thought so. Trey had never been overly preppy, or into fashion, but he'd insisted on looking his best when taking Danika out. He joked he was always glad to change out of his hockey gear, which he claimed smelled like rotten socks no matter how many times he washed it.

Danika insisted he didn't need to dress up for her, but it had made her feel special all the same. She loved seeing him in a polo or button-down when he came to pick her up. At sixteen, meeting him after moving to St. Cloud had felt like a true lifeline; she had never experienced love like that, and after coming off her father's death, it felt even more like a gift.

With Chat around, it was impossible not to fall back into those memories. It was always a sweet, bitter pain, like staring at the sun too long. It was especially difficult in moments like this, before the party, when the wine made her body and mind fluid and she was no longer in control.

"You look wonderful." She smiled as Chat came down the stairs to the foyer. He looked just like him.

"You do clean up well," Bill added, polishing off a glass of whiskey. They were both tipsy by now, grateful Chat was driving.

"Right back at you both. Though here's our real star," Chat cooed as he scooped up Max.

Danika walked to them and leaned in to kiss Max's cheek. Then, she turned to look at the three of them—herself, Chat, and Max—in the mirror at their side. For a moment, as she studied their reflection, she allowed herself to travel to an alternate life: one where Chat really *was* Trey. Where the child he held was theirs. One where death had not been licking at their heels.

27

The Crawleys hadn't yet arrived, and Augie had no choice but to get back to work. She reluctantly helped Zami rotate the crackling pig, the meat so hot it made her sick, and tried to imagine what she would say to Chat. It was pointless to prepare. There was no time to rationalize—only to act.

Above all, Augie wondered what Chat knew. Part of her hoped he was clueless—that Danika was the one lying about everything. She wouldn't let herself think he was the bad guy in all of this. Not yet. If he was, Augie would never trust her judgment again.

She had to find him.

Augie continued filling trays, clearing tables, and fetching drinks with her head on a swivel, but there was still no sign of them. It wasn't until she started up the stairs to the Club to grab supplies from the kitchen that, as she reached the top step and turned to the party from above, suddenly, there they were.

Augie swore the world slowed as the Crawleys entered in a cloud of white. They looked like royalty. Even Max and Cooper seemed like celebrities in their tiny linen shirts.

Augie rushed inside, feeling overwhelmed.

The party took on a new atmosphere from there. And as Augie

returned to the grill station, she kept watching them out of the corner of her eye. She could barely focus as she thought about how to approach Chat. She went to the lower clearing station at the base of the pool, practicing a script in her mind. Yet as she reached the cart, there he was, appearing beside her.

"Augie," Chat said, his voice focused. Above them, string lights swayed in the breeze, and to their side, kids squealed and played a duck toss game. The combination of lights and noise made the space between them feel even smaller and more intimate.

Augie stared into the bin of dirty glasses, ignoring the way her pulse pounded in her ears.

"Augie." Chat put one hand on the cart, maneuvering to try to look in her eyes. "Please, talk to me. Why haven't you messaged me back?"

Augie pinched the fake flowers around her neck. Finally, she turned to him.

He looked even more handsome than usual—his hair and eyelashes darker in the late light, his irises ablaze with copper, his white shirt and pants perfectly fitted yet loose.

"I need to talk to you," he said.

Augie felt suddenly desperate. "Chat. Are you lying to me? What is *really* going on?"

His face collapsed, taken aback. "What do you mean?"

"I know, okay?" Her voice grew louder. "About your uncle and Danika. That they were together, or in Latvia, or . . . I don't know. You tell me. Please, just tell me what's going on."

Chat went still. "What?"

"And did Trey go to hockey camp with Lyle?" She squinted. "I truly don't understand why you would hide something like that. Clearly something is going on between you and Danika. What are you not telling me?"

Augie hated to witness the guilt and terror now seeping into Chat's face. She felt lightheaded. Maybe she really had read him wrong.

"Augie." Chat reached out to her, but she pulled away. "I can explain. You have to listen to me." Yet, just as he started talking, Cooper rounded the corner—making them both jump.

"There you are," Cooper said between licks of an ice cream cone, the chocolate dripping down his wrist. "I need you to help me with the duck toss, please. It's so, so hard."

He tugged at the bottom of Chat's shirt with his free hand.

"I can't, Coop, I can't right now," Chat said as Cooper kept yanking him forward.

Chat looked at Augie, pleading.

"Can you meet me at the cage?" he said. "In ten minutes? I promise I'll tell you everything."

Augie feigned normality as she went back to the grill, checked the chafers, gave Zami a shaky thumbs-up, and headed back up the stairs to the Club. Without allowing herself to think, she went to Aida's office. She grabbed the spare key and headed to the cage.

As soon as Augie turned down the final hall, she saw Chat already there, leaning against the wall, arms crossed, cupping his elbows. Neither spoke while Augie unlocked the door.

Even as they entered the large, dim room, Chat didn't say anything. But then, in one movement, he rushed forward and kissed her.

Augie was so caught off guard, all she could do was kiss him back. She folded into him, disappearing into the smell and taste of him—how natural it always felt. He held her so tight, they began to sway, but a second later, Augie shoved him away, touching her lips as if bleeding.

"You can't do that," she said, a sharp pain in her chest.

"Augie."

She backed away, stumbling over a box.

"It's not what you think." Chat moved toward her.

"Why didn't you tell me how you really knew Danika?" For the first time ever, Augie had used her first name. "Why did you tell me you met on some sitter website? Why lie?" A new dread fell through her.

Chat slid his hand over his face.

"Augie," he sighed. "Believe me, I wanted to tell you everything from the beginning. But it wasn't about me. It's *not* about me. I *did* meet her on a sitter website. Danika has no idea who I am." His shoulders rose as he started talking faster. "She doesn't know Trey is my uncle. Trey doesn't know I'm here, either. Neither do my parents. No one does. They would freak out. They all think I'm babysitting for some family in Lakeville. It was—it is—better this way."

Augie held his gaze. She pictured him as Trey, arm slung around Lyle's shoulders.

"What do you mean? How would Danika not know? You and Trey look alike. I saw photos of him."

Chat dipped his chin. "How? And how did *you* know Danika was with Trey?"

"Don't turn this back on me. *It's not about me,*" Augie said, mocking his words.

Chat sat down on a cardboard box, shaking his head and tugging at his hair.

"Latvia," Augie finally said, quieter. "I heard Danika mention Latvia . . . when she was talking about her necklace, how she got it from an ex. Then at their house that night, you said your uncle Trey lived in Latvia, played hockey. It was a weird coincidence, so I started to put it together. Then Leah found Trey online, and she recognized him from the training photo with Lyle. And . . ."

Augie stopped and sucked in a breath.

"Chat." She held still. "Why are you really here?"

Chat hung his head. A moment later, he looked up.

"Augie, I'm going to tell you everything. But first, I need you to know that none of this has anything to do with you and me, okay? With how I feel about you. I need you to understand that. You were never part of the plan. And you were the best part of this summer. Seriously."

Augie lowered herself onto a box across from him. "Just tell me what's going on."

He started to talk.

First, he explained that Trey and Danika had been high school sweethearts. The summer they were nineteen, in college, he and Lyle had been at hockey training camp together. They'd met at a few camps before, but that summer, they were roommates.

"They were good friends," Chat said, continuing to say that after Lyle died, even though Trey got his dream to play in Europe, in Latvia—and Danika went with him—he was never the same. He became depressed; Danika left him a year later.

"The year they split was also the year Trey and I started getting close. I was only eleven, but I had started taking hockey seriously, and my dad had left for North Dakota, so yeah. We started talking a lot.

"I didn't know about Lyle or anything then . . . I didn't know how lonely Trey was, either. I was too young. Trey didn't even tell me about Lyle until last fall." Chat chewed his cheek. "I was so down after my injury, one night, he let it out. I knew he was trying to show me you could pull yourself up from the darkest of places, but I think it was also driving him mad. He needed to tell someone. He felt so guilty. He still does."

"Why would he feel guilty? It was accident."

"Yeah, but—" Chat clasped his hands together between his knees. "Augie, Trey was there that night. At The Manor. The night Lyle died."

Augie didn't move.

"He wasn't on the boat," Chat added quickly, "because he and Danika had a fight, and she came to pick him up early. But"—he paused—"what's more important is that, well, Trey thinks someone else was on the boat that night. That someone else was driving the boat. He's just never been able to prove it."

"I don't understand. What do you mean someone else? Why didn't Trey say anything?" Augie could only think of Leah then, her heart racing.

"It's . . . complicated." Chat shifted on the box. "That's why I'm here this summer, though. I'm trying to help. Ever since Trey told me everything, I've been, I don't know, obsessed. I wasn't able to stop thinking about it. So when I was looking everyone up online, and I stumbled across Danika's nanny ad, I took it as a sign. I thought, if I could get to Aldon Lakes, maybe I could find some way to help. Or, at the very least, I could tell Trey Danika was happy. He worries about her all the time, misses her. He hasn't talked to her in years."

Chat half smiled. "I really did need a job, too. For what it's worth."

Augie suddenly stood. "You need to talk to Leah. This is too much."

Chat rose to meet her.

"I know, I know. Augie, hear me out. I promise, I'm only trying to help. And, even more . . ." He turned more serious. "I know it sounds crazy, but I think I'm close to the truth . . . to being able to prove who was really driving the boat that night."

Augie's body felt lighter, as if filling with air.

"Who?"

"Joshu—"

But it was then—before he could finish—that they heard the chaos from outside.

28

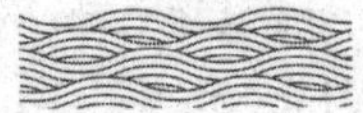

The moment Danika noticed Cooper was missing, she also knew Chat and Augie would be gone. That feeling was back again—the same one from the start of summer: a deep, blooming dread.

Danika had been tracking the two of them all night. She'd watched Augie work, watched Chat sift through the party—but she'd eventually lost track of them. She was too disoriented and drunk. Now, she set her cocktail down and stood up from her table, thinking only of Cooper. She spun in a circle, the decorations and fake animals and lights blurring around her.

She tried to be rational. She asked Bill if he'd seen him. She asked the Birches. She asked the Schmidts and Andersons and Harrisons.

"I saw Chat." Holly stepped forward. "He was talking to that girl."

Holly raised her eyebrows, and Danika knew then that despite never telling Holly about Chat and Augie, Holly sensed what was going on. Probably, she knew Danika better than she thought. Danika felt suddenly grateful for her.

"Come on," Holly said. "We'll find him. We'll find Cooper."

Danika looked out to the Club, the pool.

She screamed his name.

29

As the commotion outside grew louder, Chat took off, bursting out of the cage and down the hall, Augie close behind. They spilled onto the top of the patio into the cooling night air. Down by the pool, people were running about, tearing at decorations and pulling chairs from tables, worried voices rising.

"What's going on?" Augie stopped TC as he rushed by with a phone to his ear.

"It's that Crawley kid again. He's missing, like at the start of summer." He cringed as his phone buzzed. "Mr. Dryer is freaking out. Mrs. Crawley is absolutely losing her shit."

Chat tailed TC down the stairs to the pool deck, but Augie couldn't move. All she could do was watch as the DJ cut the music and tapped the microphone, telling everyone to please stay calm and that Cooper had last been seen near the duck toss wearing a white shirt and white pants. The announcement only seemed to incite more panic, because everyone scrambled faster, grabbing their own kids, rushing away from Mrs. Crawley—who was now in the center of it all, moving in a hurricane of white.

Augie rushed inside to help. She remembered how Cooper had

been found hiding in a closet earlier that summer, how Liss had been the one to find him.

Chat hadn't been watching Cooper. He'd been with her. Augie couldn't ignore her own budding guilt as she searched. If something happened to Cooper—she pushed the thought away.

Augie opened every closet she saw, pawing through the library and dining room and ballroom, but found nothing.

"No luck?" she said to Aida as she returned to the kitchen out of breath.

"Danika is straight up losing her mind."

Augie started to say she was sorry when TC burst through the kitchen door.

"Got him," he yelled. "Once again, our girl Liss is the Cooper whisperer!" He shook his fists in the air. "He was down in the parking lot, trying to get something from their car. It's good. He's all good. You can call off the troops."

Augie's body sank with relief. Aida clasped her hands together.

From there, the staff gathered. Aida gave a pep about salvaging the night and, after chugging Diet Cokes and coffees, everyone reluctantly returned to their posts outside. Augie stayed put.

"I don't feel well. I'm sorry, Aida. I just, I can't."

"I'm sorry, too, Aug. You do look sort of pale."

Augie didn't know how to explain. She didn't want to lie.

"Tonight is not our night, huh?" Aida sighed. "Mr. Dryer's giving a speech now and getting the DJ back on track, so if you could help clean up real quick, you can be first cut. I'm sorry to ask, but it's a disaster out there, and the sooner we get this place straightened, the better. Give it twenty or so minutes, okay?"

Augie nodded. *Twenty minutes,* she repeated to herself. All she wanted was to get out of there—to go back to her house with Leah and work through everything Chat had told her. She was glad they'd decided to sleep at her house, too, since her mom was out of town with Peter. It would be easier to talk without Lyle's photos hanging all around them. Augie knew they needed more information, though. They needed to talk to Chat again. Still, she knew it wouldn't be tonight; he wouldn't leave Danika and Cooper's side.

At least now, she understood why.

When Augie returned outside, she noticed the sky was fully dark, that last shade of blue before black. Cooper must have been missing longer than she had thought. She took a gulp of night air. *Just focus*, she told herself as she went to the cocktail tables on the upper patio, adjusting their tablecloths and votives. *Twenty minutes.*

Augie moved from table to table as the crowd below returned to chatting and drinking, yet as she crouched to the base of the table closest to the stairs—she froze. She stood up fast. Out in front of her, Mrs. Crawley was clambering up the steps.

She looked even more hysterical than earlier—even more unhinged than Augie had seen her in her closet that night. Lines of mascara ran down her face; blotches of red colored her cheeks. Her whole body radiated rage.

"You," Mrs. Crawley hissed, pummeling toward her.

Augie stumbled backward.

"*You*," she repeated as she jabbed her finger in the air, still coming closer.

Augie stuttered, so stunned, she barely noticed Chat rushing up the stairs behind Mrs. Crawley, followed by Bill. Augie looked from side to side, feeling trapped.

"What is your fucking problem? What do you fucking *want*?" Mrs. Crawley spat, leaning into Augie's face.

Augie couldn't move. Around her, the fake flowers and animals and tiki torches all bobbed back and forth in the dark night, making the whole scene feel ridiculous and fake, like they were actors in a play—though Augie's panic was real.

"All summer"—Mrs. Crawley swallowed dryly—"you've been after him." She threw one hand back toward Chat, who was coming closer. Out of the corner of her eye, Augie noticed a crowd now forming around them—the Harrisons, the Fravels. Wyatt and Leah.

"Don't you dare!" Mrs. Crawley cried, raising her palm to Chat, telling him to stop. "You stay with my children. You do your *job*.

"You." She twisted back to Augie. "You sneak over to my cabin. You sneak over to my house. You put my boys at risk—my family!" She moved closer with each phrase, until finally, her face was inches from Augie's. Augie could smell the liquor on her breath, see the veins of her eyes and the pores of her nose.

"I, I don't know—" Augie knew the door was nearby, and she imagined sprinting to it, racing inside and down the hall to the safety of the cage; the keys were still in her pocket.

But suddenly, something inside her snapped.

"You think *I'm* the one putting your boys at risk?" Augie was so surprised by the ferocity of her voice, it was like hearing someone else.

Mrs. Crawley seemed equally taken aback. She straightened, blinking.

Augie was now the one hunching forward. "*You're* the one putting your family at risk. With all your lies, your secrets." She was gaining momentum now—she enjoyed the panic on Mrs. Crawley's face.

"You're the one sneaking around! With Chat, his uncle. Your, your ex-husband?"

Mrs. Crawley stumbled.

"And you and Trey knew Lyle? What else are you hiding?" As lost as Augie felt, she also felt empowered—like she was reaching into a bag of ammo, firing one emotional bullet after another.

Mrs. Crawley stared at her, swaying like one of the blown-up animals.

"Danika," Bill said, stepping forward and stretching his arms out like a referee. He looked to his wife, then to Augie, his face twisting in confusion. "Danika, what is she talking about? What in God's name is going on?"

Augie used the distraction of Bill as a chance to escape, grateful to spot Leah behind her. Leah reached out, grabbing her hand, pulling Augie toward her.

Bill and Danika were now in the center of the crowd.

"What did she mean, 'ex-husband'?" Bill narrowed his eyes; his white shirt billowed in the breeze. "You were never married."

Before Danika could speak, Wyatt Greene stepped forward, too.

"Danika," Wyatt interrupted, his voice focused. "Was that true? You knew Lyle?"

It went quiet as a new look of horror fell over Mrs. Crawley, like a sudden shift in weather. She reached to touch her necklace. The amber pendant. Her eyes filled.

"Please, tell me," Wyatt said, his tone still measured.

"What the hell is going on?" Bill threw up his hands.

Mrs. Crawley looked to Bill, back to Wyatt.

She heaved in a breath. "Oh, what does it even matter anymore," she finally cried, leaning back as if howling. She straightened as her eyes grew wetter, redder. "You two, you're full of your own secrets, your own lies." She pointed back and forth between Bill and Wyatt.

"Danika." Bill moved toward her quickly. "Stop," he warned.

"You think I don't know?" She looked out to the crowd, searching. "My best buddy Josh Mike told me everything . . . everything you've been lying about. How you lost all that money. Our *houses*. How you've been fucking Wyatt Greene in Briar Ridge for God knows how long."

Augie stiffened. Next to her, Leah raised a hand to her mouth.

Bill and Wyatt turned ashen.

And then, out of nowhere, Joshua Mike split the group and started running down the stairs in his flamingo-pink suit.

Mrs. Crawley was the first to call his name. "Oh, don't you dare leave," she cried.

"Hey," Joshua Mike yelled while stumbling down the steps, clearly drunk. "I don't want any part of this!" He raised his hands up over his head, taking more unsteady steps down the stairs. "You all leave me out of it! Whatever this is—you are all insane!"

Despite his words, Augie registered an unfamiliar look on his face: fear.

Chat started racing down the stairs, chasing after him. A second later, Bill followed.

Bill moved faster than Augie thought possible—fueled by something unnatural—because he quickly surpassed Chat and grabbed Joshua Mike's lapels just as Josh reached for the pool gate.

Joshua Mike tripped, falling to his knees, but Bill didn't stop there. He dragged Josh Mike back to his feet and whipped him around.

"How could you tell her? You swore." His face contorted with anger—grief.

Before Joshua Mike could speak, Bill pulled back his fist and punched him square in the face—once, twice, and then over and over and over.

Augie couldn't watch as blood burst to the ground. She turned in to Leah's hot shoulder, barely looking up until the sounds of screams and sirens filled the air.

30

Augie and Leah drove home in silence. They were in shock, all the drama and confusion of the night spinning knots inside their brains. They'd left the Club as fast as possible; Augie hadn't even gone to her locker for her bag. They'd beelined straight for Leah's car.

Augie was again grateful her mom was gone and that they wouldn't need to explain themselves yet. Neither she nor Leah knew where to start.

Regardless, as soon as they changed and settled on the couch—enclosed in the dim lights of the living room, everything from Leah's shoebox spread out onto the coffee table—Augie told Leah all she'd learned from Chat: how Trey had been hockey friends with Lyle, how he'd been at The Manor that night but left early with Danika, how Trey thought Joshua Mike had been the one driving the boat—but couldn't prove it.

It was especially hard to think about Joshua Mike being involved. They realized it was likely the same year he'd inherited all that money and bought The Manor, the marina, the Minnesota Wild, though; it could make sense.

They still needed more answers. They'd both messaged Chat on LinkedIn, sending Augie's address and begging him to come over.

Augie had been warmed, despite everything, to see his apologies and pleas from the previous week. She told herself she'd think about that later.

"I don't understand why Trey wouldn't come forward," Leah said now, although they were repeating questions at this point. "It doesn't make sense. If they were friends, why wouldn't he tell the police to at least look into Josh Mike?"

"I don't get it, either." Augie again checked her phone. He still hadn't replied.

"I just feel so, I don't know. I feel so happy *and* sad." Leah traced her tattoo. "I'm vindicated to know I was right—that there is more to the story—but it makes me sick to think if Josh Mike really was on the boat, he's been lying and hiding all this time. Right in front of us."

"I know. I'm so sorry, Lee. It's twisted."

Leah pulled the blanket higher. They were sitting longways on the couch, their legs parallel, a duvet over them.

"Have you talked to your mom or dad yet?" Augie asked. At least this question had a clear answer. Augie was also beginning to realize this was another source of the worry coursing between them: Wyatt had been cheating on Robin. Augie had been so shaken to hear it and, selfishly, could not stop thinking about Julia and Micah. Her own affair.

"No. I figured it's best to give them space. I'm sure my dad is calling her right now, trying to get to her before anyone else." Leah leaned back against the couch's armrest, looking up to the ceiling.

Augie had been relieved to learn Leah already knew her dad was having an affair, that it wasn't one more massive blow from the night—though Augie was still shocked. Apparently, Robin had discovered he was cheating months ago, and in a fit of sadness, had told Leah. Still, neither had known it was with Bill.

"I'm sure she's freaking out. She's always been obsessed with keeping our family intact, not breaking it up any further. I don't know. It's probably for the best if they split up. But my dad, *Bill*." Leah covered her forehead with one hand. "I can't say I saw it coming, but I can't say I'm completely surprised, either. I just want my dad to be happy."

Augie picked at her nails. While it paled in comparison to the recent revelations, Augie knew then: She had to tell Leah about New York. They were entangled in too many lies. Augie couldn't be one more person hiding something. She owed Leah the truth.

"Lee." She cleared her throat. "There's something else I need to tell you."

Leah sat upright.

"No, it's not about Lyle or Trey or anything. It's about . . . me." Her voice grew small. "It's about something I did. In New York."

Leah leaned forward, grabbing Augie's calves over the blanket.

"Tell me. You know you can tell me anything."

Augie breathed slowly. She was terrified to face what she'd done, and for Leah to judge her, for Robin to have yet another painful reality to face—but she had to get it out. So, finally, she started talking. She came clean: New York Fuckboy was not some random thirty-year-old from her team, as she'd initially said, but forty-three-year-old Micah. Julia's husband.

Leah was quiet at first, which made Augie even more apprehensive, but she plowed forward. She told her every detail, from their first meeting at the penthouse to their first messages. That first kiss and beyond. She recounted every little gesture, every single hookup. Her voice quivered as she got to the part where it all came crashing down: the day they got caught. The day she got fired. It filled her with white-hot shame.

New York, May

Micah and Augie had established a steady routine a couple weeks after they started sleeping together. Micah would show up to Augie's apartment after work, or on weekend afternoons when Julia went to spin class, or any night she was at a work dinner or out of town. It was both predictable and unpredictable—their bodies were familiar, but the moments they could be together still appeared and disappeared like magic. As a result, the affair felt desperate; Augie craved Micah and missed him when he was gone.

One Thursday, she was especially eager to see him. Julia had been home sick for a week, and Micah hadn't been able to leave the house. They never texted much—it made Micah nervous—and Augie felt lonely. She got to the coffee bar at work extra early that day, waiting for him.

As usual, he'd kissed her against the fridge. But this time, it didn't feel right. She wanted more from him—to feel like she meant more to him.

"I don't know if I can keep doing this." Augie knew that line felt used, but she couldn't come up with anything else. Micah had buried his head in her neck, inhaling the smell of her.

"We'll be back to normal soon," he murmured. He kissed behind her ear.

"This isn't normal." Augie wriggled away. She turned to the coffee machine, pressing the button in an attempt to distract herself. She grabbed a mug.

"Oh, Augie, come on," he teased, reaching for her hand. "You know what I mean. You don't want to be *normal*. We could never be *normal*."

He pulled her into him, kissing her wetly on the mouth. Augie kissed him back for a few seconds before turning away. She didn't want to give in that easily. She'd felt so pathetic and rejected over the last week. It had made her realize, for the first time, that she'd always be in second place. She was nowhere near as special as he'd made her feel.

"Well, whatever this is, normal or not, I don't want it," she said, surprised and impressed by her response. She took her coffee and left.

Micah spent all afternoon pinging her. He apologized and apologized, telling her they'd find time to be together soon, that he missed her, too. Augie couldn't help it: She weakened. She ate it up. This was what she'd really wanted. So at seven, once most people had left, when he asked her to meet in a conference room on the fifteenth floor to apologize in person, she agreed.

As usual, she knew where it was going. But as she watched Micah close the blinds, lock the door, walk to her, and drop to his knees, tugging down her skirt, she didn't stop it.

Neither of them could have known that an hour before there had been a focus group in that conference room. Like the focus groups Augie had led with young people who had never played the lottery, a video recording device had been set up so the strategy team could watch from a room next door, follow along to take notes, list insights, ask questions.

Neither of them knew that the strategy team was still sitting there, on the other side of the wall, debating their recent findings. They didn't know that the camera was still on, taping their every move, up until the moment the VP of the company noticed the screen and lunged forward to shut the camera off.

Of course, it was already too late.

* * *

"He was friends with Micah, naturally." Augie took a breath before continuing to explain how that next day, she was called into the VP's office, and how—in what she described as the world's most condescending tone—he told her there was a merger approaching and many people were going to be let go. That he was sorry Augie had been caught up in all of it.

"There was nothing I could do. He told me I could get HR involved if I wanted, but it felt like a threat. He said it would only drag out the process and that twenty percent of the agency would be laid off. It would be more tactful to leave with the merger. He said he'd still give me a good recommendation. But I never wanted to speak to him again. I never wanted to speak to any of them again. Micah didn't stand up for me. He called me once—*one* last time, to say he was 'sorry for how things ended,' to warn me about the recording, to explain he was too far along in his career to 'blow it up now.'" Augie bit the tip of her tongue until the pain felt like relief. "It was all so horrible. I was so mortified. I *am* so mortified."

Augie closed her eyes, raw and sick with embarrassment. She pressed the heels of her hands against her eyes, blurring the spots of light behind her eyelids, as she waited for Leah to scold her—to ask how she could do such a thing, to remind her Julia and Micah were married, *family*—but she felt Leah climbing over to her. Leah knelt on the floor beside her, then leaned up to hug Augie around the shoulders.

Augie didn't know what to make of it at first, but as Leah squeezed tighter and rocked her back and forth, whispering, "I'm so sorry. I'm so sorry that happened to you," Augie began to cry.

"This is not your fault," Leah said.

Augie swallowed hard, more tears rising up her throat.

"You have to believe me."

And for the first time, Augie did.

Augie didn't know when she and Leah fell asleep, but at some point, she woke to knocking at the front door. She sat up, panicked, as she took in the dark room, and grabbed her phone. It was just after one a.m.

She had five new messages from Chat.

Augie felt like she was in a dream as she peeled herself off the couch, careful not to stir Leah. She moved over the squares of moonlight on the carpet as she walked to the door, smoothing her oversize T-shirt and sweatpants.

Chat's shoulders were scrunched to his neck, his hands in his pockets, as he shivered from the cool night. When he saw Augie, his body slackened. He didn't speak.

She moved to the side.

Neither knew what to do. The only sound was Leah snoring lightly behind them.

"Thanks for messaging," Chat whispered. "I wanted to talk to you. To both of you."

Augie searched his tired face, feeling another strange mix of tenderness and anger.

"We should wake her up." Augie stepped toward the couch.

Chat reached out suddenly and grabbed her forearm, but she kept moving away until he was holding only her fingertips.

She gently nudged Leah awake. Leah blinked twice, but as soon as she noticed Chat, she sat up. She threw off the blanket, gathered the papers from the coffee table. "Kitchen?" she said.

It was bizarre having both Chat and Leah in her house—especially in the middle of the night, especially after all that had happened—but they made their way to the breakfast nook. Augie boiled water for tea and set out mugs. She turned on a side lamp so the light wasn't harsh.

"Okay," Leah said diplomatically.

Augie could tell she was trying to remain calm.

"We need to know what you know. Everything."

Chat shifted in his seat.

"Because all I've ever known, for my whole life, is this." Leah pushed the pile of accident reports and photos of Lyle toward Chat, the papers flat and flimsy. "Lyle and Grant left The Manor, stole the keys, stole the boat. Crashed into the Arcola fucking Bridge and died."

Chat's chest rose and fell as he looked at Lyle's photo.

"I'll start at the beginning. If that's what you want."

"That's what I want. Augie told me what you told her, but I want to hear everything. From you."

Chat said okay; he understood. Then, he began.

He again explained that Danika moved to St. Cloud right after her dad died, that she and Trey were sixteen. "I was only six, and I don't remember ever meeting her," he said. "He and my dad didn't get along, which stressed my mom out, so we didn't see him much. Trey and I didn't get close until I was twelve or so and started to take hockey seriously, like I told you." He glanced to Augie. "Trey was all about hockey. He was a star in high school and college and was scouted early on. He was getting some crazy good offers, but he always wanted to go to Europe."

Chat held his mug with two hands. He tapped one finger against its side.

"So." He cleared his throat. "The summer after his freshman year of college, the year before he was hoping to sign somewhere and quit school, which my dad said was ridiculous, of course, Trey went to training camp near Minneapolis, the famous one, not far from here."

"The Hamilton arena," Leah said. "Lyle was there all the time."

"Right. So that summer, Trey and Lyle became friends. Trey, Lyle, Grant. Trey said he and Lyle had met at other camps, but they were on the same team that summer and bunked together, so yeah. On their nights off, they'd hang out. They went out, sometimes, to The Manor. Trey said it was the place to be that summer. And one night, they met the owner, Joshua Mike."

Augie took a sip of tea, feeling as if the hot water was filling her lungs.

Leah bored into Chat.

"He was part owner of the Wild, too, and Trey said he loved to show off. He was super generous, friendly. Josh Mike was only thirty at the time. They couldn't help but be impressed," Chat said with an air of defensiveness. "They were only nineteen, trying to go pro, and here was the owner buying them drinks and telling them about the NHL. He even said he had contacts for the European leagues, coaches he knew. One time, he brought Mikko Koivu along. After that, Trey said they'd always look for Joshua Mike. And, on their last night of training, he made a point to be there."

"August twenty-ninth," Leah interjected, her voice clipped.

"They were all at The Manor that night, going harder than usual. Trey said that at one point, Joshua Mike was bragging about how some guy from Chicago had just brought the latest Cigarette speedboat, the X42 series, to his marina. Which I guess was a big deal."

"The boat was worth over four hundred grand," Leah added. "It was rare. They said that's why Lyle and Grant stole it."

"Right. But according to Trey, Joshua Mike was the one who wanted to take it out. He kept saying it was fine. He knew the guy, had the keys, no one would care."

Augie watched red bloom across Leah's neck.

"Trey and Lyle said no at first, but Joshua Mike kept insisting, bragging about it, and Grant said he wanted to go. So when the bar closed, Joshua Mike convinced them. They were all wasted by that point, so they finally said, whatever. Joshua Mike didn't want to stop the party, either, so he asked the bartender for drinks to take with them. She said no, and he got mad, but he realized he had a six-pack of beer in his car. He told the boys to go wait at the boat while he grabbed the beer. The boat was right there in his marina next door. Joshua Mike told them where the key box was, gave them the code, said to meet him there."

"But the key box was broken," Leah said. "It was busted. That's why they said—"

"I know," Chat said. "I'll explain. But first, it's important to know that Trey didn't end up going on the boat. He and his girlfriend, Danika"—Chat paused, tensing—"had been fighting all night. Trey said they'd been fighting all summer because of the distance. She was scared if he went to Europe, he wouldn't take her along. She'd have to get a visa, or they'd have to get married. It would be complicated. And that night, she was losing it, so she drove down to pick him up. That was why, instead of going to the boat with Lyle and Grant, Trey walked with Joshua Mike to the parking lot, where Danika was meeting him. Joshua Mike tried to convince him to stay, but she was already on her way."

Chat looked down.

"He's tortured by it all. Trey. He wanted to stop Joshua Mike, but he was young, and dumb, and drunk. And, he didn't. He said goodbye, he walked to Danika's car." Chat suddenly turned to Augie. "She never saw Josh Mike. She didn't know he was with them. She still doesn't."

It went quiet before Chat continued.

"But, that next day, when the news came out about the accident,

Trey got a message from Joshua Mike. He wanted to talk. Trey said he was in shock, that he couldn't believe any of it. Couldn't understand it. He was back in St. Cloud with Danika by then, but Joshua Mike insisted they meet. So that afternoon, they met at a gas station halfway between them."

Chat said Joshua Mike had brought cash. Fifty thousand. He told Trey he felt bad about what happened—that he'd told the boys about the boat. He also told Trey that he felt bad he'd decided to leave right after him—that he didn't go on the boat. He said he wished he would have so he could have helped. He told Trey he'd gotten tired and driven straight home.

"Was that a bribe, then? The money? Trey had to have known he was lying," Leah said.

"He didn't know what to do. Trey said he believed him, in the moment—he wanted to believe him."

"Why not at least tell the police? At least mention Josh Mike?"

Chat lifted one shoulder.

"It was all a mess. They'd been underage drinking, and Trey knew it wouldn't change anything . . . it wouldn't bring them back. He also said that when Josh Mike put the cash in his hands that day, when he told him he heard he was a great forward, and that the coaches—his friends—in Latvia wanted to talk to him, he didn't know what else to do. All he could do was say okay. Take the money. It wasn't until later that he realized how twisted it all was."

Augie could tell Leah was trying not to cry.

"He still feels sick about it. I do too. But I can understand. What was he going to do, go up against Josh Mike, who basically owned all of Aldon Lakes, on a hunch?"

Chat shook his head.

"He should have. Because in addition to everything, when he got to Latvia, he was too depressed to play. He knew he didn't deserve it. It ruined his relationship with Danika, too. It ruined his life. He thinks misery is what he deserves."

"Maybe it is." Leah turned to the darkened windows, the wetness in her eyes threatening to brim over her bottom lashes. She took a shuddered breath, like it was climbing a ladder.

Chat's face look pained, too. He leaned forward.

"This is why"—Chat pivoted to Augie—"when I came across Danika's post this summer, I knew I had to be here. To find someone to corroborate Trey's story."

"Why can't Trey come forward now?" Leah snapped back, scowling. "And what about the key box? Why was it broken into if Joshua Mike gave them the code?"

"Exactly. Trey thinks Joshua Mike must have broken it the next morning to frame them. It's the only thing that makes sense."

"We have to go to the police." Leah stood halfway up.

"I know, I know. But look, Trey's always been worried there's not enough evidence to prove Josh Mike was on the boat."

"Well, Trey needs to do something. *We* need to do something."

"I'm trying, trust me. If I can find one more witness to support Trey's story, it might work. Even if it's too late to prosecute Josh Mike, at least it's something. I think it would set Trey free. I think it would set you . . ." He glanced to Leah but trailed off.

"It's what I've been focused on this summer," he said, talking faster. "I was hoping I could solve everything before anyone found out who I was. Trey still doesn't know I'm here. He'd be too freaked out about everything."

"What do you mean one more witness?" Augie interjected.

"Yeah, seriously, Chat." Leah was growing angrier. "How are we supposed find one more witness? No one saw them leave that night.

And the marina cameras were conveniently out." Leah went suddenly still. "Joshua Mike. Of course."

Chat nodded as Leah sat down. A second later, he spoke again.

"Trey did tell me there was one other person that knew about the boat that night, who heard Josh Mike talking about it." He paused. "Who might be able to help."

"Who?" Leah said. "Who is it?"

"The bartender," Chat said on an exhale.

Leah scoffed. "Oh great, how are we supposed to find some random bartender from The Manor from twelve years ago?"

Chat held still. "Because we know her."

Leah looked to Augie, back to Chat.

"Who?" she said, exasperated—just as it clicked in Augie's mind. At once, they all knew: Teuta.

31

The night after the luau, Danika dreamed of Trey. Even with the alcohol swirling in her head, the dream was vivid and bright, an inverse to the dark places her mind usually went when she was at her lowest. Still, the memories were fleeting, teasing.

There was the smell of fresh-cut grass, the gentle intonation of his voice. The day they drove to Millie Lacs Lake, stretched out on a blanket under the blue sky, kissed for the first time. Then, there were trips to the library; dinners with his parents; road trips to Canada; swimming at the local pool; drinking wine coolers and laughing more than she had in her life.

There was hockey, too—always hockey. The chilled, massive ice rinks; the way her fingers went numb as she cheered his name from behind scratched plexiglass. The way she wore Trey's jersey like a badge of honor.

Danika had learned to skate with him, out on the pond up north. She'd cherished twirling in the freezing Minnesota woods, the air so cold, her breath puffed out of her mouth in small gray clouds, like blowing the seeds of a dandelion. Those nights, gliding across the ice, she'd never felt more loved. It had evened out the loss of her father, in a way. With Trey, she felt whole.

Finally, there was Riga, Latvia. Their small attic apartment; the sweet, cobblestoned city. A shining amber necklace.

As if her mind knew when to stop to preserve these gifts, she woke suddenly. She didn't needed to face the end—the night, heartbroken, she'd left.

DANIKA FELT DISORIENTED as she awoke to the pale morning light, the world washed out around her. She scooted up against her pillows, her throat like sandpaper as she swallowed and noticed Bill next to her. He'd pulled a chair to her bed. His face was swollen and red, his hand bandaged and resting on his knee.

He reached for a water glass from the bedside table and handed it to her. She took a long, cool sip, the water so refreshing it felt holy.

"Danika." Bill sounded as weak as the light.

She clutched the glass tighter, remembering the night before. As if he could see her thoughts, he let his head fall down into his hands.

"I never meant for this to happen." He looked up at her, tears in the corners of his eyes. Danika realized that in all their years together, she'd never seen him cry. This thought jolted her awake.

"I've only ever wanted to build our family. To support you and the boys."

He continued from there, explaining how everything had started, hesitating before saying that he'd never wanted to accept he was attracted to men.

"You know my parents, my family. One can only imagine how they'd react. How they will react, when I tell them."

Bill kept talking as if searching for penance, explaining how one night after a golf event, he and Wyatt had gone for drinks with Joshua Mike. The whole group was going out bar crawling, and eventually, they ended up at a swingers club. Bill said Joshua Mike had tricked the group into going—he thought it was hilarious.

"I was livid," Bill continued, "but Wyatt convinced me to stay for a drink, and we got to talking as everyone paired off. It was an awful place, and I should have left right away, but we kept talking, and my cab was taking forever. We realized how much we had in common. Far more than golf . . ." He forced a small, pained smile. "I don't mean to make excuses. I need to own my actions, but I also want you to understand. I never meant to hurt you."

Bill sighed and rubbed his chin, his rare morning stubble.

"Abby, their friend, was there that night. She saw Wyatt and me together. I think she inferred something was going on. Even though nothing happened that night, I suppose we still had a connection. It wasn't until the next day at Briar Ridge . . . It feels insane to say, but Wyatt and I are right together. Maybe I shouldn't be telling you this, but it seems you've had your own share of love lost. I'm hoping you can understand."

Danika knew it would have been easier to hate him. To be angry, the scorned wife. But Bill looked so broken, and she felt so broken, and she was so tired of fighting. She believed him. Plus, he was right: She had lost love. She did understand. She'd been lying all these years, too.

"Bill." Her voice was barely audible.

"You don't have to explain," he said, retreating. "Not if you don't want to."

She leaned back into her pillow. She only wished they had come clean earlier—that she'd told him about Trey earlier, that she'd known about Wyatt. Everything made more sense now. The affair explained Bill's hot-and-cold behavior this summer, his passion and guilt conflicting. How had she missed it?

"Obviously the financial situation with the properties, and Joshua Mike, is a different issue. It all got so bad when he found out about Wyatt and me. He walked in on us one day." He looked at his hands. "But, Danika, I'm going to fix it. I promise you that. I never should have caved to him. One way or another, I promise I'm going to fix it." He held his breath. "But I'm also going to be with Wyatt. I have to. I'll always be there for you and the boys. I just have to choose him, too. I have to fix my life."

Danika felt a new, deep calm overtake her. She wasn't sure who was more surprised, her or Bill, as she scrambled over the bed, stood, and cradled his head in her arms, his tears soaking the front of her silk nightgown.

32

Chat left after three in the morning. Leah had run out of questions, and exhaustion had engulfed them all. Plus, there was only one clear next step.

They had to talk to Teuta.

Chat had tried to approach her the week prior. All summer he'd been trying to get to know her and build a rapport before he asked for her help. But when he finally told her who he was—when he asked about that night—she shut down. She told him that was her past life. She told him she didn't know anything.

"I knew her by that point. I could tell she was holding back. I knew she was scared."

Augie didn't know what to think. On top of everything, she realized this had been Chat's goal all summer: mine people for information. Had Augie only been a pawn? As she finally climbed into bed that night, she tried not to think about how many people had lied to her. Thankfully, she was so drained, she fell asleep before she could overthink further.

Chat was supposed to pick them both up to go to Hyla that morning, but as Augie woke to the sound of Leah in the kitchen, she knew she couldn't go.

"Lee?" Augie said as Leah turned to her. "I'm not sure if I should go with . . . I might only be a distraction. I think you guys should talk alone."

Leah nodded. "It's okay. I understand." She looked focused and charged with adrenaline. Augie knew she'd be fine without her; nothing was getting in her way. So when Chat pulled into the driveway at seven o'clock sharp, Augie only hugged Leah tight and said good luck.

After everything that had happened, it felt strange to be alone. It was hard to hold it all in her mind—from the luau to her New York confession to everything surfacing about Trey and Lyle. Augie could only focus on simple tasks: emptying the coffee grounds, taking a shower, trying to eat a piece of toast.

She wished she could distract herself with work, and finally—as if the world knew she needed it—her email pinged.

It was from the job in DC. For the first time all summer, Augie hadn't been actively worrying about the future, but there was a response to her application, a message from someone named Heather, an invitation to schedule a phone interview.

Are you free to talk any day this week?

Augie wasted no time in replying, her mother's words suddenly chiming in her head.

Karma isn't so black and white.

33

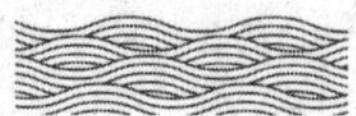

Danika felt dazed as she made her way downstairs. She was glad the boys weren't around to see her. Bill had packed them up and was taking them to the cabin.

"We need some quality time," he'd explained, "and I need to get out of here. To clear my head and think." Danika hadn't protested. She was emotionally and physically drained—and possibly, in the moment, still drunk. Bill also told her that Chat had left early that morning but said he'd be back. Danika hoped this was true.

She had to see Chat. She had to talk to him.

The kitchen was eerily quiet as Danika poured coffee. Yet even in solitude, she couldn't bring herself to relive the night. She felt ashamed for all she could and could not remember, memories pulsing in and out like a strobe light. She did remember the heavy blows: Her words to Augie. Augie's accusations. Exposing Bill and Wyatt. Bill punching Joshua Mike.

Danika steadied herself against the counter. The sun fell through the skylight in glittering ribbons, and as she sipped her coffee, she again focused on her main takeaway:

Chat knew who she was. He had known all summer.

It surprised her that while she felt another bite of betrayal, she also felt—on some level—impressed. There was more to Chat than she'd thought. It didn't outweigh her confusion, though. There was so much she wanted to know about Trey, about why Chat had sought her out this summer, and what that had to do with Lyle Greene.

Danika remembered that summer clearly. She and Trey had been fighting daily. His schedule had been intense, and while she knew it was an important training camp, she felt cast aside.

That had been the catalyst for their late August blowout. They'd been having the same fight over and over, but when they kept missing each other's calls throughout the day, when she knew training had finished and he was out drinking with the guys, she felt overwhelmed. So that evening, she got in her mom's car and drove the two hours to get him. She picked him up at The Manor.

She remembered how drunk he'd been when she arrived. As she pulled the car into the dark, mostly empty parking lot, Trey had stumbled forward alone, laughing and calling over his shoulder. But as soon as he got inside and slammed the door, he focused only on her. He leaned over the center console and caressed her cheek, kissed her.

"You're always the person I'm most happy to see. I'm no idiot," he said, pulling away and reaching for his seat belt. "I'd never leave you behind."

Danika felt giddy with relief. She'd backed out of the lot, grateful.

Of course, Danika didn't know that was the last time she'd see Trey as *Trey*—the carefree, charming, joyous person she'd fallen in love with. Everything changed after he heard about the accident.

Danika had never understood why the tragedy affected him so deeply. He and Lyle had been good friends, but they didn't see each other often, and it was a freak accident. She had hoped that once they got to Latvia and Trey's hockey dreams came true, everything would be better. But even after their courthouse wedding and moving to Riga, Trey couldn't escape his demons—an all-encompassing guilt.

This was part of the reason she'd hated interacting with the Greenes. Part of her would think, *If I had just driven them all home, if I had insisted, where would we be now?*

Now, Danika pulled her bathrobe tighter. She looked around the kitchen and opened the freezer, leaning into the cool air, the shock cutting through her headache. She leaned in farther, resting her cheek against the icy inside of the door.

What if Chat never comes back? she thought. *What if I've lost them both?*

Then she heard the garage door rising. She looked to the foyer.

When Chat turned the corner and hung the key to the Range Rover on the hook beside the door as usual, Danika loosened.

"Chat," she said. Slowly, she closed the freezer door.

He stepped into the kitchen.

"Danika," he said, his voice lined with something like acceptance or defeat.

34

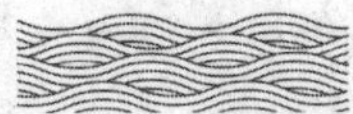

As promised, Leah called Augie as soon as she left Hyla. Augie sat at her desk but immediately closed her computer, focusing on Leah's every word.

Leah said Teuta hadn't been surprised to see them. Zami had told her about everything that had happened at the luau. She was expecting them. She already had everything prepared. Leah said Teuta was struggling not to cry as she started talking.

"Augie, you won't believe it, it makes so much sense now," Leah said.

Leah told Augie everything: how Teuta explained she'd been twenty-one that summer, bartending almost every night. She was also closing each night, which meant she was often at The Manor until three or four a.m., cleaning up. She remembered that summer, all the hockey boys. As the new owner, Joshua Mike was also there every evening, commanding the bar. That night in August started like any other, Teuta said, but as it got later, the hockey boys and Joshua Mike were getting crazier than usual. Joshua Mike had ordered bottle service and extra shots to celebrate the end of their training.

"She said she felt guilty for serving them underage, but Joshua

Mike told her to turn a blind eye. She did say she refused to give them to-go drinks at the end of the night." Leah swallowed. "Because, Augie, she heard them talking about the speedboat. She heard Joshua Mike convincing them to go, saying he would take them out."

Leah started talking rapidly: Once Joshua Mike paid and left, Teuta continued on as normal. But a few hours later, when she was leaving around four a.m., the sky still dark, she saw Joshua Mike in the parking lot. Teuta said she'd always remember how wild he looked. He was wearing a marina-branded sweatshirt and shorts—not what he'd had on earlier—and he was ghost white and limping. She saw him stuff something in the trash can before he got in his car. It was so odd that after he left, she went to look at it.

"What?" Augie leaned forward. "What was it?"

"His clothes. Augie, they were soaking wet. He had to have been on the boat."

"Why didn't she say anything?" Augie suddenly pictured Teuta at twenty-one, hiding in her car, watching Joshua Mike in the dark.

"It's like with Trey." Leah softened. "Joshua Mike tracked her down the next day. He knew she'd heard them talking, but he wanted her to know that he'd left the bar when Trey did. Then he gave her cash. He called it a tip. A *fifty-thousand-dollar* tip." Leah sighed. "We should have known no one wins that much from a scratch card."

Augie felt a flash of cold. She pictured the bulletin board.

"He had to have been the one driving, Augie. He probably got thrown from the boat, walked back, and said nothing."

Augie still felt lost as Leah said she and her parents were going to talk to their lawyer.

"Will she, will Teuta get in trouble?"

"No. It's been so long, I don't think anything will happen legally. But this"—Leah paused, the silence filled with her emotion—"this is more than I could have hoped for. I never expected . . . all these years later . . . I can't even be mad at her. You should have seen her, Augie, I'd never seen someone so upset. She kept apologizing over and over, saying she was ready to pay for everything. But you know, Aug, I'm so relieved at this point, I'm not angry. I'm angry at everything that happened, but not at her. She was our age then. He had all that power."

Augie understood. She knew now there were certain emotions that didn't make sense, instincts that didn't derive from formulas or expectations.

"She wants to see you," Leah said. "But, Aug, I have to go. I'm about to meet up with my mom. I love you."

"I love you, too."

Augie hung up, silent, and stared down at her phone. Then, before she lost her nerve, she walked straight out the front door and headed to Hyla.

35

Chat asked if they could go to the movie theater room. He said he was hot and tired and it was his favorite place in the house. Danika was surprised, but as they pushed inside the secret door, entered the windowless room, and settled into the recliners, she relaxed, too. It was as if they were closed off from the world.

They didn't speak at first; the only sound was the AC humming above. Eventually, Chat cleared his throat.

"Before you say anything, I want to tell you the full story. You deserve to know the truth, to understand what really happened with Trey."

Danika leaned back and closed her eyes, listening carefully as he relayed everything he had learned. It wasn't until he got to the part about Joshua Mike meeting Trey the day after the accident that she felt sick.

"Why didn't he tell me?" she whispered. "That Josh Mike was on the boat? That he took that money?"

Chat ran a hand down the back of his neck. "I think he felt too guilty. Once he took the money, he realized he was complicit. He was scared, and ashamed. He was a dumb nineteen-year-old."

Danika's heart lurched—she'd loved that dumb nineteen-year-old—before her mind kicked into gear. She remembered how rich they'd felt that year after receiving Trey's hockey signing bonus. Now she realized most of it had been from Joshua Mike. She'd bought a dress for their wedding with that money.

Finally, his guilt made sense. Finally, she understood.

"Did he know who I was?" Danika suddenly asked. "Joshua Mike? All this time? Is that why he'd never leave me alone?" Hearing her words aloud, she realized it was true.

Chat looked ashamed. "He helped Trey with the visa and everything. He wanted Trey settled and far away. So, yeah, he probably knew who you were."

Danika sank deeper into the chair. She hadn't known it was possible to hate Josh Mike more.

"But, Danika." Chat glanced at her through the dim room. "For what it's worth, I know Trey still cares about you. He's never gotten over you, any of it."

Danika's stomach flipped at the thought of Trey thinking about her—a feeling like an old high school crush, which was also how she'd felt after first seeing Chat's photo, his application.

"Does he know you're here?"

Chat stretched his arms over his head, letting them hang off the top of the recliner.

"I never told him, or my parents. I knew they'd tell me not to come to Aldon Lakes and stir things up. I wanted to see if I could help before I said anything."

Danika felt another swirl in her stomach as she imagined Chat telling everything to Trey. There were so many emotions now piling up inside her, she didn't know where to focus. But it was time; she had to confess, too.

"You know, Chat. I knew all along. I knew who you were from the start."

Chat turned to her, propping up on one elbow. His face remained still until he lifted half his mouth in a smile.

"I wondered. At the luau, when Augie said Trey was my uncle, you didn't react. Of everything, that didn't seem to surprise you. I had no idea before, though. I kind of feel like an idiot. Here I thought I was so smooth."

Danika couldn't help it then. It all felt so outrageous, she laughed. She laughed so hard she couldn't stop.

"Okay, I know you and Trey aren't exactly twins." She caught her breath; Chat was laughing now, too. "But come on, you look like him. *Act* like him. And your name—of course I knew. How many Chats are there? You know we've met before."

Chat gripped the recliner's armrests. "Are you sure? I feel like I would have remembered you. Even as a kid."

"Well, it was only once. Trey, your dad, you know . . . But yes, it was Halloween one year. You were about eight. Trey and I came to hand out candy while you all went trick-or-treating. You were dressed like—"

"Buzz Lightyear?" Chat sat higher.

"You do remember."

"I remember those photos—that was the only year my parents dressed up together. They were . . ."

"Woody and Jessie."

Danika and Chat studied each other. Smiled.

"Well, damn. I just figured that if you *did* know who I was, you never would have wanted me around. You never would have hired me in the first place. Trey said it ended badly, and you acted so normal and nice, I assumed you didn't have a clue."

"I'm glad you thought I was acting normal." Danika crossed her arms, hugging herself. "I was so nervous the first time I called. I worried you knew who *I* was. Bunch of liars we are, huh?"

"White liars, I'd say." They sat in companionable silence for a moment, letting the relief of the last ten minutes settle.

"I do want you to know, though," he said, lower, "everything I said in that interview was true. I really do love kids. I really did need a summer job. My friend really was a manny. And I really did have a good summer with you. I wasn't trying to be dishonest. I appreciated getting to know you. All you shared with me."

"I had a good summer with you, too, Chat."

"And, you know, Trey will want to talk to you. Once I tell him everything, I know he will. He's never wanted to intrude on your life, but he misses you."

Danika felt as if she were hovering outside her body, listening to everything unfold. Yesterday, she'd sensed her life was about to change, but she'd never expected this.

"He's still teaching English, by the way. He's a director at that program he started with after hockey. He's doing well. I'll let him tell you about it."

Danika softened, a peace coming over her.

"Chat, I—" she finally said. "I also have to apologize. About . . . Augie." She forced out the words. "For overreacting this summer. It wasn't fair and I, well, I apologize."

Danika sensed Chat's surprise.

"I know it's embarrassing," she continued, equally surprised by her admission, "but I felt threatened by her. I was afraid to lose you. To lose you . . . too."

Chat paused, but then reached out between them, opening his palm, and once again, like at the model home, they held hands. This time, she squeezed once and let go.

"I guess what I'm trying to say is"—she swung her voice—"is that of course you don't have to come to Hilton Head, if that trip is even still happening. You should stay here with her. If there's anything else I can do to make it right, please tell me."

A second later, Chat suddenly sat up. He said he did have one small favor to ask.

"Have you ever been to Noelle's?"

36

Augie got to Noelle's early. She wore her favorite blue linen dress and gold earrings. It was hard to believe this would only be her third time seeing Chat outside the Club; she wanted to impress him.

They hadn't spoken one-on-one since he arrived at her house in the middle of the night. She was desperate to figure out what, if anything, between them was real. While he had lied to her all summer, she understood now that he'd only been trying to help. In so many ways, he had succeeded.

Augie was especially grateful for the chance to connect with Teuta in a new way. The day before, they had spent hours at Hyla. Augie could tell Teuta was terrified, but as they talked and she told Augie how difficult those early years had been—as she apologized for everything—Augie finally felt closer to her. Even more so after Augie told her about New York and her relationship with Chat. It was refreshing to be honest with each other. Augie realized then that their age hadn't been their main divide; rather, it had been the fact they were both hiding from the world, and mostly, from themselves. It hadn't come down to simply being adults. After all, there didn't seem to be such a thing as grown-ups—only the act of growing up.

Noelle's was a small, rectangular shop with an order window surrounded by pastel ice cream illustrations and lists of flavors. Out front, there were pink umbrellas, wooden picnic tables, and a wide lawn pressed up against the lake. Augie loved sitting as close as possible to the water, and as she slid onto the bench of the best picnic table, sunlight illuminating the blue lake and green grass around her, she took it as a good sign. She set down her phone and watched an idling boat. She thought back to the start of summer, the boat party.

Augie was looking down at her shoulder, adjusting the strap of her dress, when she felt a new presence and shadow above her. She looked up and almost fell off the bench.

There, instead of Chat, was a nearly unrecognizable Mrs. Crawley. She wore a white baseball hat, a gray T-shirt, black leggings, sneakers. No makeup.

"I know I'm not who you were hoping to see," Mrs. Crawley said, standing at the opposite side of the table. "But can I sit?"

Augie didn't react.

Mrs. Crawley slid onto the bench across from her.

"So." She set down her tote bag and rested her forearms on the table. Despite her forced nonchalance, Augie sensed she was nervous. Augie didn't know how to feel.

"So," she repeated, as she pulled down the bill of her hat. "I'll keep this quick. I just wanted to clear the air. And, quite simply"—she cleared her throat—"to apologize. For the luau, for the Fourth, for . . . everything."

Her voice moved from rushed to assured, as if she'd practiced this before. Augie felt suspended in time. Every dynamic shifted. The woman across from her was nothing like the woman from two days ago, who had been dressed to the nines and screaming in her face. Augie couldn't bear to make eye contact and looked out at the lake.

"If I'm being honest, I was just so excited to have Chat with us this summer. I worried he'd become distracted by you. That he might leave us for you. I've never been good at sharing our private life . . ."

"Chat never would have done that, though." They both seemed to be startled by Augie's voice. "He never would have just *left* you."

Danika leaned back.

"You're right." Mrs. Crawley tilted her head. "And if I'm being honest"—she looked straight at Augie—"I was jealous of you. I was jealous of your freedom. Your possibility. Being young."

Augie couldn't help it. She laughed. "You were jealous of *me*?"

"Of course. I couldn't stop thinking about those early years with Trey." At the sound of his name, Augie suddenly pictured Danika and Trey as herself and Chat. "I couldn't stop thinking about all the choices I'd made. Everything I thought I wanted back then."

"What did you want?"

Mrs. Crawley folded her hands. "To be . . . settled. I was so eager to get married, have a family. That's the great irony of life, right? When you're young, you only want to be old and to know what your life will look like. Then, later, you look back and—" She shrugged. "It's bittersweet." She raised her eyebrows in a playful way. "I know it's pointless to tell young people that youth is wasted on the young, so I'll stop while I'm ahead."

A breeze moved over them, and Augie swiped the hair from her face and lips.

"There is one thing I wanted to ask you, though." Mrs. Crawley paused.

Augie tensed. She slid her hands under her thighs.

"How did you find out about Trey? I sense Chat didn't tell you, not from the start, anyways."

Augie clawed at the wood of the bench, buying time. There was no use lying anymore. She lifted her hand, pressed a finger to the center of her collarbone.

"Your necklace." She tapped her finger against her skin. "At the baby shower, Mrs. Cline asked if your necklace was from Latvia. I heard you tell her it was a gift from an ex. Then I remembered Chat saying he had an uncle in Latvia, and I pieced it together."

Something changed in Mrs. Crawley's demeanor then. A fresh vulnerability coupled with—admiration?

"I have a good memory, too." She lifted her necklace from under her shirt, freeing the pendant so it hung down her front. It glinted in the light. It was the same color as Chat's eyes.

Augie felt a connection tug between them.

"Sometimes, I hate my memory. How I can't forget certain things."

Augie studied her. She looked younger without makeup, lighter.

"Like the night Trey broke up with me. I've never been so heartbroken in my life. He was the one who ended it, you know. I know the story makes it sound like I left him, fled Latvia, but he made me go."

Augie stayed quiet, listening.

"I didn't explain that to Chat or Bill. Call it my ego, maybe. I don't like to talk about it. Trey basically told me he didn't deserve me. And one night, he pulled my suitcase from the closet . . . He said he couldn't give me the life I wanted. He didn't deserve happiness. He said I needed to leave, and he was sorry. Like that was enough." She glanced up at the sun. "I was devastated, but I couldn't fight him. I had no choice. I left in the middle of the night. I haven't seen him since."

Augie felt her skin tighten with sympathy.

"All I ever wanted was a family," she continued. "That safety and security. Love. My own family was such a mess."

Mrs. Crawley let out a long, low sigh.

"I'm sorry," Augie suddenly said. "I'm sorry you had to go through that."

"Thank you." Mrs. Crawley straightened. "I don't know what's gotten into me. But it feels good to finally talk about it all. I hope it helps you understand my perspective, too. How seeing Chat, being reminded of Trey, after all these years, I just . . ." Her voice dissolved.

"I get it." It was true. It made sense now, her obsession with Chat. How odd it must have been to have him in her life and home—a ghost of the past. All that pain surfacing. The sick relief of it. While Augie had never experienced such heartbreak, she knew what it was like to bury memories—and how it felt to let them out.

"I'm also sorry," Augie said as Mrs. Crawley shifted in her seat, "for this summer. For going over to your house, for the luau. For . . . spilling on you at that happy hour."

Mrs. Crawley's smile ticked higher until they were both grinning at each other.

"Apology accepted." She leaned forward. Then she tapped the table with both hands and stood up. "Well, I think that's enough. Before I go, one last thing." She picked up her tote bag and slung it onto her shoulder.

"Bill is headed to Hilton Head next week, and I'm going to the cabin with the boys to work on my design firm. The house will be empty, and Chat isn't leaving quite yet. So if you'd like to stay there with him while we're away, well, you're invited."

Augie's mind went blank, but a beat later, it filled with a supercut of her and Chat in the Crawleys' mansion: images of them snuggling in the movie theater room, swimming in the pool, laughing at the bar—spending all day in bed.

Mrs. Crawley nodded to the parking lot. "He's in the car, by the way. He's excited to see you. Probably for ice cream, too. So, Augie."

She reached into her bag and pulled out her wallet. A twenty-dollar bill. "Let me get this."

Augie stared at the money. Immediately, she thought back to the baby shower—that haphazard tip. She wasn't sure how to read this final gesture. Was this her last power play? Her final way of taking control?

But whatever it was, Augie realized she didn't care. She'd let Mrs. Crawley have this one. That felt like power, too. She'd take a free ice cream.

She plucked the cash from Mrs. Crawley's fingers.

As Augie sat back down on the bench and stared up at the clouds, steadying herself and ruminating on the rawness of the moment, she heard a voice behind her. She looked over her shoulder, her chin against her bare, tanned skin.

"I hope you don't hate me for that. For any of this," Chat said sheepishly. He stood a few yards from the bench as if afraid to come too close, a stretch of grass between them.

Augie stood up to face him.

"I don't hate you."

His eyes brightened as he stepped forward. He wore a red St. Cloud T-shirt, a reminder of the past—the truth.

"Do you still think she's a bad person?"

Augie twisted her mouth.

"Maybe like, medium bad."

Chat laughed, and Augie sensed his relief. Augie didn't want to talk about Mrs. Crawley anymore. She didn't want to talk about anyone or anything but the two of them.

"Do you think I'm a bad person?" he said.

Augie squinted at him. "What?"

"For lying to you all summer. To everyone."

Augie glanced to two birds passing overhead. "No, Chat. Though, I do want to know"—she looked directly at him—"at the boat party, were you only talking to me because of Leah? Because you wanted to learn more about Lyle and everything? Were you only using me to get close to her and Teuta?"

"Augie." Chat shook his head at the ground before looking back up her. "Do I have to remind you that you're kind of the one who jumped my bones?"

"But is that the only reason you went along with it?"

Chat took yet another step toward her.

"I didn't know Leah would be at that party. I didn't even realize who she was until I heard her name, and then, I felt so bad about everything, I just wanted to avoid her. At least until I could help. I promise, I was never using you, Augie. Not for Leah, not for Teuta, not at all. If anything, you made everything more complicated."

Augie flinched.

"Not in a bad way." Chat lifted his hands. "This whole summer, all I wanted to do was hang out with you. Talk to you. Danika was right. You *were* a distraction. You're all I thought about."

Augie's face flushed, and she couldn't stop herself: she smiled.

"I haven't liked anyone in years. And . . ." He blew air out his teeth. "I feel like an idiot saying this, but we have something, right? Because if I have this all wrong, just tell me. You don't have to feel bad. I know you were never supposed to see me again."

Augie was done talking. She went to him and slid her arms up his shoulders, her fingers fanning the back of his neck. She studied the lines of gold in his irises—pinwheel rays of sun—and finally, he hugged her into him and kissed her.

37

The last time they met at Briar Ridge, they went to the model home: 34 Aspen Lane. This time, they weren't hiding. They'd already been living together at Wyatt's new apartment downtown.

"Should we take everything out of the boxes?" Bill asked, rounding the corner of the main bedroom. "Is that more or less helpful?"

From where he crouched near the window, installing new blinds, Wyatt chuckled. He stood, lifting the screwdriver in the air.

"I feel like Danika would rather come home to piles of boxes than piles of clutter. You know she's going to find the perfect place for everything." He walked to Bill, gently grasping his elbow. "I know you want to help, but let's remember, Danika is the one with the eye."

Bill acquiesced. He set the box down outside the closet.

In reconfiguring their lives, Bill and Wyatt had decided to buy Danika the model home. While the Crawleys would have to sell their Aldon Lakes house and cabin, between that cash, the success of Briar Ridge, and the fact that Bill had moved in with Wyatt, they could afford the model home. They were back on their feet.

As chaotic as the summer had been—that fated luau—Bill realized it was the crack in the dam of lies they'd needed. Now, he and

Wyatt could finally be together. It had been so refreshing, and life changing, to discover Wyatt was hiding the same secret as he was. That night after the bar crawl, he'd told Bill he was going to leave Robin and start living his truth. Bill hadn't been able to lie. Pointedly, he'd told Wyatt he saw himself in him.

The next day at Briar Ridge, they'd kissed.

Of everyone, Robin was having the hardest time. As Wyatt explained, she'd always valued appearances and keeping their family together—two traits Bill understood—and the divorce was difficult for her. Wyatt assured Bill she would be okay, eventually. Plus, her cousin Julia from New York was also leaving her husband. They were going to Thailand together come fall.

Most importantly, with all the new information surrounding Lyle's death, the Greenes finally had closure. Even if Joshua Mike could not be prosecuted (it was past the statute of limitations), they still felt vindicated to have answers. To know what really happened. It all made more sense now, too, comparing Teuta's testimony with the initial engineering report, which supported the theory that someone else might have been driving the boat that night.

For now, Joshua Mike was gone; he'd left for one of his houses in Cabo. He had quit the Club and was selling The Manor and the marina. Without a word, he'd sold Bill back his shares of Briar Ridge for pennies.

"I think there are only a few boxes left," Bill said, entering the kitchen. He and Wyatt were moving Danika's things over slowly, staging the old house to be sold.

"We're making good time." Wyatt adjusted the orchid they had bought as a housewarming gift. Danika would move in the following week—the end of the month.

After all, August had passed in a blur: Danika had spent weeks at the cabin with the boys, Bill had taken a solo trip to Hilton Head to come out to his family (which had gone just about as well as expected), they'd all seen Chat off to Europe, and then there they were, up to their eyes in preparations to buy and sell and shuffle homes.

Still, despite it all, Bill felt at peace. And as he leaned against the counter and looked up to the ceiling, the fan spinning above, he also felt grateful. He'd never expected this summer and the affair to lead to such new lives, but here they were, everyone on a new, better path.

"You want to grab those last boxes, then get out of here?" Wyatt asked.

Bill lowered his gaze from the fan to Wyatt. He nodded.

And for the first time, they walked out the front door hand in hand.

38

Danika's new favorite room in the house was her office, the fourth bedroom transformed. While at first, she'd worried the model home was too small for her, the boys, and her business—Designs by Danika was taking off after the success of Briar Ridge—she was growing to love it. Every space felt purposeful, gorgeous. Surprisingly, Danika was also coming to enjoy the community.

It was a shocking to see how fast the boys made friends on the street—how many young families had moved in. In fact, since they'd arrived two weeks ago, they'd already been to two block parties. She hadn't even hated them. Holly came with her to one, eager to see the new house and this signature style everyone was raving about.

Danika had outdone herself with the office. It had a large, sleek walnut desk, two pale pink boucle chairs, floor-to-ceiling linen drapes. She had splurged on a new computer, with a state-of-the-art camera. When she and Trey had their daily morning video calls, it was almost like they were face-to-face. Well, at least most of the time. His computer was outdated, though he promised he'd buy a new one soon. It didn't matter. He was coming to visit in three weeks.

Danika admired her reflection on the screen as she waited for

Trey to log on, smoothing the ends of her hair and sliding the pendant of her necklace to the center of her chest.

A moment later, the video crackled to life.

"Hey, hi, you there?" she heard as Trey's handsome, now-familiar face came into view.

Danika scooted forward on her elbows, smiling wider.

"Hey, yes! Trey, can you hear me? I'm here."

Acknowledgments

I vividly remember driving along the bays of Lake Minnetonka at twenty-two—sun on the water, windows down—feeling completely stuck. I'd just graduated college and was working my first "real job" at an ad agency after five summers at the country club. But all I wanted to do was write. It was a secret dream—one I hadn't let myself accept. It felt too hard, too unknown. I was used to succeeding. I was terrified to fail.

But something shifted that day, looping along the water a month into the job: I realized if I didn't try then, in that post-grad summer season of change, I might never.

So I applied to MFA programs. I got in. I moved.

Thirteen years later, I think my twenty-two-year-old self would be proud. Because it *was* hard. I *did* fail—over and over again. I didn't give up.

I cannot simply credit my own resolve. I never would have had the inspiration or resources to keep going without my incredible friends, family, and writing community. To connect with so many people on this journey—in this life!—has been a dream in and of itself.

Danya Kukafka, I'm not sure where to start, but you were the beginning—to taking myself seriously, to honing my craft, to working my way toward this story. Thank you for never breaking up with me! For always believing in me. You are a unicorn, shooting star, daydream of a person, writer, and agent. I pinch myself every day that I get to have you in my corner.

Ariana Sinclair, maybe we knew each other in a past life, because everything about working together has felt so fated and joyous. Thank you for seeing this story more clearly than I could. Every round of edits, you picked up the wobbly parts and helped me ground them. You changed this book—and my life—in the best ways possible.

I'm wildly indebted to the rest of the Trellis and William Morrow teams. Allison Hunter and Mariah Stovall, your expert, perfectly timed suggestions made all the difference. Mary Interdonati and Amelia Wood, thank you for your genuineness and ingenuity in helping bring this book into the world; it means so much to me. And Emily Krump, I'm so grateful that an invisible Minnesota string tied us together from the start—thank you for believing in this book (and in Aldon Lakes!).

My next bout of gratitude belongs to Colleen McKeegan, my writing wife and favorite person to yap with over a martini. Since our meet-cute in the redwoods, I've never been alone in this strange writing world; you always pick me up and push me forward. I adore you.

Brittany Kerfoot—where would I be if you hadn't replied to my MFA Facebook comment back in 2013? I don't want to think about it. The yin to my yang, I couldn't ask for a better partner-in-crime. The dogs and I are obsessed with you. I cannot wait for everyone to devour *The Seven Year Rule*.

Ah-reum Han and Marissa Peronne, my MFA darlings, you are two of the best writers I know. Ah-reum, your steadfast, selfless soul is a gift. Marissa, you are one of the funniest, wittiest people I've ever met. Please send me more pages.

The best part of any writing retreat is the people I meet—the ones whose work I love, who make me laugh, who stay in touch. As a result, my writing groups have grown from true friendships, which has been a gift.

First, to my Unyoungs: Liz Riggs, you are my "Behind the Music" rockstar. Our phone calls are more comforting than *The OC*. I'm so happy we sat next to each other that day in New York. You are cool incarnate. Sheila Yasmin Marikar, your books are as delicious as your travel photos, outfits, and taste in wine. Thank you for your sage advice and quick texts back. You are goals. And Avery Carpenter Forrey, whose puns are as bright as her smile—I relish your infectious energy, unwavering support, and razor-sharp sentences. I'm always as excited to see you as I am for the bridge of "Champagne Problems."

Next, my Squark Squad! Paula Tang and Lindsey Steffes, is there a smarter or hotter duo? I think not. I love being your skating pageant mom. Our trips are some of my favorite memories. I can't wait to see you (and workshop!) again soon.

To my "On the Hinge" ladies, Rachel Taff, Alli Hoff Kosik, and Eli Raphael: What a *damn* delight to connect with you just when I needed it most. I'm so fortunate to have you as my brain trust and free therapists. (And happy 2026! Let's party!)

Next, to the other writers and editors who've been so crucial on this journey:

Heather Lazare, thank you for creating the NorCal Writers Retreat, bringing so many wonderful people into my life, and cheering me on over all these years. Your spirit is as beautiful as Pacific Grove.

On that NorCal note, I'm so appreciative of Stacy Lee Niemiec—my noir, first-edition, Maine woods queen—who has read so many of my shitty first drafts and gives the best, sharpest notes. I love meeting you at all ends of the country. And to Caro Claire Burke: I'm in awe of all you've accomplished and fight for. I cannot wait to read *Yesteryear*.

Carola Lovering—ever since I sent you that fangirl DM back in 2018, you've been nothing but a gracious role model and literary inspiration. Thank you for your early support—and for leading the charge against the Stephen DeMarcos of the world . . .

Georgia Clark—*Generation Women*, your classes, and your contagious, ambitious energy have buoyed my creative life. You are a star. We can't wait to have you in a DC show.

To my teachers and mentors, Susan Shreve, Courtney Bkric, Stephen Goodwin, Bill Miller, Kris O'Shee, and the late Alan Cheuse: You made grad school a dream. You each embody brilliance, class, generosity, and Alan's call to "read as much as you can, write as much as you can, and love as much as you can." I'd follow you anywhere.

Tita Ramirez, Drew Perry, Cassie Kircher, and Kevin Boyle: Your classes meant more to me than you'll ever know. Thank you for early encouragement—and for being so cool. Also, Tita: I'm so glad you asked me if I knew what an MFA program was. I did not.

When you move as often as I do, you have the good fortune of collecting many gems of humans along the way—and now I get to shout about them!

My Minnesota crew: Cici Sohn, Alicia Barrera, Taylor Luse, Kimberly Perl, Britni Snow, Jessica Stanchfield, and Neha Singh. From bonfires to boat parties to all our bad behavior, I cherish our "lake life" memories. I'm so happy we grew up together. I'm so proud of who everyone has become.

A special shoutout belongs to Kelly and Dave Chaplo, my MN muses. Kelly, I'm so glad you had a crush on that male nanny. I'm even more grateful for your early reads, thoughtful notes, and that we found our way back to each other. Chappy boy, I'm not sure this story would exist if you two had not been visiting Kosovo during that Hail Mary revision. I'll never forget our hour-long cab ride brainstorm—or your creative eye and big heart.

To my Elon gals, Caroline Plyer, Kathleen Donnelly, Lindsay Gabriel, Elli Broujos, and Sian Rucker: You always believed in me, always waited for this moment. Thank you for that; I always felt it.

I have so much love for friends who have become family—and my ultimate hype team: Kasim and Bob Dahl, Kelsey and Robin Shaler, Sophia Cacciatore, Ashley Haynes, Cami Viola, Laura Keiter, Verona Hasangjekaj, Sanie Beqiri, Claudio Ballesteros, Jason Wright, Erica Schumack, Kathy Barton, Yesenia Rodriguez, Sebastian Engels, Rhiannon Osman, Morgan Hite-Hoffman, Danielle Mooney, and Karin Toscano—as well as the Munirs, Magnussons, Schaefers, Leipolds, Davises, and the Cecchi girls. To those who read early drafts: I owe you a drink.

My in-laws, the Conley and Shanahan clans, have given me so much joy and support—especially Kacey, Dan, Rachael, Colleen, Christine, Anders, Teddy, Ted, and Brenda. And to Beth White, my fellow woo girl: Your early reads and enthusiasm meant the world. I'll keep bribing the bars so you can sing karaoke first, forever.

To my family, from Minneapolis to California: Your love and encouragement keep me going. To the Ojis and Lansens, it means so much you never stopped asking about the book. Dan and Becky, I owe you for continually empowering me through microgreens, live music, and espresso martinis. You're the best.

Rohit Malhotra, I didn't know where to put you. But I decided you are my work husband in the fact that you consistently answer my calls, go out of your way to help me, and make me feel special. Your creativity and selflessness know no bounds. I love you more than a

"Lake Club sandwich"! Thank you for everything and never letting me pay you back.

To my darling, real-life husband, Ryan: I'm sure the Lorde lyric "I shouldn't have kissed a writer in the dark" has echoed in your head once or twice (maybe when I've stayed at my desk for hours, cried over a rejection email middinner, or asked if I can turn your boss into a character), but I'm so glad you did. What a life! What *fun*. Lule, Toka, and I love you endlessly. The next book's for you (just let me know the plot).

Lastly, to Aaron, Mom, and Dad.

Aaron, you motivate me to chase dreams, to never settle, and to jump off cliffs (both literally and figuratively). Thank you for having my back over the years—and for not being surprised when this worked out. You are one of a kind, and I love to brag about you.

Mom, I cannot distill my love for you! No one is more chic, strong, or selfless. I'm forever indebted to you for always putting me first and championing my dreams (how rare is that?). Thank you, also, for being my best shopping buddy, travel agent, and fellow book lover—and for always reminding us "you can never have too many books." I strive to be just like you.

Dad, your brains, creativity, tenacity, and heart are unmatched. I don't know anyone else who can build a camper van from scratch, narrate audiobooks with such talent, hitchhike around the globe, work tirelessly, and still remain so kind. Thank you for overcoming so much to give me this beautiful life. I'm so proud of who you are. It's an honor to be your daughter.

And now, reader, I turn to you: We all carry many stories within us, both real and imagined. Thank you so, so much for spending time with one of mine.

About the Author

LINA PATTON is a writer, illustrator, and teacher. Originally from Maine, she moved to Minnesota at thirteen, trading the ocean for 10,000 lakes. She holds a BA from Elon University and an MFA from George Mason University. Her work has appeared in *Elle*, *The Cut*, *Narrative* magazine, and *Driftwood Press*, among others. After seven years abroad, she and her husband currently live in Washington, DC, with their two very good, very bad dogs. *The Lake Club* is her first novel.